CLEAN KILL

What Reviewers Say About
Anne Laughlin's Work

A Date to Die

"[A]n entertaining mystery with a bit of sweet romance in the background. It's got all the ingredients for an enjoyable read: mystery, plot twists and romance."—*Lez Review Books Blog*

The Acquittal—*Lambda Literary Award Finalist*

"Laughlin's other mysteries—*Veritas, Sometimes Quickly, Runaway*—have been stand-alones, but one hopes (I hope) that *The Acquittal* is the beginning of a Josie Harper series. Josie is a terrific character, written with verve and depth. She's immensely likable and the issues she's dealing with are presented forthrightly and sensitively without bogging down the mystery plot. With *The Acquittal*, Laughlin has added another strong mystery to her retinue as well as a fabulous new character I hope we see more of."—*Lambda Literary Review*

Runaway—*Lambda Literary Award Finalist*

"Anne Laughlin is one of those authors that I just enjoy reading." —*C-Spot Reviews*

"[*Runaway*] is an easy read, with the story zig-zagging between Maddy and Jan. The second half of the book, working towards the final events in Idaho, keeps the pages turning. ...Some of the word selection and observations are sublime."—*Lesbian Review*

Veritas

"*Veritas* is a fun, well-paced and intriguing mystery with all the components readers of classic and competent cozies seeks. (It) is perfect reading for a cold winter night in front of the fire."—*Lambda Literary Review*

Visit us at www.boldstrokesbooks.com

By the Author

Sometimes Quickly

Veritas

Runaway

The Acquittal

A Date to Die

Money Creek

Clean Kill

CLEAN KILL

by

Anne Laughlin

2024

CLEAN KILL
© 2024 By Anne Laughlin. All Rights Reserved.

ISBN 13: 978-1-63679-634-5

This Trade Paperback Original Is Published By
Bold Strokes Books, Inc.
P.O. Box 249
Valley Falls, NY 12185

First Edition: May 2024

Credits
Editor: Cindy Cresap
Production Design: Susan Ramundo
Cover Design By Tammy Seidick

Acknowledgments

Many thanks to those who gave *Clean Kill* a first read and provided valuable feedback: Linda Braasch, Ann Stanford, Joan Larkin, Patricia Barber, Ann Farlee, and probably a few others I'm forgetting. I'm seriously indebted to my writing group, who shepherded the book through conception to final draft. Thank you Amin Ahmad and Claudine Guertin-Ceric. You are book doctors extraordinaire and my good friends. It was Claudine who came up with the title *Clean Kill*.

Thanks to Dr. Steven Bines who helped with medical questions and Detective (Ret) Jim Hennigan for all things law enforcement.

Thanks, as always, to my editor, Cindy Cresap, who reins in my shaky grammar and provides insightful suggestions of a more substantive nature. Bold Strokes Books has been my publisher for fifteen years now and I'm so grateful to them for giving my work a home.

I'd never miss an opportunity to thank my wife, Linda Braasch, for all her support for my writing. She reads, she listens, she advises, she encourages. I can't imagine doing any of this without her.

PROLOGUE

It was muscle memory, it really was. The woman hadn't meant to enter Simon's Tavern, but the blue neon sign outside was lit up, and it beckoned to her like a lighthouse in the darkness of the deep Chicago winter: *Here, here, here.*

The woman thought she'd pop in for a moment, just to see if she recognized anyone. She walked in, smelling the air thick and sour with booze, and was turning to leave when an old drinking buddy waved to her from the long mahogany bar.

The woman—mousy brown hair, big black puffer coat—had been sober for six months, an eternity for her. Now she spent the evening fiercely getting drunk to forget the fact that she was getting drunk. If she showed up intoxicated at her halfway house, she'd be kicked out, and so her plan—formulated sometime close to midnight—was to sleep in her car. Wherever her car was.

The woman had always been able to drink for hours without seeming drunk, but by one a.m., it was an hour past that time. When she left Simon's Tavern, the blue neon sign outside had been switched off. Where was her rusty old blue Taurus? She staggered across North Clark Street and a car almost hit her before vanishing into the dark mouth of an alley. Ah, yes, now she remembered: she'd parked illegally in the alley behind a hardware store, too broke to pay for a metered space on North Clark.

The alley was brightly lit at first, darker farther in. The woman—puffer coat clutched shut with both hands—walked deeper into the gloom. Rats skittered around the dumpsters. The El squealed to a stop somewhere close by, scaring her. It's just an alley, just a Chicago alley. She was thinking dimly about the next day—her spot at the halfway house gone, back to her old routine of waiting for the bars to open, scraping together money for the booze—when she slipped on a patch of black ice and fell. Her ankle twisted under her, and her face bled hotly from where it had scraped against the asphalt. *Hell.* Already her plan was coming undone. But it was still okay, wasn't it? She'd held on to her car keys, and the Taurus was right there, within sight. Still, her face hurt, and she began to cry.

"Hey, you need some help?"

The woman looked up and gasped.

Strong hands pulled her up, and as she was lifted, she glimpsed a figure in a black balaclava and a long, beige duster. It wasn't cold enough for a balaclava, she thought, and anyway, who wore those scary things these days—and she knew then something was wrong, and reached down, scrabbling for her handbag, thinking she could swing it as a weapon.

Her fingers had just closed over the strap when the figure moved closer and metal glinted.

A sharp pain pierced the woman's chest, so awful she almost passed out—but she was still conscious when she hit the asphalt again, conscious enough to feel the grit pressing into her cheek, the awful sprawl of her body, something warm leaking from her chest.

This time, she knew there was no hope of getting up.

CHAPTER ONE

Nicky dropped her suitcase in the foyer of Olive Street House and went to the kitchen to put a pot of coffee on. Visiting her sister was the only vacation she could afford on her pathetic salary, but it was good to get away from the house for a week. Leaving ten newly sober women unsupervised was a gamble, but for the most part they were a good crew, trying their best to live a completely different sort of life. She started to look for evidence of any disaster that might have occurred while she was away.

Olive Street House was a large frame home on a tree-lined street in Chicago's Andersonville neighborhood. It was owned by a recovery services company that ran halfway houses, outpatient, and inpatient programs, for people trying to get and stay sober. The house needed a new coat of paint, and everything was a tad run-down. The stairs to the front door were a dirty white, one of the gutters was hanging over the eave, the metal fence in front was spotted with rust. Inside there were scads of oak—window and wall trimming, flooring, cabinets, stairs, banisters. It wasn't to Nicky's taste, but she didn't complain. She was grateful to have a roof over her head.

The kitchen shared an open space with the family room where the women spent most of their time. It was tricked out with an enormous television, courtesy of a resident's wealthy parents. Fights regularly broke out over control of the remote and were smoothed over as quickly as they began. It was like living with fractious children who quarreled and made up over and over. When Nicky went into the kitchen for her coffee, she saw Diane and Susan snuggled up to one another on the couch in front of the TV. They had come to the house around the same time and became a couple almost instantly. Residents weren't supposed to have sex with each other, but Nicky had neither the desire nor the energy to put a stop to it. They were adults. Instead, she tried to keep them from gross displays of affection when they were around the other women. No one wanted to see that.

"Nicky, you're back!" Susan said, disentangling herself and getting up from the couch. Diane followed her into the kitchen.

"How were things while I was away?" Nicky was surprised at the welcome.

"No problems, boss," Diane said. "You should go away more often."

"I wish. What are you up to?"

"Just leaving. We're going to Clark Street for some coffee. Want to come?"

She'd never been asked to do anything by a resident since she started the job four years ago. She wondered if they were up to something.

"I have to get to work, but thanks."

"You may want to check on Darlene upstairs. We heard some banging coming from her room," Susan said.

Banging could be anything, but probably nothing good.

She took her bag upstairs and heard the noise coming from the end of the hall. Oli and Darlene shared the room and Nicky knew Oli would be at her day job. Darlene was a meth addict, new to the house and completely antisocial. When Nicky knocked on the door the bumping stopped. There was still no response when she knocked a second time. She opened the door and found Darlene sitting upright in her bed, clutching her chest and breathing heavily. There was a crack in the wall where she'd been banging her head. She was hugely overweight, and Nicky thought she might be having a heart attack. She'd seen enough meth overdoses while in uniform to know what she was looking at. A person in the throes of meth was capable of doing a lot of damage.

The instant Darlene's eyes came into focus she jumped from the bed with surprising agility and barreled toward Nicky as if to tackle her. Nicky easily sidestepped the attack and Darlene banged into the doorframe. She gave a blood-curdling scream as she turned around and grabbed Nicky's collar. Her punch grazed Nicky's chin, but it had weight to it and she stumbled back a few steps. Darlene grabbed her again and tried a roundhouse punch that missed Nicky entirely and spun her around. Nicky stepped in and roughly pulled her arms behind her back, longing for the handcuffs she'd once carried every day. Darlene struggled and Nicky yanked her arms upward, causing a loud yelp and an end to the struggling.

"Do you need some help, Nicky?"

Lou stood at the door, her large frame blocking the doorway. She was also new to the house and didn't interact much with the other residents, but she seemed to want sobriety. She did the work required without complaint and pitched in around the house.

"Call 911 and tell them we have a meth overdose." Nicky held on to Darlene, who'd started struggling again. When Lou finished the call she looked to Nicky for further instruction. She had on her Starbucks uniform, the sleeves rolled up to display her elaborate and colorful tattoos. She wore a lip ring, and nose ring, and multiple earrings. Nicky had yet to see her smile.

"Let's get her onto the bed." Nicky considered using her belt to restrain Darlene, but it seemed cruel.

Lou took over holding her hands behind her back, her size and strength making it easy work. Darlene was panting and her eyes were glazed. She let go of her arms as they sat her on the bed. Nicky worried the ambulance wouldn't make it on time.

Lou went downstairs to wait for the ambulance. Nicky tried to get Darlene to breathe deeply, but she was unreachable. Soon she heard sirens and the sound of men clomping up the stairs. She followed behind the EMTs as they strained to bring Darlene down on a stretcher.

Lou closed the door behind them and looked to Nicky.

"I'll have to go to the hospital," Nicky said. "The house must be empty or they'd all be down here watching the show."

"There's no one else here."

"Let's keep this to ourselves, at least until we know how she's doing."

"Sure."

All Nicky knew about Lou was in her office file. She had a small income from her Starbucks job, which she'd managed to hang onto despite bottoming out on alcohol. She had a meth arrest and two DUIs on record, all of which had been dismissed. Two years prior she'd graduated from Northwestern University, so she was no dummy. It would have taken weeks to get all that out of Lou, who wasn't a sharer. But now she stood next to Nicky almost as if she wanted to hang out. That was something new.

"Let's have a cup of coffee before I go to the hospital." Nicky led the way into the kitchen and poured them both a cup before heading to the patio in the back of the house. The air was warm and sweet. They took seats on the metal wicker chairs and Lou looked at her expectantly.

"What happens to Darlene now?" Lou asked.

"She'll be removed from the house." Nicky sipped her coffee. She hadn't put enough cream in and frowned. Coffee was one of the few substances she could still enjoy, and she wanted each cup to be perfect. "I know it seems harsh, but it's to protect the other women in the house. This has to be a safe place."

"No, I get it. It's a little scary is all. I used to do meth. I finally pulled back on it after having a few too many experiences like hers."

"You were able to do that on your own?"

"I hit the booze harder instead. Pick your poison." Lou's big body shifted in her narrow chair.

"How did you do while I was away? I'm sorry I left town so soon after you arrived at Olive Street."

"It's cool. No one bothered me."

Being a loner worked against Lou as she tried to stay sober. Newcomers were too close to their old thinking and when left alone with it they usually went back to their old ways. Talking to other recovering alcoholics was what made not drinking or using start to feel attainable. She hoped Lou would open up more.

"What've you been doing with your time?"

"What am I supposed to do? I work, go to meetings, do chores, and still there are huge gaps of time to fill."

"That's a problem in the beginning. For me, drinking was a full-time vocation, something I did every moment I wasn't working or sleeping. Take the drinking away and time becomes a wasteland. Do you have any friends in Chicago?"

"I thought we weren't supposed to hang out with friends?" Lou sounded frustrated trying to understand the new guidelines.

"It's good to ditch your drinking friends, but what about others?"

"I don't have any of those."

Nicky drank more coffee and tried not to feel sorry for Lou. There was no making it easier for her. Getting sober was fucking hard, which was why so few made it.

"Did you get to know the other residents while I was away?"

Lou pulled her WNBA hat low on her brow. "They were nice and everything, but I have a hard time talking to anyone without a bar underneath my elbow."

"It'll get better, Lou."

"I hope so. I want this to work."

"It will if you put in the time. I need to go to the hospital, but we can talk more later if you like."

Lou looked pleased. Nicky would do whatever she could to help her, but it was an inside job. Lou would have to find her own way.

At the Swedish Covenant ER, Nicky spoke with a resident about Darlene. They were admitting her because of the heart involvement which gave her until the next day to evict her from Olive Street House. She felt she should have done more for Darlene by helping her integrate into the group. The women in the house became like family to each other, a powerful motivator to keep sober and not disappoint your peers. She stayed to talk briefly with Darlene, saving news of her upcoming eviction for a later time when she was less likely to have a heart attack.

As she walked back through the emergency room, she noticed a cluster of people gathered at the triage desk. There were no uniforms, but they were unmistakably cops. She'd spent countless hours in hospitals as a detective, waiting to interview injured witnesses and suspects, occasionally checking in on a fallen comrade. She knew the look. A woman in the group had her back to her but turned just as Nicky was passing by. Their eyes met briefly before she turned back to her discussion. Nicky felt a little flare of attraction, a feeling she'd not had for so long she'd forgotten the pleasure of it. She was tall like

Nikki, dressed in the requisite pant suit, with shoulder length auburn hair, an aquiline nose, pronounced cheekbones, and dark eyes. She took it all in in a flash and felt a loss when the woman turned away from her.

Before returning to Olive Street, she drove her terrible old car down to the Uptown neighborhood and parked in front of a modest bungalow near the lake. It was too late in the day to hope to see Laura leaving or entering the house. Instead, she pictured her with crutches and braces off, sitting up in her foster family's living room, hoping she was loved as if she were a daughter. Nicky hadn't come by the house for a week and let her guilt layer itself into something cloaking, as it did whenever she visited Laura's house. There were times she could barely breathe with it. There were also times, like now, when she couldn't bear to actually see Laura. She'd come by when there was no chance of seeing her struggling to get to the school bus. Each visit brought her past as a cop vividly to life.

She often longed for her old life as a homicide detective. She'd loved almost everything about it until that one moment changed everything. She'd been on her way back to the station one afternoon driving an unmarked vehicle when a Mazda passed her on Broadway, weaving between the lines, bumping against curbs. She flipped on her lights and siren and called for backup on a traffic stop. The car didn't immediately pull over and she cursed when the driver sped away. When she finally managed to pull him over she got out of her car with her hand on her weapon and approached with caution. Before she walked two steps, a man burst out of the Mazda and fired at her. She dropped to a crouch and returned fire, hitting him once square in the chest and a second time a little to the right, traveling straight through his body and into the vehicle. Also in the car was the man's ten-year-old daughter, Laura, who caught the second bullet in the spine. Nicky's life wasn't the same from that moment. Within a month she'd resigned from the police department and concentrated on making her already heavy drinking into a full-time job.

The department tried to keep her. No one blamed her for the errant shot that injured the girl. There were no relatives to initiate a civil suit against the police. But Nicky knew she'd lost her effectiveness as a cop. In any stressful situation she'd think of Laura and seize up. The thought of hurting someone else was paralyzing.

For two years Nicky drank and lived off the occasional security gig plus whatever cash her mother would give her. She drank from the stroke of noon until she passed out every night, like it was a job and those were her hours. She didn't think her life could get any darker after she shot Laura, but bottoming out on alcohol made it bleaker still. By the time she entered rehab there wasn't a shade of light in her soul. She was friendless, penniless, homeless, and purposeless. She was desperate enough to accept some help. She hadn't had a drink since, a miracle she sometimes still found hard to believe.

When Nicky returned from the hospital she headed straight to her office. The office was a perk in a job with not much in the way of perks. It was barely big enough for a desk, visitor chair, and file cabinet, but it was all hers. The only thing she'd done to personalize the space was display her 24-hour coin from the day she stopped drinking, hardly radical decorating in a sober living home. She kept an open door and welcomed it when residents sought her out to unburden themselves, as Lou had just done.

As soon as she touched the office doorknob, she could tell it was unlocked. She took her hand off as if it was on fire, her crime scene training making her feel she'd already contaminated this one. The door was never left unlocked, especially while she was on vacation. She put her coffee cup on the floor and used the bottom of her T-Shirt to wrap around the knob, opening the door slowly as if a perp were in the room. She wanted her gun and her shield. Before snapping on the overhead light she took a look behind the door. No one was there.

Her heart sank when she saw a desk drawer yawning open, its lock heavily scratched, almost clawed at. She sank into her chair before bending over and peering in, hoping against hope the two locked cash boxes would be there. Of course, they weren't. No one was jamming open a locked desk to steal Post-it notes. Her mind raced through the ten women living in the house with her. Who among them would do this? She couldn't think of a single one who seemed likely, while at the same time they all were capable of it.

The AA treasury box was a complicated loss. She was entrusted to hold the funds raised by seven different AA meetings held at Olive Street. She pulled out a ledger from another drawer and ran her eyes down a column. There was close to three thousand dollars in the large cash box. She didn't care about the petty cash box. That money belonged to Reardon Malloy, the company that owned the sober house, five hundred dollars at the most. They wouldn't miss it, but in AA, every dollar counted.

She could call the police first, but that would mean detectives and interviews with all of the residents and probably an arrest. She didn't want that, not yet. She knew her boss, Gerri Thomas, was supposed to have been in the house the previous day to leave grocery money. Nicky called her, half hoping she wouldn't pick up. Seldom was a conversation with Gerri a pleasant one.

"Welcome home, Nicky. I have to say I'm glad you're back," Gerri said.

"Someone broke into my office while I was away. They took the two cash boxes out of the desk."

"What?"

"Yeah, it's bad. The desk was forced open."

"I was just there yesterday and everything was fine. I saw both of the boxes."

"That's what I wanted to check with you. Was everything locked when you got here?"

"Yes. The door, the desk, the petty cash box. I used keys on all of them. I didn't pay attention to the other cash box."

"And you locked everything up when you left?" Nicky asked.

"Of course." Nicky could hear the defensiveness in Gerri's voice, but that didn't surprise her. Gerri was defensive about everything. "I distinctly remember locking the cash box and the desk, because both of those locks were a little tricky."

"And the door?"

"I can see you're putting your detective hat on, Nicky."

"That may be. But tell me about the door."

There was a moment's silence. "I can't say I specifically remember locking the office door. I just assume I did, really. Why wouldn't I?"

"No reason. But if you neglected to, it would be good to know." She cringed when the word neglected left her mouth.

"Any neglect on my part would not be an open invitation to steal, would it, Nicky?"

"It would not. It's simply information I'll give to the police."

"Wait. Let's think about this a minute. The police will turn the house upside down, don't you think?" Gerri had that "let's work together" tone in her voice, which meant she fully intended to get what she wanted. In this case, Nicky thought, it might be what she wanted too—no police.

"We need to find out who took the money," Nicky said.

"Agreed. But I think you're the best person to do that. You were a detective, right? I'm authorizing you to investigate. In fact, I'm ordering you to do so as the house manager. It's likely to be easy to solve, right? We know it happened between the time I was there yesterday afternoon and right now."

Gerri sounded like the matter was taken care of and she could wash her hands of it. Nicky knew the stink of it would be all over hers. Still, she'd rather investigate herself than have cops crawling all over the place.

"Fine," Nicky said. "I don't like it, but I'll do it. We'll have to talk about how to replace the three thousand dollars if we can't recover it."

Gerri laughed. "Nicky, be real. Would we have insurance to cover the theft of AA money in a house full of addicts and alcoholics? Let's just cross that bridge later."

Gerri hung up. Nicky threw her phone on the desk and stared at it blindly. Her resentment of Gerri grew every time she talked to her. She never got the feeling Gerri cared about the residents in the slightest. For Nicky, helping the women was the only reason to stay in a job that paid about the same as a car wash attendant.

She walked through the living room to get more coffee when the front door opened and her sponsor, Sheila, walked in. Nicky almost ducked around a corner, but Sheila spotted her and joined her on the way to the kitchen. Like many in recovery, Nicky revered her sponsor and avoided her in equal measure. In the beginning of sobriety, a sponsor was a lifeline. They explained the mysteries of the program, checked up on you, guided you through AA's Big Book and steps, encouraged you to clean up your apartment and get a job. They tried to see what made you tick when you had no idea yourself. In return, the sponsee was supposed to be in regular touch, do their assigned step work, and, most importantly, call their sponsor when they were tempted to drink.

Nicky was only a few months sober when she started working with Sheila, still in a fog, living in a friend's basement. Sheila encouraged her to get a job, any job, in order to get some structure back into her life. She tugged her along to group dinners after the meetings to help her make friends in the community. She kept telling her things would get better if she just held on. There was no doubt Sheila had helped her stay sober, but she was all about the talking. Processing this, unpacking that. Everything needed to be explored to see how it helped or hindered her recovery. Nicky only had so much talking in her, not enough as far as Sheila was concerned. They got along well, but this was a point of some friction.

Sheila smiled as she leaned in for a hug. She was about ten years older than Nicky's own forty years and she looked like it had been a long time since her last drink. She struck Nicky as the most serene person in the world. Everything about her was relaxed. Her round face was warm and welcoming. She was dressed sharply in leggings and a tunic that showed off her strong and slender frame.

"Hey, there," Nicky said. Her lips were a straight line across her face.

"Hey, yourself. Everything okay?"

"Not even close. How could you tell?"

Sheila chuckled. "You look like you're about to pop."

"Something bad happened."

They went into Nicky's office. "Tell me about it."

"No, I better not. I shouldn't, anyway."

"Nicky, you know whatever we talk about won't go beyond me, don't you?"

Nicky nodded and reluctantly took a seat. "I know I can trust you. I just don't know if talking's going to help very much."

"Try it. It's probably not going to hurt any."

Nicky told her about the theft. Sheila wasn't shocked at the news of the theft. It wasn't as if this never happened in AA. Not everyone became honest once they stopped drinking, or any less desperate.

"I'll have to talk to them all one at a time. They're not going to like it."

"What are the alternatives? Do you want the police to come in? Or your boss?"

Nicky smiled. "Can't I resent it and accept it at the same time?"

"You can. I don't know if it does you any good."

She stood up and looked at Sheila. "Thanks for the ear. Let me know if you hear anything useful, okay?"

"You've hardly told me a thing. Don't keep this all to yourself."

"I won't. Why don't we have dinner tomorrow night? I don't want you to think I don't appreciate you." She had to spend some time with her sponsor. It was a relationship she couldn't afford to screw up.

Sheila's smile lit up her face. "I'd love that. Should we meet and leave from here?"

"Perfect."

Nicky watched her leave before she picked up the phone and called Deb, the woman she'd recently started dating and a perfect diversion from the mess at the house. She'd start the investigation in the morning. They'd been out a couple of times but hadn't slept together. Nicky couldn't envision how that would come about. She had so little experience with women in sobriety. Deb answered the phone before she thought about what she was going to say.

"Nicky! I was wondering when I'd hear from you." They'd had dinner the week before. Was she supposed to be checking in with her?

"I just got back into town and thought I'd call."

"Do you want to come over?" Deb said.

It was hard to misinterpret that message. She wasn't being invited over for coffee and a Danish.

"Uh, sure. I'll walk over. Should I bring anything?"

"Just your sweet self."

She was about to have her first sex as a sober person, and nearly the first sex she'd had when not drunk. Hadn't she put it off as long as possible? At five years, her celibacy was teetering on pathological. It was time to hitch up her pants and then go take them off with someone. With Deb. And why not Deb? She was nice, she was pretty, and she seemed to like Nicky. The last point alone made her girlfriend material. She ran up to take a quick shower and change into a good pair of jeans. She pulled her old slouchy boots on and buttoned up a new shirt. She was so tall her image barely fit in the mirror. Her tallness was a bane while growing up but extremely useful as a volleyball player. She won a full-ride scholarship to play at Illinois State University. Still, six two made her a little freakish. Her sleek black hair was pulled back in a ponytail as usual and her long legs looked good in the tight jeans. She didn't wear makeup, but her smooth complexion allowed her to get away with it. She was still able to get away with a lot.

Deb lived four blocks away in the heart of Andersonville. The neighborhood felt as familiar as a small hometown to Nicky. Once the home of the city's Swedish population, it had long since morphed into a destination neighborhood, its residential streets wrapped around the main commercial strip on Clark Street, where the restaurants and shops drew people from all over the city. Nicky seldom felt any need to leave the neighborhood. She had everything she needed, even a girlfriend.

When she reached Deb's building she hesitated for several long moments before pushing the buzzer, trying to calm her jangly nerves. When the door clicked open, Nicky grimly mounted the stairs. Deb opened her door, reached out, and pulled Nicky in by the front of her shirt, closing the door with a foot and then pushing her up against it. She held her lips a mere inch away.

"Can I kiss you?"

Nicky was relieved that Deb had no interest in the awkward preliminaries. Her bold first move made things easy. She pulled Deb closer and kissed her soundly, and in that instant her fear left and she felt desire. They kissed for a long time while leaning against the door, Nicky's sense of urgency rocketing upward. Her body was making it quite clear what she was supposed to do next. They went into the bedroom to do exactly that.

"I've wanted this since the moment I saw you," Deb said during the pillow talk afterward.

"Really? You mean our first date?"

"Before that. When I first saw you at the Friday step meeting. Maybe a couple of months ago."

"Huh. I didn't know that." She only knew she'd seen Deb a few weeks in a row at the meeting and then one night Deb asked her out. She didn't know much about her other than she was sober and went to meetings.

"How much time do you have?" Nicky asked. In AA parlance, time meant the amount of sober time a person had. Why had she forgotten to ask Deb this before? What if she was only a couple of months sober? It would be like sleeping with one of her residents—not only wrong, but a bit creepy. The recovery equivalent of the Mann Act was to not sleep with anyone who hadn't been sober a year. Nicky had no interest in breaking that unofficial rule, but seemed to have conveniently forgotten to check she wasn't.

Deb shifted a bit and snuggled into Nicky's shoulder. "A bit under two years."

Safe, but still not much time. In the grand scheme of putting your life back together, two years was the equivalent of toddler age.

"I know you're an old-timer," Deb said. "I was there on your fifth anniversary."

Nicky laughed. "I am definitely not an old-timer. I'm just old."

"You are not. How old are you?"

"Forty. Old."

"I'm thirty-seven. You've probably had lots of girlfriends since you quit drinking, right?"

"What makes you say that?"

"Because you're so hot. I've heard other women talk about you. I assumed you'd gotten around."

Nicky lay there mutely, stunned at the idea women would think she's hot, that they talked about her. She could only hope what was said about her was more flattering than it had been in her drinking years. It would almost have to be.

❖

The day before

Gerri Thomas steered her company car onto Lake Shore Drive and headed north toward Andersonville. Lake Michigan gleamed to her right, the late afternoon sun turning the water into an ocean blue. It made no impression on her. She wanted to take care of business at Olive Street as quickly as possible and get out.

As Reardon Malloy's regional director for outpatient recovery services in the Midwest, Gerri oversaw operations in all outpatient and resident facilities in her area. Another manager had the good fortune to be in charge of the inpatient facilities and Gerri coveted his job. Patients in the hospital were very easily controlled and there was a minimum of drama, unlike the daily soap opera that took place in each of the halfway houses in her charge. R-M was one of the largest recovery companies in the country, a for-profit that mined the vast potential customer base of people suffering from alcohol and drug addiction. She knew how clever a business model it was; the vast majority of patients seeking treatment were potential repeat customers. Relapse was part of the disease of alcoholism, but for R-M it insured a healthy profit as patients cycled in and out of rehab.

The trip to Olive Street House was necessary because of another fight between residents while Nicky Sullivan was on vacation. She vowed to never again approve vacation time. It was too much of a burden on her to play backup. She also needed to give petty cash to one of the residents for groceries. She wondered when it was that every single thing about her job became unpleasant.

The three women she'd been called about sat waiting for her in the AA meeting room that had once been a parlor. Two sat together and the third sat far away.

"Okay, which one of you called me?" Gerri walked to the front of the room and sat at the secretary's desk. She glared at them.

The woman sitting on her own stood. "That was me."

"And you are?"

"Maria." Her hands twisted around each other.

"And you're claiming these two," she pointed at the others without looking at them, "are having sex with each other?"

"Well, they are. My room's right next to theirs. I can hear them."

Gerri turned to the other two.

"What are your names?"

The two stood, which pleased Gerri. She felt like a judge.

"I'm Diane and this is Susan." Diane had stepped forward, as if she were about to take a bullet for Susan. Gerri directed her gaze at Susan.

"What do you say to Maria's claim, Susan? Do you deny it?"

Susan and Diane exchanged looks and Susan nodded.

"We don't deny it," Diane said. "We're in love."

Gerri barely contained a snort. "Of course you are. And I'm the Queen of Sheba."

She picked up the gavel sitting on the table and gave it an experimental whack. Now all she needed was a black robe. "No, what you girls are is barely sober, living in a house that has rules to help you stay that way. Sex with other residents is against the rules and I can throw you out for it."

Gerri saw the look of alarm on Susan's face, the defiance on Diane's, and the smugness on Maria's. If they were any more transparent, she'd literally be able to see right through them. She turned to Maria.

"Does Nicky know about this?"

"I don't know. I wasn't sure about it until after she left on vacation. But I think she might."

Diane glared at Maria before turning to Gerri. "Listen, you don't have the right to legislate our feelings. It's not something we can control."

"Honey, I'm not interested in your feelings. You all signed off on the rules and regulations when you came here. The question now is what to do about you breaking them."

"Please don't kick us out," Susan said. "I don't have anywhere to go."

The truth was Gerri didn't give a damn if they slept together. It happened all the time, whether the women were straight or gay. She supposed it was like boarding school or prison. She was annoyed not by the act, but by it being reported and forcing her to do something about it.

"There are a lot of women who would kill to have your spot in the house. Why shouldn't I kick you out?" She smiled when she saw the anguish on their faces.

"Please let us stay," Susan said, her normally confident tone now sounded like pleading. "We'll stop what we're doing."

Throwing them out would mean more work for Gerri. There were reports to write and new residents to bring in. The last thing she wanted was more work.

"Here's what we're going to do. Maria's going to move in with Susan and Diane will move in with Maria's roommate. And no one is going to have sex."

Maria began to protest, but Gerri raised her hand to silence her. "I want this all done by lights out tonight, understood?"

Gerri gathered her bag and left the room, the sound of arguing voices erupting as soon as she cleared the door. Nicky could deal with the fallout when she got back from vacation, which was the next day, thank God.

Her phone buzzed as she walked toward Nicky's office, and she let it lie at the bottom of her purse. She was avoiding the astounding number of calls she was getting from Bank of America. She was two months behind on her mortgage, thanks to her unemployed husband. Why the bank felt five calls a day would produce money from her when one call didn't was beyond her. It pissed her off. Why did they call her and not her husband? He was the one who'd lost his job, not her.

She found the right key for the office door, after trying at least six others. She snapped on the overhead fluorescent and wedged herself between a wall and the desk before falling into the creaky wood chair. On top of everything else, she needed to lose twenty pounds, which would soon be thirty if she didn't stop eating herself into a sugar coma every evening. Her phone buzzed again, and she fished it out of her purse. It was the bank and she hit the Ignore button. She saw the other call had been from her husband, Jeff.

After stabbing another three keys into the locked cabinet door in the desk, she opened it and pulled out the petty cash box. She took out a couple of hundred and filled out the receipt form. She'd have to find Angela, the most senior resident in the house, who was doing the grocery shopping this week while Nicky was gone. When she leaned over to slide the petty cash box back into the cabinet, she noticed another metal box tucked in the rear. She put the petty cash box back on the desk and pulled out the larger one. She knew it had to be the treasury box for the AA meetings; all of her halfway houses had one.

The box was locked. Gerri riffled through her Olive Street key ring and found one that fit into the larger box. It was about the size of a shoe box and stuffed to the gills with cash. Someone had faced all of the bills and tried to put them in some sort of order, probably Nicky, and it looked like about half were singles and the other larger denominations.

A plan formed instantly. She left the boxes on the desk and stepped out of the office, locking the door behind her, and went upstairs to find Angela who was in her room studying for her exam as a certified alcohol counselor. Gerri wanted to warn her against her new career, but she didn't have time or the interest to bother. She gave Angela the grocery money and tried to say a few chatty things before leaving the room. She went downstairs and walked casually out the door of the house and retrieved a tote bag from her car. She brought it into Nicky's office and closed and locked the door behind her before slipping the treasury box into the tote. After a moment's thought she put the petty cash box in with it. It wouldn't make sense that a thief would take one without the other, and she had to think like a thief. The house was full of potential thieves and that provided wonderful cover. One of them was sure to be blamed. There were so few advantages to working with newly sober addicts and alcoholics, but at least this was one. She took advantage when she could.

Gerri reached into her purse and found her Swiss army knife, which had resided in her bag untouched since she'd received it as a gift from R-M. She locked the cabinet door and then used the knife's blades and screwdriver to mangle the lock on the desk cabinet enough to pop it open and leave it looking very much tampered with. She then left the office door closed but unlocked behind her and walked out of the house with her tote bag and purse. The unlocked office door would be temptation beyond resisting to one of the residents, or so everyone would think, even the residents themselves. It was pretty damn clever, she thought.

She drove downtown to finish out her day. She had an office in the company's main building, an old brick house in the city's near north side. She thought it wise to be seen this afternoon. She wouldn't be able to deny being at Olive Street House, but she wanted her visit to appear as unremarkable as possible. Quick, to the point, and back to work downtown. It wouldn't occur to anyone she'd been jimmying locks and stealing crumpled dollar bills from recovering alcoholics.

Her phone buzzed and it was Jeff again. She sighed and took the call.

"Hey, babe," Jeff said. He still called her babe, twenty years after they were married.

"Three calls from the bank today," she said, in what had become a fairly standard greeting.

"That's not bad," Jeff said. "They must be slacking off."

"The day's not over yet."

"Listen, I'm going to pick Liam up and head to a meeting. I left dinner for you in the fridge."

"Fine." This was good news. Gerri loved an evening home to herself. "Are you going out afterward?"

"Yeah, probably."

"That's fine, too." Gerri waited for him to say more, but he didn't. "What went on today?"

Jeff laughed. "You shouldn't try to be coy. Ask me what I did to find a job today. That's what you want to know, isn't it?"

"Well?"

"The usual. I sent out resumes, I checked the websites, I tried to think of more people to call, but frankly, I've tapped every resource I've ever had."

"Any hits?"

"Don't you think I'd lead with it if there had been?"

"I'm not sure I know. You don't seem to feel any sense of urgency about this."

Jeff stayed quiet for a moment. Gerri knew he was probably saying the Serenity Prayer or counting to ten. There'd been a lot of these silences lately.

"We handle things differently, babe. I'm going about this as diligently as I possibly can. The fact that I'm not riddled with anxiety doesn't mean I'm not taking it seriously."

"You're right we're different." She didn't feel like fighting. She felt like counting the money in the lock box to see how much time it would buy her with the bank. "I'll see you when you get home."

She hung up and pulled into the rear parking lot of Reardon-Molloy. She'd count the money at home, while Jeff was away, and hope it was enough to get them current.

CHAPTER TWO

Nicky would have to search every bedroom in Olive Street House. If the cash boxes were stolen by a resident, it seemed unlikely she'd still have them hidden in her room, given a search was inevitable. But it's possible the thief didn't know when Nicky was getting home and thought she had more time.

She started her search in the two bedrooms in the basement. They were larger than the ones upstairs, but the casement windows that ran along the top of the wall cast only meager light. They made her think of a teenager's room, and Rhonda and Tory's looked like one. They were the youngest women in the house, both barely twenty. It was a hard age to get sober, and it wasn't the first attempt for either of them.

The room was festooned with posters and postcards from bands she hadn't the slightest familiarity with, but the beds were made. That was a rule of the house that Nicky hated enforcing. It was meant to foster a sense of responsibility, but it made her feel like a camp counselor or a drill sergeant, depending on how much in their faces Nicky had to get.

Another rule of the house was the house manager had access to the residents' rooms at all times, including to conduct searches. It brought home the reality that Olive Street was not a boarding house or a dorm. In order to keep the house safe for people trying to stay sober, the manager had free rein if she thought anyone might be holding drugs or alcohol or had committed a crime. Nicky appreciated the fact she didn't need a warrant to enter, but it still wasn't something she enjoyed. She was always afraid of what she would find, of who she'd have to kick out.

There were advantages to having spent time as a uniformed cop. She'd picked through her share of dumpsters and shooting galleries, Porta Potties and abandoned tenements. Sifting through the dirty laundry in Rhonda and Tory's closet was a cakewalk in comparison. She didn't find anything in the room that shouldn't be there. They both kept diaries, but Nicky wouldn't read those. She would take her mandate only so far. She saw Rhonda's three-month sobriety coin on the nightstand by her bed.

She climbed to the second floor. Her own bedroom was at one end, the only single room in the house and the only one with a lock on the door. The doors to the three other rooms on the floor were all closed. Nicky wondered if Lou was still here, brooding alone in her room.

Nicky knocked on the door closest to her own. Angela shared the room with Denise and Nicky had no expectation she'd find anything that didn't belong there. Angela and Denise were the good girls in the house. They had the longest amount of sober time, they volunteered for service work, they offered to help the new girls in the house, they cooked the best meals. They also raised their hands during the house meetings to rat out the other residents when they did something wrong. Nicky was surprised no one had taken a swing at one of them. Their room was spotless, the beds crisply made, and their personal items squared off on all of the surfaces. It took Nicky less than five minutes to get through it, turning up nothing more than a worn copy of *The Story of O* and a miniature vibrator under Denise's mattress. She wondered when Denise ever got a chance to use it.

The next room had been Diane and Susan's, but now was Diane and Maria's. She'd heard all about Gerri shifting around room assignments and needed to smooth things over, but that had now fallen off the radar. Kerry was asleep in the third room. She had an overnight shift job at a hospital, so Nicky moved on to the last bedroom on the floor, which Lou shared with a wiry, nervous woman named Zoey. Nicky was surprised Zoey and Lou hadn't struck up some kind of friendship. They both shared a punk aesthetic, but Nicky had yet to see them together in the TV room or hanging together anywhere else. She tapped lightly on the door, hoping Lou had gone out, not wanting to have to explain what she was doing. There was no response. She eased open the door and went in.

As usual, Zoey's stuff was strewn around her bed as if it were a moat keeping people away. She was very often on extra dishwashing duty because of her slovenliness, which didn't seem to disturb her at all. Lou's half of the room, however, was tidy and spartan. Other than some books on her nightstand, there was nothing personal of Lou's visible. Nicky glanced at the titles. *Middlemarch* and *Jude the Obscure* anchored the pile with their imposing weight, and atop them were volumes by Jeanette Winterson, and some other women authors she'd never heard of. Lou was a puzzle.

Nicky started on Zoey's side of the room, wading through clothes and jewelry and art supplies, but finding nothing she would get in trouble for. Lou's side took less time. She only had a few pairs of pants, some shirts, her Starbucks uniform, and a pair of shit-kicking boots in the closet. There was nothing in her dresser drawers other than underwear and T-Shirts, not even a journal. Nicky lowered herself to check under the bed and stopped dead. She reached in and pulled out a snow-white box with the Apple logo on it. When she opened it she saw a brand-new MacBook with the cords and accessories still in their clear packaging, untouched. She couldn't tell if the laptop itself had been opened and turned on, but it looked pristine. A receipt from the Apple store was tucked into one of the compartments. Nicky grabbed it and searched for the date of sale—it had been purchased the evening before, at six fifteen, a cash payment of almost two thousand dollars. She scoured the room for the one thousand that would be left over but came up empty. She put the computer back as she'd found it and left the room, a queasiness beginning in her gut.

It was ten in the morning. She didn't know where Lou had gone or how long she'd be. Nicky went back into her office and locked the door behind her. She wanted a drink. She wanted to be able to do the same thing she'd always done when she felt overwhelmed—lock the door and take out a bottle. For now, she'd just lock the door. The urge to drink had largely left her, so when it hit now it was terrifying. The idea of living with white-knuckled cravings was a recovering person's nightmare. She went into the kitchen and grabbed a Diet Coke, another sanctioned vise.

There were things to do. She needed to talk to each resident individually, she needed to find out where everyone was between the time Gerri left and the time she discovered the theft. She wished she could dust the office door and the desk for fingerprints. At least half of the women in the house would have prints on file from their various arrests. Maybe she'd get some help from one of the few cops she still knew. They might find it amusing to help Nicky play detective in her new career as head drunk in a house of drunks.

It was not a job she'd ever imagined for herself, but she was glad to have it. Her name had been passed along to Gerri from the woman who ran Nicky's rehab program. For some reason, the director thought Nicky a good candidate to run the house, maybe because of her law enforcement background.

Each woman in the house had motive and opportunity to steal the money. The office door had been unlocked an entire day, with no way to pinpoint when the theft occurred. Nicky assumed all the residents knew that money was kept in the office. They saw Nicky take charge of the collection after every meeting, saw her go into her office with it. And each one of them needed money. Even those who came from well-to-do families were now living with virtually no money of their own after being cut off. Many women had lost their jobs, their homes, their cars. They came into Olive Street in financial ruin. Three thousand dollars would look like a fortune to any one of them. But did that make them thieves? Nicky couldn't think of one who'd she peg for it. Of course, she wouldn't have guessed Denise as being a fan of *The Story of O*. You never knew what went on in a person's life. So much was hidden.

She would take all the steps necessary to conduct a thorough investigation, but she knew she was unlikely to come up with anything as damning as the computer in Lou's room. She realized she wasn't only an investigator now; she was state's attorney, judge, and jury. But she wasn't ready to bring charges against Lou. She'd put it off by calling a house meeting for five thirty that evening and then talking to each of the house residents alone. Everyone was going to be pissed off.

❖

Gerri drove to the office early Thursday for the monthly meeting with the Reardon-Malloy vice president in charge of recovery services. After she left Olive Street on Tuesday with her tote bag full of cash, she began to realize how little she'd thought the whole thing through. She'd completely forgotten Nicky Sullivan had been a police detective. A disgraced one, for sure, but probably still with more investigation skills than Gerri was comfortable with. Their phone conversation had made her uneasy. She seemed to be doing things lately as if she had no control over her own actions. This wasn't her first bit of thievery, and she blamed her financial peril for it. She felt her back against the wall.

She wasn't going to be able to do much with the money. She'd counted the bills at home, before Jeff returned from his AA meeting, and it took much longer than she thought possible. Counting the dirty, crumpled singles was simply depressing and didn't amount to much once they'd all been totted up. When she added them to the fives, tens, and twenties in the box, it was under three thousand dollars, plus another three hundred from the petty cash. What did she expect? She had robbed a halfway house, not a bank. Even so, it would get them current on the mortgage. Then it dawned on her she wouldn't be able to deposit the money. If any investigation became official, a look at her bank account would be a big arrow pointing her way.

She'd put the boxes in the rear of her closet, behind the pile of old clothes she intended to take to Goodwill but never got around to doing. The idea of going there always repelled her. When did that happen? She used to work with agencies like Goodwill early in her social work career and thought they were great. Those days seemed like a lifetime ago.

Jeff had a separate closet, so he was unlikely to stumble upon the boxes in Gerri's. They lived separate lives, and she wasn't sure when that had happened or whether she cared. She just wanted him to get a job.

Her phone rang and she picked up when she saw it was her boss. "Gerri, it's Dave."

His voice was high and tight, like something had grabbed onto a vocal chord and wouldn't let go. It was irritating as hell.

"Are we still on for the meeting today?" She sent up a prayer he was canceling it.

"Absolutely. And it's an important one. I'm making sure you're able to be there."

That didn't sound good. "Why wouldn't I be?"

"No reason. I'm calling everyone. This is a priority today—I don't want other business taking anyone away."

"Anything you can tell me now? You've got me curious."

He did his version of a chuckle, an alarming squeak that made her grip the phone tighter.

"We'll all be together in an hour. I'll fill you in then."

He hung up and Gerri stared at the phone before reaching for the envelope full of cash. She went to a currency exchange to get a money order for the bank. Handing over the wad of cash, Gerri prayed no one would see her paying her bills like a day laborer.

CHAPTER THREE

Gerri had driven home immediately after the company meeting, arriving at her small Bucktown cottage before six o'clock. She quickly changed into her pajamas, grabbed a bottle of wine and a bag of cookies, and locked herself in the guest bedroom, which was morphing into her own bedroom. She found she was sleeping there more nights of the week than not. When she told Jeff she was having trouble sleeping, she intended for him to get the message she'd continue to have trouble sleeping until he got a job, though she couldn't see it was having any effect on him. He didn't bother to knock on the guest bedroom door when he got home later that evening.

Now it was Thursday, and she woke up with a sugar hangover, as well as the dry, stale mouth that came from the half bottle of wine she'd drunk. She stared above her at the hideous popcorn ceiling, a style of the 60s, when the old house was last renovated. She and Jeff had managed to put in a new kitchen and bath after they bought the house five years ago, at the absolute height of the market. Now they couldn't afford to do the additional work they should do to get the house ready to be sold. The fact was, they couldn't even afford to sell it. It was worth far less now than what they paid for it. They were as underwater on their mortgage as she felt she was in her life. She kept kicking to the surface for air and someone's boot kept pushing her back down. She was exhausted.

The most recent shove came from her boss, Dave Edmundson, at the meeting yesterday. While all of the area directors and managers sat around the conference table trying to hide their fear, Dave presented a series of charts and graphs that would have been dead boring were they not so terrifying. Reardon-Malloy was on the verge of a crisis. Census at all of the inpatient and outpatient facilities was way down over the past six quarters, though not because there was a decrease in alcoholism and drug addiction. If anything, that was on the rise. But there were far fewer means for people to pay for treatment. Insurance coverage, which had been shrinking for years, was now questionable for even the shortest of detox hospital stays. Operating costs were steadily rising in the form of property taxes, insurance coverage, fuel, food, and, he emphasized with a look, salaries. Without serious intervention in the form of cost-cutting, the company would have no choice but to begin laying off personnel at all levels. Gerri felt her heart constrict when he uttered the words.

The first order of business was a series of internal audits of all R-M facilities. She could expect the accounts to be reviewed for each of the three outpatient programs and four halfway houses she oversaw. After the company audit was complete, the executives would determine the hierarchy of cost-cutting. As far as she knew, that had never been done in the fifteen years she'd been with the company, and it immediately presented a serious problem. How well hidden was the small but steady trickle of funds she'd been taking out of Reardon-Malloy?

After the meeting, Gerri wore a serious but confident face and thanked Dave for giving them such a generous heads-up. She spoke reassuringly to colleagues who looked like their spleens had ruptured. Once in her car, she felt acid burn its way through her stomach. She called Jeff.

"What are you up to?" she asked.

"And how are you? I'm fine, thanks for asking."

Gerri sighed. This was how Jeff tried to get to her. He appealed to some polite, compassionate, and friendly side of Gerri he continued to pretend existed. Even Gerri had said good-bye to that a long time ago.

"Okay, Jeff. How are you? Did you have a good day? Did you have time to stop and smell the roses?"

"You know I always take time for that," he said.

"What I know is while you were busy not working, I was sitting in a meeting listening to how I'm going to be laid off."

"What? Seriously?"

"Kind of puts the fear of God in you, doesn't it? Without me working we'll have…nothing. Smell that."

"Jesus. I mean, did they actually lay you off? Or was it more like a threat?"

"I think we both know in this climate, once a company starts talking layoffs, it's all but a done deal."

Jeff paused. "It doesn't necessarily mean you'll be laid off. You're high up the chain, right?"

"I'm a forty-five-year-old middle manager, which is what you are. Or were. I'll be the first to go."

"It hasn't happened yet. Let's not assume it will. That's negative thinking inviting a negative outcome."

"Oh, please. I really can't stomach your platitudes right now."

Gerri was pulling into the alley behind their house. She pressed the garage door opener and saw Jeff's car was gone.

"Where are you?" she asked.

"Downtown. I told you last night. I have an interview at six."

Gerri turned her car off and closed the garage door behind her while she sat in the front seat.

"Get that fucking job, Jeff. You shouldn't even come home if you don't get that fucking job."

She cut him off and tossed the phone in her purse. She momentarily contemplated turning the engine back on and letting the carbon monoxide do its thing, but she wasn't quite ready to commit violence on herself. The idea had a future, though.

She went into the kitchen, grabbed the half bottle of wine and half bag of cookies left over from the previous night, and retired to the guest room. An hour later Jeff came home and started banging pots and pans around as he cooked dinner. She returned to the kitchen.

"How'd the interview go?" she said, heading for the refrigerator.

He turned to her and leaned back against the counter, crossing his arms across his chest.

"It went very well." He looked pleased.

"Did you get the job?"

"Gerri, you know it doesn't work like that. I'll have to go back for I don't know how many interviews before they make a decision."

She stood in front of the window looking over the backyard. It was postage-stamp-sized, and Jeff had stuffed it with flower beds and containers. She had no idea what any of the plants were called. He made a tentative move toward her, standing behind her and putting his hands gently on her shoulders.

"We'll be okay," he said. "You have to stay positive."

"You're dreaming, Jeff. We're not going to be okay."

❖

Angela sat in the chair on the other side of Nicky's desk and glared at her.

"Angela, I'm not accusing you of anything. I'm talking to everyone in the house about this," Nicky said.

"Asking for my whereabouts for the past twenty-four hours is the same as accusing me."

Nicky wanted to scream. She knew of no group of people more sensitive than the newly sober alcoholic. It was making the interview process not only tedious, but unproductive as well.

"You know how on TV the detectives always talk to everyone who was around the scene of the crime? That's all this is. It's routine."

"You don't have to patronize me." She sat with her chin up, as if daring Nicky to arrest her. Her chin was long and sharpened to a point. She wore a pink St. Mary's T-Shirt over leggings and poofy slippers.

"Just tell me about Tuesday afternoon. Gerri Thomas was here to give you the grocery money, correct?"

"That was all there was to it. She knocked on my door and handed me the money and then she was gone."

"She didn't say anything?"

"She told me to spend the money wisely and left. She's not real friendly."

Nicky smiled. "That's true. And you said that was about two in the afternoon?"

"Yeah."

"Okay, Angela. You can go."

She hesitated a moment. "As the most senior girl here at Olive Street House, I'm speaking for all of us to formally protest the searches through our personal belongings. You had no right to do that."

"Actually, I did. It's in the paperwork you signed when you moved in here." Nicky remained impassive.

"It undermines the sense of trust we're trying to build," Angela said. "Particularly with those of us who never do anything wrong, like Denise and me. It's just not right."

"Duly noted."

Angela got up to leave.

"You've been living here over a year now," Nicky said. "Have you thought at all about when you'll be ready to leave? Maybe it's time you were more in control of your life."

Nicky couldn't miss the alarm in Angela's eyes. "You're not going to kick me out, are you?"

"No, I'm not. But you can't stay here forever. Maybe it's something you should start thinking about."

"Duly noted," she said, the sarcasm clear, closing the door a little too forcefully behind her.

That left the interview with Lou, the one Nicky most dreaded. It would be far more painful than the ones with Diane and Susan, who refused to talk about anything but how Gerri had switched their rooms around. Nicky finally allowed them to move back in with each other, just to shut them up. She sternly suggested they learn how to eliminate any noise that might be heard by others, or she'd have no choice but to break them apart permanently.

Lou would be getting home from her shift at Starbucks in the next few minutes, and they were scheduled to talk. She hadn't reacted in any particular way when Nicky requested the appointment, not compared to most of the other women. If she was scared, Nicky didn't think she'd be able to hide it. Lou knew the laptop had to have been discovered and that also scored points for her. If she were guilty of stealing the cash and then using it to buy the computer, wouldn't she have hidden the computer elsewhere or accounted for it in some way? The fact she hadn't sought Nicky out to explain why she had a brand-new, expensive laptop told her Lou didn't think it needed to be explained away. Either that, or Lou was much cagier than she was giving her credit for.

Nicky made more coffee and returned to her office with a fresh cup. She saw Lou come in through the front door.

"I'm here whenever you're ready, Lou. Take your time."

"Let's do it now," she said. Nicky watched as Lou walked toward her and thought how the simple Starbucks uniform suited her well. Nicky could see with a little more hair on her head, Lou would be good-looking. She had presence—a stillness that spoke of confidence, even though she probably had little of that in her new recovery. She was an unquestionably butch, attractive woman. The world could always use more of those.

Lou carefully placed her backpack on the floor and took the guest chair in the office.

"Coffee?" Nicky asked.

"God, no. I just did four hours at Starbucks."

Nicky sat at her desk and leaned back in her chair. "Lou, you know we're here to talk about the theft discovered yesterday."

"Obviously."

"And you know after I discovered the theft, I did a search of everyone's rooms."

"Yeah, I know. It kind of sucks, but I understand."

"What I'm wondering is how you can explain the brand-new laptop I found hiding under your bed."

Lou's head tilted to one side, as if she'd heard a funny noise. "What do you mean 'explain' it? It's a laptop."

Now Nicky leaned forward, resting her arms on her desk. "The receipt in the box shows it was bought Tuesday evening."

Lou looked perplexed. "You think I stole that money?"

"I don't think anything. I'm asking questions."

Nicky saw the first flash of anger in Lou's eyes. "Man, I am not a thief. I've done some shit, but I've never stolen. That's not me."

"Tell me where the laptop came from. Maybe we can clear this up."

Lou crossed her arms and leaned back. The anger was clearly there, and so was fear. Nicky felt like she was clubbing a baby seal.

"It was a gift from my brother," she finally said. "He gave it to me Tuesday night. Surprised the hell out of me."

"Where'd he give it to you?"

"Out back, in the alley. He called me after dinner Tuesday and said he had something for me and I should meet him in back. I was worried he was going to ask me to hold something for him. But he gave me a laptop."

"You're telling me that on Tuesday, the day the theft most likely occurred here, your brother suddenly called you and came by to give you a laptop, out of the blue. That he paid cash for."

"He pays cash for everything," Lou said, as if that explained it.

Nicky frowned. "You better walk me through this. Start with what you were doing on Tuesday."

Lou looked at her smartphone, a purchase from a more prosperous time.

"I worked the early shift at Starbucks on Tuesday. Six 'til noon and then I came back here."

"For the rest of the day? Didn't you go out again?"

"It's not like there's much else I can do. I don't have any money. Would you rather I'd been sitting in a bar?" She didn't seem aware she was denying herself an alibi.

"Did you talk to anyone else while you were here all afternoon?"

"I saw Angela when I went into the kitchen for something to eat. That was it."

"Did you and Angela talk at all?"

"We said hello."

Nicky already knew Angela had been in the house. She would have been interested had Lou mentioned seeing anyone else. All the other residents claimed they were away all afternoon.

"Now tell me about your brother," Nicky said.

Lou reached down and picked up her backpack, slinging it over her shoulder as she stood. "I don't have to tell you shit. I didn't steal the fucking money."

Nicky stood and took a step toward the door, as if to block Lou if she tried to leave.

"Are you keeping me here against my will?" Lou asked. They stood within inches of each other. Lou was nearly as tall as Nicky and a lot stockier.

"Don't walk out, Lou. That's going to make things look bad." She stepped back until she could feel a wall behind her, clearing herself out of Lou's personal space. "I haven't accused you of anything and I don't want to. But you have to help me out here."

Lou hesitated before she dropped her bag where she stood and sat down again. She waited patiently for Nicky to get settled.

"You said you were surprised to hear from your brother. Why is that?"

"I haven't seen my brother much during the last few years. He just turns up once in a while and I never know when it's going to be."

"Is your brother involved in drugs? Is that why you said he might ask you to hold something for him?"

Lou squirmed in her chair.

"Lou, I'm not interested in turning your brother in. I'm trying to figure out what kind of guy stops by and gives his sister a two-thousand-dollar computer on the spur of the moment."

"Jack is that kind of guy."

"Maybe I should call him."

"You can't call him! There's no way you can call him. He'd kill me if I gave out his number or had anyone call him."

Lou was agitated, her hands gripping the edge of the desk.

"Is your brother some kind of major player? Are you afraid of him?"

"No, I'm not afraid of him. I know what his rules are, and I won't break them. I can't."

"Can you get him to call me?"

Lou hesitated. "I guess. I'm not sure he will."

Nicky jotted her cell number down and pushed it toward Lou.

"See if you can convince him to talk to me. It's important."

Lou took the number and stood to leave. "I know this probably doesn't look good, but you have to believe me I didn't steal that money. I like it here. And I have nowhere to go if you kick me out."

Nicky looked at her and nodded, staring at the door after Lou closed it behind her. She did believe her. Lou didn't feel right for a burglary, and like most cops, she trusted her intuition. She wished like hell Lou had a better cover story.

❖

Nicky closed her office door, hoping none of the residents would come harangue her any further. She was exhausted. Her job was on the line if she didn't find the thief. She'd no doubt Gerri would blame her for the debacle, and with no money saved, that was a dire threat. Her parents lived in town, but she couldn't crash with them. At forty, it was too humiliating. She'd be right back where she was the day she got sober, which was dirt poor.

A gentle knock on the door startled her.

"Nicky? It's Sheila."

Nicky barely suppressed a groan. She'd texted Sheila earlier to cancel their dinner date and now here she was. She got up from her desk and opened the door. Sheila held up a bag from Potbelly.

"Thought I'd bring you a sandwich since we had to miss dinner," Sheila said.

"Huh." Nicky opened the door wider. "Thanks. I guess I was getting a little hungry."

She motioned Sheila toward the guest chair and went into the kitchen to grab plates and a couple of sodas. Sheila was spreading the food over the desktop when she returned.

"If you're not in the mood for company, say so," Sheila said. "I can take my sandwich and get out of your way."

"You're not in my way," Nicky said. She smiled at Sheila. It was a closed-mouth smile, not the fifty-watt smile she trotted out on occasion. "I appreciate the thought, but I'm lousy company tonight."

"Do you want to talk about it?"

"Not even a little bit."

"I'm worried about you."

Nicky grimaced. "You're right. I guess I'm pushing you away."

"Gee, thanks. How's your investigation going?"

Nicky put her sandwich down and grabbed some chips, debating what to say.

"The short answer is it's a mess. I don't have anything conclusive that says anyone did it, and I don't have anything that eliminates a single resident as a possibility. Any of the women could have grabbed it in that time period."

"Do you have something less than conclusive that says someone in particular may have done it?"

Nicky looked at her. "Are you sure you're a librarian and not a lawyer? That was pretty sharp."

Sheila smiled brightly. "The words 'anything conclusive' leaped out at me."

"I don't know how much I can tell you," Nicky said. "Honestly, I don't know if there's any standard of confidentiality I'm supposed to adhere to in a situation like this. It's new to me."

"Nicky, I'm not going to plead with you to tell me what's happened. If you feel like sorting it out with me, then go ahead. You know it won't go beyond here."

"I know. But there's nothing much to tell you. The investigation is ongoing, as they say." She sensed she'd disappointed Sheila.

"Do you want to hang around for a while?" Nicky asked. "The Bears game starts in a little bit. Thursday Night Football. I'm sure it's on in the back."

"Do you have to stay here this evening? I'm not much for football, but we could go over to the bookstore. There's a reading there at seven thirty."

"I'm not much for readings. Besides, I need to stay here for a while, at least until curfew. I thought I'd go over to Deb's after that." She hadn't called Deb yet, but hoped she'd be open to another night together.

"Deb's?"

"Yeah. Deb Alvarez. We've seen each other a few times. Didn't I tell you?"

"No, you hadn't mentioned it. That's big news, coming from you."

"Why?"

"Because you haven't had a real relationship since you've gotten sober. I know you told me that much."

"True, but I can't live like a nun forever. Hell, nuns probably have had more sex than I've had in the last five years."

"You're having sex with her?"

Nicky cocked her head. "I'm not going to her place at eleven at night to play Yahtzee. What's the matter? Did you think I didn't have it in me?"

Sheila started folding up her sandwich wrapping, her meal half eaten. "Oh, I'm sure you know what you're doing, Nicky. But be careful."

"Why? Is there something about Deb I should know?"

"All I know about Deb is she's young, beautiful, and works at some high-paying job downtown. I've seen her power suits at meetings. She's a catch. But I tell everyone to be careful about getting into a relationship."

"That's because you're still getting over Nora." Nicky had heard plenty about that break-up. Sheila had fallen in love with a middle-aged Lotharia who cheated on her regularly. She'd finally ended it a year ago which seemed to not matter at all to her lover but for Sheila was devastating. "You'll be fine, Sheila. You're too good a person to not have women lining up for you."

Sheila got up and stuffed garbage into the bag. "I guess I'll head over to the bookstore, if you're sure you won't come."

"Not tonight. I bet a reading is a great place to meet women."

"Right. The lesbian equivalent of a bath house."

Nicky walked Sheila to the door and stepped onto the porch with her. "Thanks for coming by. It means a lot you checked up on me." When she settled back in her office, the phone rang. Deb. She must have read her mind.

"How are you, Deb?"

"Excited. I have some fun things for us to do this weekend and I wanted to go over them with you."

Nicky's desire for distraction drained away. She felt like someone was pulling on her collar from behind. "I'm sorry. Had we made plans for the weekend?"

"We didn't make plans exactly. But why wouldn't we spend some time together?"

"I have a crisis in the house. I can't make plans."

Deb was silent for a moment. "You can't or you don't want to?"

"I don't want to because of the crisis. I'm a little concerned you'd presume we'd be spending the weekend together."

"If you don't want to be with me, say so."

Nicky pulled the phone from her ear and stared at it as if it would help her understand what Deb was saying. Did having sex one night automatically make you a couple? It was old-school lesbian to think so, something she didn't expect from Deb.

"I'm afraid I can't make plans right now. I didn't know you'd expect that."

Deb hung up on her before she could explain further. What the hell? Nicky knew she had poor relationship skills, but this hadn't yet become a relationship. She couldn't help but think she'd dodged a bullet on an already shitty day.

She went up to her room, grabbing a Diet Coke on her way. The room depressed her in its sparseness and shabbiness, but it was her refuge and she closed the door with relief. Lying on the bed propped up against the headboard, she wondered what to do with herself—stare mindlessly at her phone? Read her book? Call a friend? Nothing sounded appealing so she stared at the window and tried to loosen her tight grip on the investigation, knowing there was so little she could control. All she could do was be as fair as possible.

CHAPTER FOUR

Gerri escaped into her office after being pinned down by other Reardon-Malloy employees frantic about their jobs. The usual Friday morning chitchat about what everyone was watching on Netflix had been replaced with the most dire predictions from staff at every level. They were solely focused on losing their jobs, while Gerri had that and more to worry about. Everything that had been slowly changing for the worse seemed to now be in freefall.

When she'd been promoted to regional director six years ago, she still loved what she did. She'd been in the recovery field for over fifteen years, working first as a counselor in treatment programs, and then, once she joined Reardon-Malloy, slowly being promoted through the administrative ranks. She cared for her patients, listened to their stories with great empathy, even puzzled over how best to help them when she wasn't on the job.

She'd met Jeff when he was in a hospital inpatient program and she was one of the counselors. Their attraction was immediate, but Gerri had been conscientious then. She didn't speak of it to Jeff or anyone else until he'd been out of the program and still sober for a year. Then she tracked him down and they were married within six months.

Many of their years together were good, even very good. Jeff had lots of friends from AA, and they spent the majority of their social time with them. The fact that Gerri could not attend their meetings didn't bother her. She'd meet the gang afterward for dinner. She was content with her career, their friends, and a faithful husband who made a good living as some sort of manager in the logistics industry. She didn't have a clear idea of what it was he did, but she didn't care either.

She couldn't say exactly when things started to change. She could point to when Jeff lost his job as the time when the pressure started to mount. But that came long after she started to find Jeff's friends tedious, their constant laughter and kindness and gratitude irritating beyond belief. She pulled away from them. Alcoholics became for her the commodity her company dealt in and the people her husband preferred over her. She grew to loathe them.

After Jeff lost his job, Gerri put into place a system at Olive Street House she hoped to expand to her other halfway houses. She fired the company that did all the landscaping and snow removal work and told Nicky she would have to assign residents to the tasks. She substituted a dummy company into her budget, making it look like she'd hired a new landscaper at a lower rate. The checks cut by Reardon-Malloy to pay the bogus landscaping company went into a bank account controlled by Gerri. The money didn't amount to much, certainly not anything Reardon couldn't afford, and she added a little to that by continuing to skim the monthly petty cash she distributed to the houses. It wasn't much, but it was free, and it made a big difference with Jeff out of work.

She thought it was a clever plan, but when word of the internal audits came, she wondered if it was clever enough. A hint of panic started in her gut and she quickly shut it down. She couldn't afford to panic.

She also had to worry about the theft at Olive Street House drawing some attention from the auditors, since about three hundred dollars in petty cash was taken. She didn't need them looking too closely at the houses' finances. It was best they didn't know about the Olive Street theft, since company policy required the police be called in such cases.

Gerri closed the door to her office and picked up her phone. It was time to call Nicky Sullivan and find out how her investigation was going.

❖

Nicky was in line in the Andersonville Starbucks when Gerri called. Lou was working at the counter, and she didn't look particularly happy Nicky was there. She took her phone outside and sat on a bench in front.

"I'm calling for a report on your investigation," Gerri said. "You've had a couple days."

Gerri had a way of making Nicky feel she'd somehow come up short on everything that was asked of her.

"I'm afraid I don't have anything to tell you. None of the women in the house admitted to anything, and I conducted a thorough search of each bedroom."

"That's all you did?" There was no mistaking the tone. Gerri thought she was pitiful.

"No. I also held a house meeting and interviewed each resident individually. Short of dusting the room for fingerprints, I did everything the police were likely to do."

Gerri paused. "It has to be someone in the house. You've failed to find the evidence."

"Who's to say it wasn't someone from outside the house?" Nicky countered. "You say it's possible you left the office door unlocked. Isn't it also possible you left the front door unlocked? It doesn't lock on its own, and you may have forgotten that."

"Trying to shift the blame to me is not winning you any points, Nicky."

"I wasn't aware there were points at stake here. I'm simply looking at all the possibilities, as any investigator would."

"Or you may be trying to redirect attention. There's nothing to say you didn't take the money."

Suddenly, the bench Nicky was sitting on felt like the San Andreas Fault, shifting noticeably below her.

"Think about it," Gerri continued, as if warming to the idea. "If the three things you cops look for are motive, means, and opportunity, you, more than anyone, had the means and opportunity. The motive is money, something all of you are desperate for. I know what we pay you, Nicky, so don't bother denying it."

Nicky felt her vision blurring. The only thing she could see clearly was Gerri intended to pin the theft on her and fire her from Olive Street House.

"You can't be serious," Nicky said.

"I'm very serious. Unless you can give me reason to think otherwise, I'm holding you responsible for the theft, knowing you either did it yourself or were responsible for preventing it on your watch."

"But I was out of town. It wasn't on my watch." This couldn't be happening.

"You could easily have taken the money," Gerri said.

"This is wrong. You can't blame this on me." Nicky knew she sounded more desperate than confident.

"I don't see why not," Gerri said, "I'm going to have to consider terminating you, Nicky. And don't expect there to be good references from Reardon-Molloy."

The door to Starbucks opened up behind her and Lou walked out, her backpack slung over her shoulder and her cap pulled down low. She headed in the direction of Olive Street House. Nicky squeezed her eyes shut before speaking again. She needed her job and knew Gerri wasn't bluffing.

"There's something I haven't told you about the investigation." She felt ill.

"Interesting," Gerri said. "Let's have it."

"I did find a recently purchased laptop in a resident's room. It looks like it was purchased within a day of when we think the theft happened."

"You saw a receipt?"

"Yes."

"I'm trying to understand why you didn't tell me this earlier. You've been wasting my time," Gerri said.

"I didn't tell you because I don't believe this resident would have stolen the money."

"I'm sure you want to believe all your girls are angels. But we know they're not."

Nicky didn't respond. All she could think about was losing her job and not being able to find another one. She felt feral, concentrated on survival only. Memories of being homeless and without a cent were still fresh, even after five years of sobriety. She'd been evicted from her apartment her last year of drinking and slept in her car when she wasn't waking up in a stranger's bed. None of her friends wanted anything to do with her and she wouldn't go home to her mother. She was too ashamed of what her life had become. Desperation drove her to asking for handouts at an intersection far from her usual stomping grounds. The humiliation of holding a paper cup out as she walked along lines of cars stopped at a light was crippling. Now Gerri was threatening to throw her back over the thin line between employment and poverty. It chilled her to her toes.

"Who is the resident?" Gerri asked.

"Lou Hansen." It was out of her mouth before she could stop it.

"Did Lou have an explanation for how she came to have a brand-new laptop? Isn't she the girl whose parents are paying her rehab costs but have cut off all contact?" Gerri said that as if it were something unusual. It was not.

"She said her brother bought if for her and dropped it by the house Tuesday evening."

"Did the receipt have his name on it?"

"It was a cash purchase."

"Jesus, Nicky. Why would you think she didn't use the stolen money to buy the laptop? It seems cut-and-dry to me. No wonder they got rid of you at the police department."

Nicky had never liked Gerri, or thought she was a particularly good administrator, but she'd never seen her as cutting as this. She was taking little bits out of Nicky now, but she was about to slice Lou right open. Nicky felt like she was handing her over on a cutting board.

"I don't feel it's enough evidence to take any action against Lou. It's all circumstantial. Even the police have to follow certain minimum standards."

Gerri laughed. "They might, but I don't. This is a halfway house, Nicky. It's not the real world. These women are lucky to have a place to stay while they get their acts together, and they only retain that privilege if they're beyond reproach. I don't feel Lou can be trusted and I want her out of the house. By tonight."

"Please don't do this. Lou will be devastated." Nicky desperately tried to come up with an idea of how to stop this train wreck and keep her job at the same time. "What if I get a statement from Lou's brother that he bought the laptop? Or from the Apple clerk that sold it to him."

"How does that help? Lou probably gave him the cash to make the purchase," Gerri said.

"You have to reconsider this. Please."

"Get Lou out by tonight. I'll have someone new over there within a day or two. There are plenty of women who need our help."

Gerri hung up. Nicky stared stupidly at the ground, as if she'd been given a strong narcotic and wasn't quite sure what was going on. She slowly raised her head and looked across the street at the restaurant on the corner, Lady Gregory's. She could see the pub side through the windows—the long mahogany bar, the bottles and glasses sparkling behind it. They sold a hundred different whiskeys, and Nicky figured she could make it through half of those by midnight if she got a start now. To one side of the bar was an area fitted out to look like a library. There were easy chairs, a fireplace, books along the walls. She would pay almost anything to be able to sit there now, chatting up whoever else was drinking in the middle of the afternoon. She would pretend she was someone else entirely. She used to do that whenever she happened to be drinking where no one knew her, like an airport bar. She would become a lawyer, a pilot, an intelligence analyst, a race car driver. She was anyone but Nicky Sullivan, the last person she wanted to be.

She got up from the curb and started walking toward Olive Street House, wondering how she was going to tell Lou she'd been kicked out. It wouldn't be any easier for either of them if she kept putting it off. As she walked up the stairs to Lou's room, she tried to be the automaton she'd been when she was drinking, when real emotions seldom reared their ugly heads.

She knocked on the door.

"Come in."

Nicky opened the door and saw Lou propped up on her bed, closing the lid of her laptop. Her face was still, but her eyes were intently on Nicky's, as if searching for a clue. Nicky sat on Zoey's bed on the other side of the small room.

"Lou, I have some bad news."

Lou closed her eyes.

"Based on the facts I presented to my boss, she has made the determination you be removed from the house." Nicky realized that sounded like Lou was going to be taken out in handcuffs. How much worse could she make this?

Lou didn't respond beyond opening her eyes again and looking straight at Nicky.

"If this were my decision, I'd have you stay. I don't think you took the money," Nicky said. "Unfortunately, I have to follow orders."

Lou took a deep breath. Nicky thought she looked like a kid trying to be brave, trying not to cry. She'd expected anger, some screaming, maybe something thrown against the wall. The laptop, perhaps, or Nicky herself.

"I'll be out within the hour," Lou said. Her voice was surprisingly strong.

"Let me see what I can do for you. I can probably find you a place in another house."

"No, thank you."

Nicky didn't imagine that sounded like a good offer at the moment.

"Do you have any money? I can give you a little."

"According to you, I should have about a thousand dollars," Lou said. Nicky could hear the anger coming, somehow channeled into sarcasm.

"I told you, Lou. I don't think you did this. My boss couldn't see around that fucking laptop suddenly appearing."

Lou swung her legs off the bed and got up. She opened the door and stood next to it, her hand on the knob, ready to shut it after Nicky.

"If you'll excuse me," she said. "I have some packing to do."

Nicky got up and joined her at the door. "Will you at least let me know where you're going?"

Lou looked at her with eyes like stone. "No."

This was much harder to deal with than histrionics would be. All Nicky could feel was Lou's disappointment in her. Not in Gerri or Olive Street House, but in Nicky.

"You should talk to your sponsor," Nicky said. "It's important you do that."

"Yes, everything you've suggested has worked out so well."

She swept her hand toward the hallway, trying to shoo Nicky out. Nicky walked through and turned, the door already halfway closed.

"Stay in touch, Lou. You know how to reach us."

The door shut in her face. Nicky stood silently in the hallway. Within a minute she heard Lou trying to stifle sobs. She returned to her own bedroom and started crying herself. She felt like a monster trampling on the little people below. It made her ill to think how much Lou must hate her. Once again she was responsible for ruining a person's life without any consequence to her own outside the persistent belief she was a terrible person. It felt like she'd murdered someone.

CHAPTER FIVE

Nicky locked the door to her room and threw herself onto the twin bed. A dull throb took up residence in her head, but she was unable to rouse herself enough to get aspirin. Thoughts of dumping Lou onto the streets coursed through her like a rush of adrenaline.

There was a soft tap at her door.

"Who is it?" Nicky didn't keep the annoyance out of her voice.

"Sheila."

There was a pause before Nicky opened her door. The last thing she wanted was a supportive friend. She deserved to be condemned, not soothed. Sheila was a great one for soothing.

"Were you sleeping?" Sheila asked.

"No." She looked at Sheila for a moment. "What do you want?"

Sheila looked past Nicky's shoulder into the tiny bedroom. There was the twin bed along the same wall as the door, a small dresser along the opposite wall, and a broken-down reading chair next to it. The open closet door showed the suits she wore as a detective, clothes no one in her present life had seen her wear. On the nightstand by her bed was a tottering pile of books with titles from Sarah Waters, Emma Donoghue, and Carol Anshaw, contemporary lesbian authors who didn't write enough books as far as Nicky was concerned. Not that she had much time to read with affairs of the house running on a twenty-four-hour cycle.

"Can I come in? I want to ask you about something."

Nicky was still annoyed, but she opened the door further and let Sheila in, pointing her to the reading chair. She sat on the bed facing her.

"What's this about?"

"Lou didn't show up for our sponsorship meeting. I talked to Zoey downstairs and she said all of her things are gone. What's happened?"

"She got kicked out of the house tonight. Or I should say, I kicked her out."

"Why? Is she the one who took the treasury money?"

"I fucked up. I ended up telling my boss about something I found in Lou's room, and she took it as evidence Lou was the thief. It's my fault." Nicky told her the whole story.

"You make it sound like you finding the laptop was the problem, not that the laptop was there. Suspiciously so," Sheila said.

"She had an explanation and I believed her. Then I sold her out."

"It's a ridiculous coincidence Lou's mystery brother would have dropped off a brand-new laptop on that of all days. It's not your fault your boss made the decision she did."

Nicky stood up. If there had been room to pace, she would have. Instead, she leaned over and braced her arms on her legs, as if she were in a football huddle, as if she was trying to keep from throwing up.

"I told Gerri about the laptop when she threatened my job."

Sheila got up and put a gentle hand on Nicky's shoulder. "Would any of us have done any differently? I doubt I would have."

"I know you would have. You wouldn't have betrayed her." Nicky was sure of that. Sheila wasn't the wimp she was.

"Look, Nicky, you're too close to this now to get any perspective on it. Let me convince you later you're not the piece of shit you seem to think you are. Right now we should concentrate on Lou."

Nicky straightened and looked at Sheila. "You're right. I'm making this all about me. Again."

"Do you have any idea where she might have gone?" Sheila asked.

"None at all. She wouldn't say a word, and she wouldn't let me help her get into another house. I don't know where to start."

"You're the detective here. You're going to have to do a little better than that."

"I'm not a fucking detective," Nicky said.

"Well, you're more of one than I am. Lou can be in real trouble out there."

Nicky felt a surge of energy. "You're right. We must find her," she said.

She led the way downstairs and pulled Lou's file out of a cabinet in her office.

"She must have an emergency contact in there," Sheila said.

"That's what I'm looking for." She ran her finger down the intake form. "It's her parents. Looks like they live downtown."

"Where exactly?"

Nicky gave her the address on Dearborn Street.

"They must have lots of money to live there," Sheila said. "Are you going to call?"

Nicky was still skimming the file. "No, let's drive down there. It's always better to see people face to face. They talk more."

"That's the experience we need," Sheila said.

Nicky jotted down the address. "Do you have a car?"

"It's a piece of shit, but I do have a car. It's out front."

Nicky led the way out of the house, and when Sheila offered her the car keys, she took them. As soon as she started driving the old Sentra, the car began to howl in protest. She looked at Sheila.

"She's terminal," Sheila said. "But I'm told she has a bit of time left. We should make it downtown okay."

"It sounds like someone's screaming." Nicky started to relax a bit as she drove toward Lake Shore Drive. "Thanks for coming with," she said. "I appreciate it."

"I sponsor Lou. I want to know she's safe."

"So do I."

❖

Nicky turned north on Dearborn from Division and they prowled up the street looking for the right address. It was as dark as anywhere in the city could be. There were too many streetlights, too much glow from all the buildings for it ever to be truly dark. They rolled past turn-of-the-century rowhouses and mid-century high-rises until they found the house on the corner of Dearborn and Goethe. It was lit up on every floor.

"Looks like they're home," Sheila said.

Nicky parked in the closest tow zone, knowing it was hopeless to find anything legal. When they opened the gate to the house she could see there was a party going on. Well-dressed people were milling around behind the big front window on the first floor. Nicky rang the doorbell, and a bristly middle-aged woman answered the door. She wore a brown cotton shift dress and a dour expression.

"Mrs. Hansen?" Nicky asked.

The woman frowned. "I am the Hansen's housekeeper. May I help you?"

"We need to speak with Mr. and Mrs. Hansen, please."

"As you can see, this isn't a convenient time. Perhaps you could phone them tomorrow?"

Nicky could see she was a formidable gatekeeper.

"This is urgent," Nicky said. "It concerns their daughter."

The housekeeper's expression did not change. "Has there been an accident?"

"Please tell them we need to speak with them."

The housekeeper closed the door without a word.

"Is that her way of dismissing us?" Sheila asked.

"They'll come out," Nicky said. "But I guarantee they won't let us in."

After several minutes, the door opened again to a large man with graying blond hair and ruddy cheeks. He was barrel-chested with stumpy legs and when he stepped onto the door stoop and closed the door behind him, Sheila and Nicky moved back a few steps.

"Who are you?" he said, without any attempt to be polite. He wasn't entirely steady on his feet.

"Mr. Hansen, my name is Nicky Sullivan. I'm the resident manager of the house where your daughter Lou has been living."

"And?"

He was impatient, as if he were talking to an incompetent employee.

"She's left the house and we're concerned about her. I wanted to know if she's here."

"What do you mean she left the house? We paid for the place through the end of the year."

Nicky could feel Sheila tense beside her and she hoped she wouldn't say anything to him.

"I take it she hasn't come home?" Nicky said.

"This hasn't been her home for a long time. I have no idea where she is."

He turned as the door opened. Nicky assumed it was Lou's mother standing there, a glass of wine in one hand. She was reed thin and wore a clinging silk dress, tottering a bit in three-inch heels.

"Eric, what's going on?" She didn't look at Nicky and Sheila.

"It's Lou again," he said. "These people tell me she's left the house we put her in."

Nicky held herself in check. She'd had years of interviewing people she'd just as soon punch in the nose.

"We can't deal with this now," Mrs. Hansen said. She looked back to the house, clearly anxious to get back inside.

"We can't deal with this at all," Mr. Hansen said. "Lou knows quite well this was it, our last contribution to saving her ass. We're done."

"I'm not here asking you for money or anything else for Lou. We'd like to find her to make sure she's okay. Do you have any idea where she may have gone?"

"None whatsoever," Mrs. Hansen said. "She's a complete mystery to us. Always has been."

Nicky took a notebook and pen out of her pocket. "Can you at least give us the names of her friends?"

"Her friends? You have to understand Lou hasn't lived with us since she left for college. I have no idea who her friends are. I can only imagine what they're like." Mrs. Hansen drank some wine.

"How about any college friends?" Sheila asked. "Maybe she kept in touch with some of them."

Mrs. Hansen was becoming exasperated. "I'm sure she hasn't. The only two I remember are Ariel Hastings and Georgia Emmer. We know their parents. Now if you'll excuse us we must get back to our guests."

Nicky wrote the names down as she spoke. "One more question. Can you give me your son's contact information. It's possible Lou has gone to him."

She saw Mr. Hansen look at her sharply. "How do you know about my son?"

"People at Olive Street House aren't in lockdown, Mr. Hansen, we talk to each other. Is it surprising Lou would mention she has a brother?"

Mrs. Hansen opened the door and went back into the house, closing it sharply behind her.

"I have no contact information for Jack. Your guess is as good as mine where he is." He turned abruptly and followed his wife into the house.

They stood staring at the door for a few moments.

"Holy shit," Sheila said.

"Apparently, the Hansen children have been a bit of a disappointment to them." Nicky started down the steps.

"What do we do now?" Sheila asked.

"I think we call it a night and regroup tomorrow. We can try to track down these college friends, though I'm not optimistic that will turn up any leads. And I'll call the inpatient program tomorrow and see if I can get any insight from Lou's counselor."

Sheila took the wheel and drove north to Olive Street House. "Will you call me tomorrow? I want to be in this with you."

"Sure. I'll call."

"You know what you're doing, Nicky. You'll find her."

Nicky doubted that was true. "Do you think she's drinking?"

Sheila paused. "I'm worried she doesn't have any money, anyplace to go, and she'll end up somewhere where it's going to be easy for her to relapse."

Sheila dropped Nicky at the house. It was still early on a Friday night. She couldn't stand the idea of being cooped up inside, so she walked along the side of the house to the garage in back and got into her car. It was in worse shape than Sheila's, a junker she'd barely been able to afford when she got her first crap job after she got sober. Somehow it had hung together for five years, but it was an embarrassment. She would never pick up a date in it. She didn't even want Sheila to see it, though she was letting Sheila see a lot.

She headed out to the first gay bar she could think of that Lou might have gone to. As part of her recovery Nicky had stayed away from bars as if they were plague-infested, but now she parked in front of the bar in Andersonville that trended lesbian and queer, hoping to find Lou, or at least some hint as to where she might be.

Donna's was huge by lesbian bar standards, with three large rooms and an outdoor patio. Nicky had spent a fair amount of time there when she wasn't in a cop bar, usually when she thought it would be a good idea to hook up with someone. She'd treated the bar not so much as a drinking establishment but rather as a sort of 7-Eleven for sex, a place to stop on the way home to pick up what she needed. She usually succeeded. She found if she went there late enough, most of the women were too drunk to notice how wasted she was and her odds went up accordingly.

The main room of the place featured a charmless bar that looked to be constructed of plywood and Formica. She imagined the tool-belted crew of lesbians building the bar in exchange for beer. All the spindly stools were occupied. Nicky stood awkwardly, trying to decide where to settle.

Two women pulled away from the bar and headed toward the dance music in the back room. Nicky slipped into a spot and instantly felt at home as the heels of her boots clicked into place on the lower rung of the stool and she leaned forward with her elbows on the bar. It was a single, fluid movement that gave her a sense of comfort, as if a muscle memory was exercised. Straight ahead were bottles arranged along the back wall, the top shelf stuff she never drank. A bartender appeared in front of her and grabbed a bottle of vodka from the well, the sound of glass clanging against the metal bringing an ocean of memory over her. She fully expected a shot to appear in front of her, next to a bottle of Pabst.

The bartender was new since Nicky had last been there. Donna must have been taking the night off.

"What'll you have?" she asked.

"Coffee," Nicky said.

She wasn't surprised to get a cup of undrinkable sludge, worse than anything she'd had at the station house. But it served its purpose of not looking like any of the drinks around her, to prevent her accidentally picking up the wrong glass. It's not that she wanted a drink, but she didn't entirely trust herself to not find one magically in her hand.

She took her time to look around the room. There was no one she recognized, and she wondered if a whole generation of patrons had come and gone from the place. A woman about Nicky's age sat on the empty stool next to her. She looked familiar to Nicky, but there was no memory attached. She had short dark hair, an athletic body, and a face that was handsome but pockmarked. She ordered a beer and waited for it before turning to Nicky. She looked at her for a moment.

"Do I know you?" she said.

"You might. You look familiar to me," Nicky said.

"Me too," she said. "But I haven't a clue where we met."

They were silent for a bit, Nicky staring at her mug of coffee, the other woman downing her beer.

"I'm Colleen," she said.

"Nicky."

"Were you ever on the softball team?" Colleen was sitting sideways on her stool, studying Nicky.

"Never."

"Dykes on Bikes?"

Nicky grinned. "No."

Colleen finished her drink and ordered another before turning back to Nicky.

"Did we sleep together?"

Nicky didn't know if they had, but it seemed the most likely way they knew each other, and it wouldn't surprise her at all.

"I'm sure if we did, I'd remember it."

Colleen shrugged. "I don't know. No offense, of course. But I'm not so young anymore, and there've been a lot of girls."

Nicky guessed there'd been a lot of booze, too, but no sense mentioning that. The thought of sleeping with her drifted through her mind. Colleen ordered a shot and offered Nicky one.

"No, thanks. I'm good."

She nodded at Nicky's coffee cup. "Not drinking tonight?"

How easy it would be to order a beer. There wasn't a soul in the bar that knew Nicky had quit, and one who would be delighted to buy her a drink. It seemed the most natural thing in the world to say yes.

"I'm afraid I drank up my quota of booze. Now I stay away."

"One day at a time, right?"

"That's what they say."

"Then why come to a bar?"

"I'm here trying to find someone," Nicky said. "Maybe you know her."

Colleen started peeling the label off her beer bottle. "Did you lose a girlfriend or something?"

"No. It's someone I'm worried about. Her name is Lou," Nicky said.

"Don't know anyone named Lou."

"She's big. About six feet, stocky, buzz cut."

"Sounds charming," Colleen said. "But I don't think I've seen her here. Not that I noticed."

A woman wormed her way to the bar on the other side of Colleen, giving her a kiss on the cheek and Nicky knew she'd lost her. She gave up her barstool and wandered to the back room to look at the dancers. She thought it was as likely she'd see a grizzly bear on the dance floor as Lou, but she'd learned long ago to be thorough.

There was a billiards room off to the side of the dance floor. She slipped by the dancers and swung the door open, the noise from the music nearly disappearing as soon as the door swung shut behind her. Every head turned to her as if she'd just walked into a western saloon with her shooting hand on her gun belt. The room had a small bar and three pool tables set up end to end. She moved to the bar with as much cool as she could muster and sat at the end. Two other women sat at the other end and Nicky could feel them looking at her as she ordered a soda from the bored bartender.

The pool tables were all occupied, with players and spectators continually shuffling around to get out of the way of the shooters. She didn't see Lou, but she saw women who looked like Lou. Same age, same surface toughness, the same buzz cut. They all glanced at her before turning back with indifference. She waited patiently until one of the players came up to the bar for a refill. She was a shorter version of Lou, with a serious look on her face. Nicky wondered if she was not having any fun, or if that was the tough look she thought she should project. The "don't fuck with me" mask. It looked exhausting to haul it around everywhere.

"Another beer, TJ?" the bartender said.

"Make it three." TJ turned to Nicky as she waited for the drinks. She didn't as much look her over as size her up.

"Can I ask you something?" Nicky said.

"I guess." TJ dug a wallet out of the thigh pocket of her cargo pants and threw a bill on the bar. "What do you want?"

"I'm looking for a woman named Lou. Maybe you know her."

TJ looked puzzled, and suspicious. "Why would I know her?"

"I'm not saying you do."

TJ shrugged and grabbed the beers with one hand. "Well, I don't." She walked back to her pool table and put the beers on a shelf by the cue rack. Her friends huddled around her, and a couple glanced at Nicky. After a while, one of them detached herself from the pack, like a jet peeling away from formation, and made her way to the bar. She was tall and thin, perhaps even younger than Lou. Her hair looked more greasy than gelled. She wore dirty jeans and had a biker's wallet chained from her belt loop to her back pocket. When she stopped in front of Nicky, she leaned against the pool cue she was holding. She was clearly high on something and used her pool cue to keep herself upright.

"You know Lou?" she asked.

"I do. I take it you do, too?" Nicky wasn't happy the first person she'd found who knew Lou looked like a meth head.

"I haven't seen her for a long time and wanted to know if she was okay."

"That's what I'm trying to find out." Nicky pulled the stool out next to her. "Why don't you sit down?"

The woman sat, still using the cue as a crutch of sorts. She glanced at her friends before turning back to Nicky.

"Who are you?" she asked.

"Nicky. Lou and I live in the same place and she suddenly disappeared. I'm worried about her."

"Yeah? I heard Lou had gone into rehab. Is that where you know her from?"

"Sort of," Nicky said. "What's your name?"

"Dana."

Dana was being cooperative for a meth user if that's what she was. Nicky didn't want to lose her.

"You knew Lou from before she went into rehab, when she was still using?"

"Yeah. We had some of the same friends. Then she was gone."

"What do you mean?"

Dana shrugged. "You know. She didn't show up, answer her calls. We figured she either got busted or went into rehab."

"What would she have been busted for?"

Dana looked at her as if she were a dolt. "Like I'm going to give you any specifics."

"Dana, I'm not a cop. This is important. She might make her way back to your friends."

"I haven't seen her. I don't know what more I can say."

Nicky paused and considered her next move. If she asked too much, Dana would back away. But she couldn't ask too little.

"Can I buy you a drink?" Nicky asked.

Dana straightened a little and put her pool cue against the bar. "Sure. I never turn down a free drink."

Nicky motioned to the bartender for Dana's beer. "Can you tell me who some of her other friends are? Are any of them here with you?"

Dana shook her head. "No way."

"I understand." Nicky wrote her number down and tore the sheet from her notebook. "Will you call me if you hear anything about her?"

Dana smiled. "Probably not." She took a drink from her beer. "Maybe. I liked Lou."

Nicky winced at the past tense. "She's not dead, but I'm worried she'll start drinking or using again."

"Are you like her sponsor or something?" Nicky could hear the sarcasm. She saw Dana glance at her friends, nervous they'd wonder what she was doing.

"You're familiar with the term?" Nicky asked.

"Yeah." Dana drank down her beer. "I have family who've been in and out of AA, NA, all that shit."

Nicky suspected Dana had been in an AA meeting at some point. "Then you know how easy it is for people to slip."

"I'll say this about Lou," Dana said. "She was a hard partier and not the friendliest person in the room, but you could tell she was real, do you know what I mean? Like she'd never fuck you over. I appreciated that."

Dana stood, collecting her pool cue and beer bottle.

"Call me," Nicky said. "For whatever reason."

Dana went back to her friends without saying more. Nicky threw some bills on the bar and got out of Donna's, relieved to be away. She knew she'd be back, though. She knew trying to find Lou was going to take her places she never wanted to see again.

CHAPTER SIX

Saturdays were a day off for most Olive Street residents, but not for Nicky. It was the day she made sure the chores assigned to the women for that week had been done and harangued them if they hadn't. She inventoried the food supply, planned a menu for the upcoming communal meals, and drew up a grocery list. She made herself available to any of the women who needed to talk, and she tried to spend more time in the kitchen and family room to make herself approachable.

She also supervised work that needed to be done outside of the house. Gerri had gotten rid of the company that did all the mowing, raking, sweeping, pruning, and snow shoveling, and then dumped all the work on Nicky to take care of however she saw fit. Nicky found a way to squeeze more duty into the elaborate chart she'd created on her computer, but she had no formula for getting the women to do their chores without being asked multiple times. She'd been told in rehab that addicts and alcoholics had the emotional maturity of the age when their addiction kicked in, which explained a lot about herself. It also explained why she felt she lived in a house with ten teenagers.

This Saturday was especially busy. Nicky was bombarded with questions as the news of Lou's departure raced through the house.

"I knew it was Lou who stole the money," Angela said. She'd cornered Nicky in the kitchen as she poured her first cup of coffee of the day.

"I haven't said that she did."

"Why else would she be thrown out?"

"I didn't say she'd been thrown out, either. In fact, I haven't said anything about Lou." She looked at Angela over her cup, thinking that though Angela never got into trouble, she was by far the biggest pain in her ass among all the women.

"Well, what did happen?" She wasn't going to leave it.

Nicky sighed and headed out of the kitchen. "I'm not saying, Angela. I'm not sure what part of that isn't clear."

She went through the family room and out the patio doors to see how the raking crew was doing. The first leaves of autumn were starting to fall from the big oak tree at the back of the yard. Diane and Susan had volunteered to keep up with raking the front and back yards, but Nicky found them out back huddled together over a pile of leaves, smooching. She felt envious, even knowing it wasn't the wisest thing for them to be doing. A new relationship in early sobriety could become a drug on its own. It feels so good and makes everything else feel less bad. She hadn't felt all smoochy and intoxicated with Deb. Her primary emotion had been relief to finally have sex, like a normal person. But there was no giddy feeling. Nicky would like to feel a little bit giddy.

She didn't bother to break Susan and Diane apart but headed to the garage instead and started up her horrendous junker. It came roaring to life for a clamorous moment before dying with a noise that sounded like someone being strangled. It made her think of Sheila. If they took the best parts of each of their cars and put them together, they might have a halfway decent automobile.

She started the car again and drove to Target to get leaf bags and other supplies for the house, expecting to see half the gays in Andersonville at the store, Saturday being what it was. Another reason for the trip was to get out of the house and make a call. She forced herself to lift the phone to her ear and call Quinn, her ex-partner in homicide.

"Nicky, is that you?" He hadn't bothered saying hello.

"I'm still in your cell phone's contact list? I'm surprised," Nicky said.

She tried to keep her voice light. She hadn't talked to Quinn since she left the police department. For years before that they'd spoken to each other nearly every day. They were the top team in the homicide division, closing cases most detectives would give up on. Quinn was her opposite in many ways. He was black and lived with his family in Bronzeville on the city's south side, was always the first to leave the bar while Nicky was always the last, and he tried to save her from her most destructive behavior. He was known to come back to whatever tavern she was in to take her home to sleep it off in his basement guest room. He tried to talk her out of resigning after the shooting, but no one could have reached her. She was hell-bent on punishing herself.

"Of course, you are. And I've thought of calling you more than once."

"It's okay, Quinn. I wouldn't have called me if I were you."

"No, it's not that. I figured if you wanted to talk about anything, you'd give me a call. I didn't want to..."

"Embarrass me?" Nicky said.

"Not at all." Quinn was silent for a moment. "How are you?"

"Sober." Nicky wondered why she was teetering on sounding like a bitch when she'd called Quinn for a favor. She sometimes wondered if she'd made any progress at all in five years.

"That's great, Nicky. I'm glad to hear it." Quinn sounded genuinely happy. His affection for her had always been a puzzle.

"You're probably wondering why I'm calling after all this time."

"I don't care why, but I'm glad you did."

"I need a little help tracking someone down."

"Let me hear it."

"My new career is playing mama to a group of women in a halfway house. You know Olive Street House?"

"Sure, I know it. Do you like it there?"

"It's okay. Pay sucks, though."

"I can imagine," Quinn said.

"Anyway, I had to kick out one of the residents last night, and I'm worried she's gotten herself in trouble."

"That happens, Nicky. You can't chase down everyone who leaves Olive Street."

"I feel responsible for this woman. She was accused of a theft I don't think she committed, and I didn't protect her. She was barely sober as it is."

"How do you want me to help?"

"Could you keep an eye out if she gets picked up for anything. Her name is Lou Hansen." She gave him a physical description.

"Not a problem."

"And there's something else," Nicky said. "Lou's brother Jack—presumably Jack Hansen—is a dealer of some kind. I'm certain she's going to contact him. Can you tell me what you guys have on him?"

"I can call someone in narcotics, see if they know anything. I haven't heard of him."

"Can you run his sheet for me?"

Quinn paused and Nicky thought she'd pushed her luck too far. "I'll run it, but I'll only give it to you if you meet me for coffee."

She was startled. "Why would you want to do that?"

"To see you, you dingbat. I missed you. I mean, I don't miss you as much now, because you've been gone so long. But I missed you a lot."

"I was a terrible cop and you know it."

"That's how you remember it. I remember a good cop and a good friend. What do you say?"

Nicky was pulling into a parking space at Target. "Well, sure. If it'll get me the information on Jack Hansen, then count me in."

Quinn laughed. "I'll call you later. Hopefully have something for you today."

"Thanks, Quinn," she said and disconnected.

Nicky felt a little dazed. The reason she hadn't called him before was her deep mortification. Even before the shooting, her drinking had been an embarrassment. Like the time she crashed his oldest kid's birthday party and fell against the grill, sending it and all the food to the ground. Or the time she wanted to arrest a woman to get to know her better. Countless things like that.

She hadn't expected Quinn to be kind. She hadn't even expected him to agree to help. Her sponsor told her until she showed her whole self to the world, good and bad, she would never believe people loved her for who she was, which still sounded like bullshit. But Quinn was the only one, other than Sheila, who knew how disgraceful a person she was, and neither of them seemed to hate her.

She was in the gardening section of Target when a call came in from Sheila.

"I tracked down the two college friends the Hansens told us about," Sheila said.

"How?"

"Have you forgotten I'm a crack librarian? There's almost nothing we can't uncover."

"I did forget you were a librarian," Nicky said.

"I suppose I should be hurt, but I'll let it go."

"Sorry, Sheila. I'm preoccupied, I guess. I know you'd be crack at whatever you did."

"Don't worry about it. I don't talk about being a librarian very often. People's eyes tend to glaze over. And they have peculiar opinions of our sex lives."

"They do?" Nicky didn't want to think about Sheila's sex life.

"Honestly. There is this deep, seemingly implacable view of librarians as being prim. Which couldn't be further from the truth, of course."

"That's a relief," Nicky said. It fell out of her mouth, but she caught its meaning as soon as it was said.

There was a slight pause. "Is it?"

"Is it what?"

"Is it a relief I'm not really prim?" Sheila sounded more curious than flirty, thank God.

"I've never considered prim to be a good thing. But come to think of it, it's probably what I've been ever since I've been sober. I mean, I haven't even had a sex life."

"But you do have a sex life," Sheila said. "Haven't you been sleeping with Deb?"

"That's over."

"Ah. I won't grill you about that just now. Later, though. Anyway, one of Lou's friends lives in the suburbs and the other has been in Germany the last several years. Would you like me to call the woman here?"

"Why don't we drive out and talk to her together? What suburb is she in?"

"She's up in Highland Park, somewhere close to Ravinia."

Nicky thought for a moment. Highland Park was a wealthy suburb on Chicago's North Shore, a place she'd been to perhaps two times before. "There's a great Italian restaurant in Highwood, north of Highland Park. It's cheap. Why don't we have lunch there?"

"That would be great. Text me tomorrow when you're ready to go."

Nicky finished her shopping and stopped for gas and a car wash on her way home. She put some quarters in the vacuum machine and cleaned the floors and seats of the old car, throwing away coffee cups she'd tossed in the back. She felt energized by having something to do to find Lou, even knowing the Highland Park woman probably wouldn't be of any help. That's what investigations were—a series of small actions until a clear picture emerged. She could only hope this interview would lead to another.

Gerri set her laptop up on the old wooden desk in the basement of her house. She'd fashioned an office of sorts in a corner of what the previous owners had called the recreation room. It was a low-ceilinged, asbestos-tiled room with a tiki bar and knotty pine paneling. There were damp splotches and warping along the bottom of the paneling where water had seeped in during the ferocious summer storms that flooded basements across the city. Everything seemed to change when they bought the house. The real estate market went to hell, and they were growing poorer by the minute. Her husband had become someone who lived rent free in her house, and her ability to stomach her job was reaching an end. She pulled a bag of cookies out of her brief bag and booted up the computer.

As a rule, Gerri didn't work on weekends. They got entirely too much of her time during the week to have her willingly give them anymore. But she was intent on finding a replacement at Olive Street House for the spot opened by Lou Hansen's departure. She suspected the overly earnest Nicky Sullivan would follow this up with some move to get Lou reinstated, which she had to guard against. With Lou gone, it was much more likely the theft from the house would be put to rest. And if a new woman was sleeping in Lou's bed, it was even more unlikely Lou would be returned to Olive Street.

Gerri had already put a call in to the Reardon-Malloy inpatient rehab downtown. There was always at least one of the staff social workers on duty on Saturdays. That social worker was now looking into who was close to discharge who might need or want to move into a sober house. It was more correct these days to call it a sober living home rather than a halfway house. Dave Edmundson had given her a look when she'd used the old term during the last meeting, as if she'd uttered a racial epithet. If he hadn't just been talking about the layoffs that were going to occur, she probably would have said something snarky. Snark was oozing out of her lately, and it was practically a full-time job to keep it reined in.

She opened her web browser and started looking through Amazon for some new romance novels. She ate some cookies. With some reluctance, she opened her email and looked at the new messages through slitted eyes. It seemed like half were from her bank, some of them low balance alerts, the rest part of the never-ending warnings about what would happen if they didn't bring their mortgage payments current. The idea of losing the house was beginning to have appeal, she had to admit. They bought the place based on both of their incomes, with Jeff making considerably more than her. Without his salary, the mortgage payment took over half of hers. It wasn't sustainable. And fuck them, anyway.

CHAPTER SEVEN

Nicky found most of the residents in the family room when she came into the kitchen for her morning coffee. The women were talking quietly, and Nicky poured a cup and joined them. Zoey scootched over to make room. All eyes were on her and she couldn't guess their mood. Usually, it was friendly. The women took care of each other and had formed their own family of choice, fiercely defending each other as well as having innumerable spats. When they were upset they found their sharp tongues and let Nicky know about it.

"How are you, Nicky?" Carmen said. She was the mother hen of the group, older than the others, with four kids waiting for her to get back home.

"I'm good. What are you all talking about?"

"Lou, mostly. Do you know whether she's okay?" Oli said. She was the only Black resident in the house, but the census changed constantly. Before she'd bottomed out, she'd been an accomplished cellist.

Nicky glanced around at the concerned faces. A few didn't hide their indifference. Angela sat forward, her back ramrod straight, her face resembling a ferret about to steal some lettuce.

"I don't know, but I'm trying to find her," Nicky said. "I'd appreciate hearing anything you know that could help me."

"I roomed with Lou and I couldn't tell you the first thing about her," Zoey said. "It was like she didn't know how to talk, like a moot."

"That's mute," Angela said disdainfully. "Moot is an entirely different word."

Nicky sighed. It was like having fractious children.

"She was shy," Carmen said. "We should have done more to welcome her."

Most of the women nodded agreement. Nicky doubted Lou would have been receptive to their overtures, but she was pleased they were thinking about their own part in it.

Later that morning she picked up Sheila for their trip up to Highland Park. She climbed into the car, arranging herself and her giant tote bag in the passenger seat. Nicky wondered what could be in it that would be needed on their trip. Probably nothing. Nicky traveled lean—her phone and her wallet were all she carried, while others brought along a subset of their worldly possessions everywhere they went.

"Did you let this woman know we're coming?" Nicky asked.

"I called her yesterday. She should be there when we arrive. Maybe we'll get some coffee and muffins."

Nicky grinned. "You're not accustomed to interviews like this. Normally all we get is attitude. People talking to cops are either belligerent or they're completely intimidated. Rarely do coffee and muffins make an appearance."

"But we're not cops."

"More's the pity. We'll see what we can get out of her."

The drive to Highland Park was forty-five minutes, most of which was spent talking about Lou, but also about Sheila's mother, who was ailing, and Nicky's mother, who was just home from a hiking trip to the Grand Canyon.

Nicky left the interstate and followed Google Maps into Highland Park to the home of Ariel Hastings. The house was large like all the houses on the street, a Tudor sitting on a big lawn between a Georgian and a Victorian. Ariel had clearly taken a much different path than Lou following their graduation from Northwestern. Nicky pushed the doorbell, which set off the sound of church bells cascading thought the house. Soon a young woman answered the door. She wore Lululemon workout clothes, her face was fresh and bright, and her hair was piled on top of her head, strands falling from it as if they were perfectly arranged to give a charmingly disheveled look.

"Good morning, Ms. Hastings," Sheila said. "I called you yesterday about Lou Hansen?"

"Please, it's Ariel. Come in."

She led them through a living room with ceilings so high Nicky couldn't figure out how the light bulbs ever got changed. They passed through a formal dining room and into a kitchen the size of a small gymnasium. At one end was a six-person table laid with a coffee service and a plate of scones. Sheila gave Nicky a smug look as they sat at the table.

"Thank you for seeing us, Ariel," Nicky said. "As Sheila told you, we're interested in talking to you about Lou Hansen, who has gone missing. We're very worried about her."

Ariel busied herself pouring coffee and passing the scones around. "I hope I can help you, but Lou and I have drifted apart in the two years since college. I don't know anything about her now."

"I understand. We're looking to get some background."

"I did run into her downtown earlier this year. I was there for a shopping trip and saw her walking down Michigan Avenue."

"Did you speak?"

"Yes, we stopped for a minute. We hadn't been super close in college, but we ran with the same people. We were close enough to hug when we saw each other."

Nicky tried to imagine a Lou who hugged people. She knew nothing about her at all. "What did you talk about?"

"Me mostly. I told her I'd married and moved to Highland Park, and I was working as an analyst at Goldman Sachs. We chatted a little about other people in our gang and then went on our way."

"She didn't say anything about what she was up to?" Sheila said.

"No, she seemed a little anxious to go."

Nicky opened a small notebook she kept in her jacket pocket, the same notebook she'd used when she was a detective. Once in a while she'd flip through the pages and be reminded of cases she'd worked on. Regret always washed over her when she did. "We'll need a list of the names of your college friends before we leave here. Will that be possible?"

"I don't know. I'm a little uncomfortable giving names out." Ariel sipped her black coffee and eschewed the scones.

"Ariel, Lou could be in real trouble. If these people were friends of hers, wouldn't they want to help?"

"No, you're right. I'll make a list. I don't have everyone's contact information, though."

"Don't worry about that," Sheila said.

"Before you do that, can you tell us a little about Lou in college? What was she like? Were there any incidents or events that stand out for you?" Nicky said.

Ariel sipped her coffee and put the mug onto the table in front of her, moving it incrementally until it was in the right spot. "Lou was a riot, life of the party, but only if you were drinking with her. Otherwise, she was kind of quiet. She's super smart and could have gotten excellent grades. I think hers were mediocre, probably because of the drinking. Such a waste."

Nicky could hear the faint tone of judgment. "Was she particularly close to anyone? Boyfriend, girlfriend, friend friend?"

Ariel shifted around until she was seated in a meditation pose on her kitchen chair. "Lou was out before she came to Northwestern and she never had a problem finding girlfriends. It was one after another until she met Portia. They went out all of junior year and most of senior."

Sheila swallowed a bite of scone. "What happened senior year?"

"Portia broke her heart. Lou assumed they'd live together after graduation, but Portia announced she wasn't sure she was a lesbian and she wanted the freedom to explore her sexuality. Lou was a mess. Her drinking was already bad, but it got much worse after the breakup. Frankly, I don't know how she managed to get her degree. Northwestern is a hard school. She pulled a lot of all-nighters, I guess."

Nicky pushed her notebook and pen toward Ariel. "If you'd jot down the names of Lou's college friends, we'll get out of your hair. We also need Portia's last name."

Ariel picked up the pen and looked deadly serious, as if she were about to take her GREs. After several minutes of careful writing, she pushed them back toward Nicky. "That's the best I can do. If you can avoid telling any of them it was me that gave you their name, I'd appreciate it. I don't want to be tagged as a gossip."

They said their good-byes and returned to Nicky's car. No doubt the neighbors thought it belonged to a household servant. She hadn't been helped much by Ariel Hastings, though hearing Lou was the life of the party was surprising. The girlfriend story made her feel even more badly for her. Nicky had lost plenty of girlfriends, usually when they got fed up with her drinking and realized they had a full-blown alcoholic on their hands. Toward the end of her drinking, she went out with Kristen, a woman who spent as much time in the bars as she did. She thought her drinking was safe with her. When Kristen ended their relationship because Nicky drank too much, the writing on the wall got harder to ignore.

Quinn wanted to meet at Coffee Studio so she dropped Sheila off in Rogers Park and headed back to Andersonville. The café had a modern European feel to it, with a few tables along the wall and in back. It smelled like coffee and someone's overpowering perfume. Quinn was already there, sitting with a woman whose back was toward her. Nicky frowned. Who the hell was she? Was she the one with the perfume? Quinn waved her over as the woman turned to look at Nicky, a smile on her rather stunning face. It was the woman from the emergency room and Nicky saw a flash of recognition in her eye.

Quinn stood when Nicky reached the table and opened his arms for a hug. She reluctantly let herself be clasped to his broad chest. He was a big man, in size and heart, and she nearly cried when his arms wrapped around her. She turned from him to look at the woman as Quinn did the introductions.

"Nicky, this is Joanne Parker, my partner. Everyone calls her Parker. I thought she might shed some light for us."

Parker reached out her hand for a shake. "It's a pleasure meeting you, Nicky. Quinn has told me about you, though I feel I've seen you before."

Nicky didn't want to admit she remembered her from such a brief exchange at the hospital. A glance, really. She shook her hand briefly and took a seat.

"Do you want to get some coffee?" Quinn said.

"I'm fine. Curious what you have for me, or is this a purely social visit?"

Quinn's smile faded. "Not strictly social, no. I picked up some information this morning you're not going to like. A white female turned up dead last night."

Nicky's throat closed as if in anaphylactic shock. Jesus, no, please let it not be Lou, but she knew in every fiber it was.

"It was Lou Hansen?"

Quinn bowed his head. "It was. I'm sorry, Nicky."

"Give me the details." She squeezed the words out of her voice box. Her face felt flaming hot.

"It was in this morning's report. She was found by a man in the alley opening his garage door. I talked to the detectives who processed the scene and now the case has been assigned to Parker and me."

Nicky nodded, trying to process the information. "What happened to her?"

Quinn glanced at Parker, who opened a notebook and read. "The victim was found in an alley behind Beacon Street in Uptown. The medical examiner on the scene said she'd been stabbed in the heart. She wouldn't have suffered."

"Was her stuff gone? She had a backpack and laptop with her."

"The backpack was there. No mention of a laptop with her."

Parker locked eyes on her. Her voice was sympathetic. "Who was Lou to you?"

Nicky felt reluctant to tell her, which would be admitting she worked as a manager at a sober house. Surely Parker would think she should have been further along in life at her age. It was embarrassing, but there were more important things now. "She's a young woman who got kicked out of the recovery house I manage. I was afraid she was going to relapse and get herself killed. It looks like half of that came true."

"All of it, I'm sorry to say. She had some meth on her and a forty-ounce can of beer," Quinn said.

"Oh, no."

"Why was she kicked out?" Parker asked.

Oh, Christ. She was forced to put her worst foot forward in front of this woman. "There was a theft in the house and convincing evidence Lou was the thief. It wasn't conclusive, though, and I argued against her being kicked out. But there you have it."

"Do you feel responsible in some way?" Parker said. "Because it doesn't sound like it's your fault."

Nicky stared at her for a minute and decided to not answer the question. It felt too probing, as if Parker were trying to access her psyche. No one was allowed access to the inner workings of her brain and personality, not even Nicky herself. She turned to Quinn instead. "What did you find on Jack Hansen?"

"Not a whole lot. He had a couple of juvenile pops for selling drugs in high school. As an adult he was picked up once for carrying a concealed weapon. He could have served some time for that, but some good lawyering got him off with probation."

"His parents are well off. I'm not sure they'd provide lawyers for him today. It seems the Hansen parents have written off both of their children." Nicky stared at the spot on the table where a cup of coffee should be.

A shadow fell across the table and she could feel a presence over her left shoulder. She turned to look and found Meg Antinou beaming down at her.

"Nicky! Even with your back turned I could tell it was you. I've been wondering how you are."

For the love of Christ, the last person she wanted to see was Meg. Now Parker and Quinn would think she was a friend and Nicky wanted no association with her. It took her a moment to find her tongue to reply.

"Aren't you going to introduce me to your friends?"

"This is a business meeting, Meg. We were right in the middle of something." She could feel Parker's cool gaze on her, while Quinn looked amused.

Meg reached her hand out to Parker. "Hi, I'm Meg, an old friend of Nicky's. Pleased to meet you."

Parker gave her a quick shake. "Joanne Parker."

Quinn warmly shook Meg's hand. "Always happy to meet a friend of Nicky's."

Nicky stood and faced Meg. "As I said, we're in a business meeting. Maybe we could talk some other time?"

"Oh, I'd love that! I'll give you a call to set it up." She looked at Parker and Quinn. "Lovely to meet you. I'll get out of your hair now." She leaned over and gave Nicky a kiss on each cheek and left. Nicky sat down and buried her face in her hands.

"You seemed awfully anxious to get rid of your friend. We could have asked her to sit down, but then I thought she might be another of your disastrous ex-girlfriends and I should follow your lead."

"She's not an ex-girlfriend, though she wanted more than I had any interest in giving her." What she didn't say was Meg gave her the creeps and she felt unsettled after every encounter with her.

"Who is she then?" Quinn asked.

"Just someone I was in rehab with." She didn't want to point out her alcoholism to Parker, who was a virtual stranger, but she knew it already. Nicky wasn't in rehab to learn basket weaving and she wasn't living in a sober home because she liked the decor. She shouldn't care what Parker might think about her. And yet, she did.

She and Meg had been in rehab together five years before and hit it off, at least at first. Meg was an attorney who'd blown her high-flying career through her devotion to Vicodin and champagne. She had a sense of humor about it all, to the point where Nicky wondered if she appreciated the desperate situation she was in. Humility didn't come easily to Meg. She had a plain face made-up to perfection, elegantly styled hair, and clothes that had taken some thought to put together. As far as Nicky knew, she was practicing law again, so there was plenty of money for clothing and spa treatments. It must be nice.

While in rehab they'd teamed up to do their fourth steps together, sharing work sessions as they listed all their fears and resentments, dredged up their sexual history, and painfully reviewed all the wrongs they'd done to people. They were too newly sober to be thorough, too lacking perspective, but Nicky gave it her best. Meg seemed to have fun doing hers, recounting stories as if they were funny and not sad and pathetic. Nicky started to put some distance between them as it became clear Meg was not only cavalier about sobriety, but also had a thing for her. She'd sit next to Nicky at every group therapy session, every meal, every in-house AA meeting. She'd tried to get her room changed to share with her. Teagan and the others teased her about it.

Nicky liked rehab, found it a relief and an opportunity, a needed rest after battering her body for so long. The only pea under the mattress was Meg and her unwanted attentions. Every time she heard from Meg in the years since she was surprised she was still sober, but not curious enough to agree to see her. She feared she'd encourage her attentions if she did.

"Where were we?" Nicky said, anxious to get the conversation back on track.

"One of the reasons I wanted Parker here is she used to work narcotics."

"And I know of Jack Hansen," Parker said. "We've had our eye on him for some time. He runs a well-organized and staffed drug operation that's grown a lot over the last two years. His crew is intensely loyal. No one's been able to turn any of them against him. He's a businessman, and like all business people he doesn't like risk and exposure, though high risk is inherent in his line of work."

"What about location? Ideally, I'd be able to find him and talk to him."

"He switches up every six months or so, moving locations when he thinks he's become too well known in the neighborhood. He's run his operation all over the north side, from Ukrainian Village, New Town, Uptown, Roscoe Village, and others, I'm sure."

"What about now?" Quinn asked.

"I checked in with a cop I used to work with in narcotics. He says Hansen is operating out of Rogers Park now, but for how much longer is anyone's guess."

"Nothing more specific?" Nicky said.

"We want to talk to him, Nicky," Quinn said. "We'll find him." She could feel Parker's attention on her like a powerful flashlight.

Parker leaned back in her chair. "Of course. I'm happy to help anyone who means something to Quinn, and you definitely fit in that category. For a while I wondered if I'd ever measure up to the legendary Nicky Sullivan."

Nicky wondered if they were talking about the same person. "You would have done that on day one."

"What are you talking about? He told me about the time you saved his ass during a shoot-out."

Nicky looked at Quinn as if he'd betrayed her. He put his hands up in defense. "Don't be mad. She was going to hear that story one way or another once she joined homicide. Who better to tell it than me?"

"Please don't tell this story. I beg you." He didn't seem to realize she was serious. She hated hearing people talk about her.

"What happened again?" Parker asked, her eyes dancing, putting Nicky on the spot. Quinn picked up the story.

"It was a Sunday night and we were on our way back from an interview when a call went out for all units to respond to an armed robbery at a 7-Eleven in Uptown, the one on Wilson and Sheridan. We were first on the scene and when we pulled into the parking lot a guy with a ski mask came out of the store carrying a plastic bag and a gun. As soon as he saw us he started shooting. Nicky opened her door and returned fire. My side of the car was facing him and I couldn't get out without being a huge target. He kept shooting and Nicky got him in the shoulder. He went down just as the patrol cars got there and made the arrest. He would have shot me for sure if Nicky hadn't been there to draw the fire."

"I don't understand why you make a big deal out of that story. Any cop would have done the same." She turned to Parker. "Wouldn't you?"

"I'd like to think so, but I've never been in anything close to that situation. It's hard to know what I'm capable of."

"You two can have a good chuckle. I think I'll go out and try to find out who murdered Lou Hansen."

"We'll need to talk to you formally," Quinn said. "Is tomorrow at Olive Street House good for you?"

"I don't want police in the house. I'll come to you."

"Great," he said. He put his hands on the table and leaned toward Nicky. "You're a detective at heart and you're going to want to find the killer yourself. She meant something to you. Let us do our jobs, Nicky. I don't want to come across witnesses you've already spoiled for information."

Nicky stood and put her phone in her jacket pocket. Parker slid a business card over to her. "My cell's on there. Call me anytime if you think I can help, or for any reason."

Nicky didn't doubt Parker would work hard to find Lou's killer. She struck her as that sort of cop. And there was the sisterhood of cops in play. Was that the little extra she felt as she stared at Parker's elegant hand holding the business card?

❖

Sunday nights at Olive Street House were for movies. All the residents and Nicky gathered in the family room and fought over which title they would pick from the small library of DVDs. Romcoms and action movies were frequent winners, though the collection offered nothing more recent than *Bridesmaids* and *Hangover 3*. They had cable TV but no streaming services, an expense her bosses weren't willing to pick up.

Nicky liked the sense of community movie nights gave the residents. There was no way she was going to tell them about Lou's death. She wasn't ready for the uproar. She'd tell them at the weekly meeting the next day.

Nicky settled into one of the two armchairs in the room. Her mind was elsewhere, but she wanted everything to appear normal to the women. Angela had snagged the other armchair. In between the chairs was a long sofa crammed with residents while others sat on the floor. She took control of the remote and started the movie. Her cell phone beeped almost at the same time and she saw the call was from Gerri. Her finger hovered over the red button that would reject the call, but she needed to tell her about Lou. She hit the green button and walked out of the family room toward her office.

"Gerri?"

"Oh, good, I caught you. I have a body for you. I'm sending her over to you this evening."

Christ. Would this day never end? "Who is it?"

"Her name is Madison Frey. She's coming to us from Northwestern's inpatient program. I talked the place up, so be sure to make her feel welcome."

"When does she get here?"

"Anytime. We got everything signed off a little while ago. They're putting her in an Uber."

"We're all gathered for a movie. She can meet everyone at once."

"Excellent!

She was standing in her office with the phone to her ear when she heard the doorbell chime. "I think your woman has arrived. I need to get off the phone."

"Go, go. Give me a full report on her tomorrow."

Nicky disconnected and hurried to open the door. A tiny woman stood on the stoop, two large suitcases next to her. There was no smile on her heart-shaped face. She was barely in her twenties and dressed like she followed a TikTok influencer—every article of clothing and accessory was picked precisely to look like they didn't go together. Her makeup was expertly applied. Most of the other residents had only what they could grab before going into rehab. This woman's wardrobe would be scrutinized and resented by the others.

"Madison?" Nicky said.

"Yes, I'm Madison. I've been shipped off to this place." She didn't look any too pleased about it. She was so much shorter than Nicky her gaze rested at chest level.

"Well, come in. Let's get you settled." Nicky reached for one of the suitcases and led Madison through the door. "We'll go up and put these in your room and then I'd like you to meet everyone. We're all in the family room watching a movie."

"Sounds delightful. I can never get enough of group activities." There was no mistaking the sarcasm in her voice. Nicky's mood plunged even further. The last thing she wanted was a difficult new resident. She didn't have the bandwidth for it now.

"Follow me," Nicky said.

They climbed the creaky stairs to the second floor, along the hallway to Lou's old room. Zoey's mess had migrated to the other half of the small space. Dirty clothes were tossed on top of Lou's old bed, used towels and other discarded clothing lay in the space between the beds. She should have had Zoey come up and clean first, but there'd been no time. "You'll be rooming with Zoey, who you can see is not a neat person. I'll have her clean all this up and this half of the room will be solely yours."

Madison looked around. "You're kidding me with this, aren't you?"

"What do you mean?"

"The lady who came to Northwestern told me this was a nice house with nice rooms and she clearly lied. This place is a dump."

Nicky felt her cheeks flush at the insult and took a deep breath. "Listen, you're here now, so let's make the best of it. This place will keep you sober, and that's what's important, right?"

"So everyone keeps telling me. I can't say it's all it's cracked up to be."

"Why did you decide to live in a sober house, then? No one's forcing you."

"My parents are. They won't take me back."

"Well, you're very welcome here. I think you'll grow to like it. Now, leave your bags here and let's go say hello to everyone."

Nicky pointed out the meeting room and kitchen as they made their way to the family room. Someone had turned the lights out and it was very dark but for the glow from the giant TV. She flipped the lights on and everyone groaned.

"Whoever has the remote needs to pause the film." Angela pointed the remote at the screen. "Everyone, a new resident has arrived and I want you to meet her." Nicky pulled Madison a little farther into the room. "This is Madison. You'll have a chance to chat with her after the movie and I expect you all to make her feel welcome. Zoey, you need to go upstairs and clean up your room, right now."

"During the movie?"

"That's the price you pay for being a slob."

Zoey hauled herself up from the sofa and left, grumbling audibly when she passed Nicky and Madison. The rest of the women stared at Madison with blank faces. Angela stood with the remote in her hand, a reminder to all of who was in charge. "Welcome, Madison. Would you like to join us for the rest of the movie?"

"What are you watching?" The frozen image on the screen could be from anything.

"*Guardians of the Galaxy*. You'll love it."

"It's a little lowbrow for me, actually," Madison said.

The smile left Angela's face and she sat down. Nicky could see a few of the women narrowing their eyes. Nicky and Madison left the room and went to the office. "Sit down for a minute. We have some paperwork to do." She reached into a file cabinet and took out a few forms. "These are liability waivers and rules and regulations. You can sign the waivers now and take the rules and regs with you."

"Are we free to come and go from the house or is it more like a prison?"

Nicky kept herself from retorting in kind. She didn't want to make an enemy of her this quickly when it seemed certain it would happen on its own soon enough.

"Most of the women have jobs, so they come and go. There's nothing stopping you from going out at any time, as long as your responsibilities are taken care of and you're back by the eleven o'clock curfew. This is not a prison. We do safeguard the women's sobriety, though. Anything you do that affects the well-being of others will be taken seriously."

They stared at each other for a moment before Madison signed the forms and picked up the rules and regs. "If it's okay with you, I'll go up to my room now, meet my roommate." Nicky nodded and she left, closing the door behind her.

The light was harsh from the overhead fixture and Nicky flipped it off, turning on her desk lamp. She settled into her chair, thankful for the quiet and solitude. Did Gerri purposefully pick the most unpleasant woman available to send to Olive Street House? She wouldn't put it past her.

CHAPTER EIGHT

After the movie ended, when everyone had gone upstairs and the house was quiet, Nicky locked all the doors and windows and turned out the lights. She climbed the stairs slowly, an old knee injury acting up as it often did when she was having a bad day. She locked the door and flung herself onto her bed, exhausted and buzzy at the same time. Sleep felt very far away. She reached for her phone to play some Spider Solitaire when it vibrated in her back pocket. It was an unknown number, but she answered it in case there was news about Lou.

"This is Nicky."

There was a moment's pause. "Nicky, it's Joanne Parker. We met earlier today with Detective Quinn."

Nicky nearly dropped the phone. Thoughts of Parker had drifted through her brain throughout the day. Her antennae had quivered when she was introduced, as it would with any attractive woman. She had eyes in her head. But this seemed a little sharper, her interest more finely tuned than mere physical appearance could explain. Nerves blossomed in her belly as her grip on the phone tightened.

"Of course. How are you?" And why are you calling?

"I hope it's okay to call. I was thinking about what you said today and wanted to check in with you."

That was a little weird with someone you didn't know. "Okay. What did I say exactly?"

"I got the sense you feel responsible for Lou, that it's somehow your fault."

"I should never have allowed her to be kicked out." Agitation now lay on top of the nerves that were already there. She wanted to get off the phone.

"But did you have any choice? I don't know your situation there, but my guess is you were forced to remove her from the house. How is that your fault?"

Nicky didn't want to share the details of how she was the one who told Gerri about the laptop, and if she hadn't, Lou would still be alive.

"It just is. You'll have to take my word for it."

"It's clear how much Lou's death means to you. I'll give it my everything to find who killed her." Nicky heard the clunk of ice on the other end of the line. Was Parker a drinker?

"I don't doubt it. If Quinn's happy with you as his partner, then you must be good police."

"I'm surprised we never crossed paths while you were still on the job." Parker's voice had become lighter, more conversational. "Where did you work out of while you were a detective?"

They chatted easily about cop stuff—assignments, promotions, particularly egregious male behavior. The female detectives were still far outnumbered by the males, a significant percentage of which seemed to be stuck in 1950 with their attitude toward women.

"Well, I should let you get on with your evening," Parker said.

"I'm glad you called." Nicky tried to sound warm and not squeaky.

"Good. I know you're unofficially on the case, but I look forward to working with you. We'll find who did this. Against the three of us, he doesn't stand a chance."

Nicky laughed. "I hope so. Lou was just starting her new life before it was taken from her. I can't let that stand."

"It won't. Good night, Nicky."

They hung up and Nicky's grip on the phone remained tight. What the hell was that? It was so hard to sort out. Was Parker just a super nice person who wanted to lend support? A fellow female cop who wanted to swap stories? Or were thoughts of Nicky drifting through Parker's mind as well, with the call signaling her interest in her? She felt herself blushing at the thought someone as together as

Parker could be interested in her. It was a good thought to fall asleep to.

❖

The phone rang in the middle of the night and woke Nicky from a deep sleep. Earlier in the day she'd called an old confidential informant from her detective days. Griffith Sutton had been a lieutenant to a major drug dealer on the north side, but when they had a falling out he moved from being a drug dealer to a drug user. When Nicky approached him about working for her, he was desperate enough to agree. Drug addicts didn't necessarily bring the most reliable information to their handlers, but Nicky was impressed with what he'd come up with. He was very knowledgeable about the Chicago drug market and kept up his contacts despite his reduced circumstances. She'd made at least three arrests based on information he'd provided. She hoped the call was from him.

"Hey, Detective Sullivan. It's been a long time, thought you'd forgotten me."

"I'm not with the department anymore."

"No shit? I'm surprised I hadn't heard that. How long?"

"About five years. I hadn't forgotten you, though. Thanks for getting back to me."

Nicky could hear a Zippo lighter clack shut and the deep inhalation that came after. She'd kill for a cigarette and resented having to give up everything that had served to calm her jangly nerves. "What can I do to help?"

"I'm looking for a dealer named Jack Hansen. Do you know him?"

"I know who he is, I know some of the guys who work for him."

"Can you get a message to him?"

"Probably."

"I need to talk to him about his sister Lou. Tell him it's important."

"That's something he might respond to. I won't tell him you're an ex-cop."

They ended the call with Griffith's promise to get word to Hansen in exchange for one hundred dollars electronically transferred into his account. That was the way modern CIs operated. Griffith was a junkie, but he was a very functional one and she trusted he'd do what he said. Now she had to stay awake to see if Jack Hansen was going to respond to her message. She was restless and unable to pass the time with anything constructive. Even solitaire demanded too much focus.

It was almost one in the morning before Griffith called her back. He told her Hansen would meet her at two at the Honey Bear restaurant in Rogers Park, an all-night diner popular with cops. It was an odd choice, but she was simply glad he'd agreed to see her. She settled into a booth before he arrived, trying to imagine what Hansen would look like. Probably big like Lou, possibly as tattooed and pierced. At two fifteen, a man entered and slid into the booth opposite her.

He wasn't as big as Lou and he didn't have any visible markings or adornments. He was dressed in a polo shirt and khaki pants, like he worked at Best Buy. Nicky didn't know what to make of him.

"Word is you want to talk to me about my sister." His voice was gravelly, as if something was permanently caught in his throat. "Who are you again?" He didn't seem suspicious but merely curious.

"I'm the resident manager of the sober living house Lou was in."

"You're the one who kicked her out?"

"You could say that, but it's complicated. When did you last talk to her?"

A server came by and took their order. Nicky stayed with the cold cup of coffee in front of her. Jack went for a full breakfast.

"Lou got hold of me the night she got evicted," he said.

"What did she say?"

"Said you believed she'd stolen money from the house because she had a brand-new laptop, which is bullshit because I'm the one who bought it for her."

Nicky's stomach turned sour. She'd believed Lou, but hearing her side of the story confirmed made her sick with guilt.

"Lou was found dead Sunday morning. She was murdered."

Jack's eyes narrowed and he lowered his coffee cup to the table. "Who did it?" He didn't seem especially surprised, murder being a more common currency in his world. Nicky recognized his immediate interest in the killer. Men in his position had people taken from them on a regular basis, and while families were usually off-limits, it had been known to happen. It was worth looking into whether Lou's death was connected to her brother's business.

"The police have no idea who did it. Do you?"

Jack sat very still and looked her in the eye. "No, there's no one I can think of. But I'm not done thinking yet."

"Tell me more about when you saw Lou," Nicky said.

"I told her she could stay at my place for the time being, but she wasn't interested. She and my girlfriend don't get along. She gave me back the laptop and I gave her some money for it."

"Did she say where she planned to go?"

The food arrived and Jack was quiet as he stared at his Meat Lover's Skillet. "She didn't say exactly, only that she'd find temporary housing until she could figure something out."

"What kind of temporary housing? A refrigerator box in an alley can be temporary housing." The smell of his breakfast made her queasy.

"I think she was headed for an SRO. That's no place for her. They're filled with addicts and homeless people and losers in general. Lou was not a loser."

"No, she wasn't. I think Lou was turning a corner in her recovery."

"She didn't belong in that house anyway. Nothing but a bunch of AA Nazis in those places."

Nicky's eyebrows went up. She hated the misconception that AA was filled with sobriety evangelists, which simply isn't true. "I'd like to think what we have at our house is anything but sobriety fascism. Lou liked it there until things blew up."

Jack chewed and then swallowed some coffee. "She asked me for some meth. I don't know how sober that made her."

Nicky's heart sank. "Did you give it to her?"

"Of course. I could never say no to her." Suddenly, Jack's face squeezed shut and he held his hand to his eyes, pushing back tears.

"I should leave you alone."

"Do my parents know?"

"I don't know. Probably."

"Fuckers. This is their fault as much as anyone's."

Nicky wasn't looking for anyone to blame beyond herself, though Lou's shitty parents bore some responsibility.

Jack sat motionless. "I'll find who did this."

"Only if I don't find him first. Or the police, for that matter. They're only starting their investigation. If you give me your number we can stay in touch about it."

"Why would I?"

"Because I cared about Lou and it seems precious few did."

He gave her the number and pushed his plate away. It seemed a good time to make her exit.

CHAPTER NINE

Monday was vacuuming day at Olive Street House, and this week it was Diane and Susan's turn to do the upstairs and downstairs rugs and carpets. Nicky's eyes flew open as the ancient Oreck roared to life outside her bedroom door. It was eight in the morning, and she'd finally fallen asleep around four. No point staying in bed. As far as Reardon-Malloy was concerned, she was officially on duty.

She got dressed and left her room. Diane gave her a grin as she continued to push the machine back and forth down the hallway. She knew she was waking Nicky up and enjoyed every second of it. Nicky slid past her and down the stairs, only to find Susan with their second rickety vacuum cleaner working on the living room rug.

She went to the kitchen and made coffee and toast and brought them to her office. An elaborate spreadsheet lay on her desk. It contained the work schedules of all the women—both their jobs inside and outside the house. The only way to run the house fairly was to monitor the schedule closely to see the women were doing their assigned chores. If one slacked off it was hard on all the others and a lot of resentment got generated. She stared at the dense numbers and letters as if there was wisdom to be found there.

Someone knocked at the open door and Oli Sasser stepped into the room. She was an exceptionally tall woman, almost as tall as Nicky, and model thin. She was not model pretty, but she was striking with her large eyes and prematurely gray hair cut almost to the scalp. She was good friends with one or two of the women, but she kept her head low. Nicky rarely had to deal with her one-on-one. She'd been drummed out of the Chicago Symphony Orchestra when the effects of her drinking overshadowed her beautiful cello playing. She hoped she'd find her way back to music.

"Nicky, I'm not going to be able to get my drug test this week. I've got training at work and can't get out of it."

All the residents were required to get a drug test once a week and it was a major bone of contention. Very few of them worked downtown, but that was where they had to go, a specific lab in the Loop. It took a couple of hours to travel to the lab and back to the house. It had to be done during the business day or on Saturdays and they bitterly resented it. Every week someone said they couldn't get tested, and it was Nicky's job to see they got to the lab. She offered to drive Oli down to the lab on Saturday and she couldn't find a reason that wouldn't work. She left the office deflated.

Nicky understood why Reardon-Malloy wanted drug tests, but once a week was onerous. She hoped to talk Gerri into backing off to every other week. Her phone rang.

"Nicky, it's Gerri. How are you this morning?"

"Not good." Nicky was still furious at Gerri over Lou's eviction. She fought off the urge to tell her I told you so, but it seemed disrespectful of Lou.

"What's wrong?"

"Lou Hansen was murdered, that's what. We threw her out on the streets with no support and someone took the opportunity to stab her in the heart."

There was a brief silence before Gerri said, "I'm sorry to hear it, but it has nothing to do with us. She's the one who stole the money. What else could we have done?"

"She didn't steal the money. I talked to her brother and he confirmed he'd bought the laptop for her. You evicted her for no reason and now she's dead."

"Whoa there. No one is responsible for Lou's death. Certainly not me."

Nicky threw a pencil onto the desk in disgust. There was no point in trying to get Gerri to accept any responsibility. She had a better chance getting her to dance a jig at the Monday night house meeting. "What are you calling about?"

"Yes, down to business. We're instituting two time a week drug testing starting this week. Same routine, twice over. See they comply by Saturday."

Nicky was nearly speechless. "I can barely get them all to do one test, and they bitch about it all the time. If they have to go twice there's going to be an uprising."

"Oh, poor girls. They're going to have to dig deep if they want to remain in their nice, safe, warm home. Two times a week or they're out."

"No, I can't do it. It's asking too much of them and it's not necessary. We don't have a problem with drug use in the house, and believe me, I'm on the lookout for it."

"What about the meth overdose the other day?"

"That was the rare exception to the rule."

"This is company policy, Nicky. Are you saying you're not going to comply with a direct order?"

Nicky paused. Once again, her job was threatened by her not going along with one of Gerri's schemes. One of these days she supposed she'd have to call her bluff and threaten to quit. Chances were good Gerri would accept her resignation gleefully and Nicky wasn't financially prepared for that yet. She couldn't face the idea of being penniless, and she refused to get help from her parents, who already thought of her as a wastrel.

"Don't we need to be somewhat competitive with other houses? Two time a week drug testing is not a selling point."

"I wouldn't worry about that. Plenty of sober houses have it. Now, can I count on you?"

"I can't guarantee they'll do this."

"They have to, Nicky. You need to impress that on them. I want a report next Monday showing everyone's testing from this week, and it better be perfect."

Gerri hung up. Nicky lowered her forehead to the desktop. Tonight was the weekly house meeting and she'd have to tell them then about the new testing as well as Lou's death. She knew which one they'd be most upset about. Administering the testing would be a nightmare, but even worse would be the change in mood in the house. It was not going to be pretty.

❖

Gerri pulled her car into the Reardon-Malloy parking lot and made her way to her office. She'd just gotten off the phone with Nicky Sullivan and her stomach was in knots. Her entire scheme depended on Nicky administering the twice weekly testing and she didn't like her lack of enthusiasm. What Nicky seemed to keep forgetting was she worked for R-M, not the women in her house. If she became unwilling to follow orders, Gerri would get rid of her. She considered firing her now—she'd find some pretense to do it—to avoid future problems, but she didn't feel up to finding and hiring a replacement. She didn't feel up to much of anything these days.

The one thing Gerri was interested in was keeping her job. A healthy bottom line was always the best deterrent to being laid off so she tried to think of other ways to increase the house revenue. Her boss had initially been reluctant to increase the drug testing. He was momentarily hampered by concern for the women at the sober houses, but when she explained how much money they could make every week by changing the policy, he grew warm to the idea.

The math was simple. The tests didn't cost more than ten dollars to administer but were billed to the insurance company at one thousand dollars. Half went to the company giving the tests, the rest stayed with R-M. It wasn't exactly legal, but plenty of outpatient facilities did it. There were precious few income streams in the recovery business. When she calculated the income the testing would produce from all her sober houses and gave Dave the figure, his hesitation ended. All he said was, "Get it done."

At least she was coming up with ideas, which had to put her in a better position than all of her paralyzed colleagues. Maybe they weren't as motivated. They didn't have an unemployed spouse and an impending foreclosure, which felt like the sword of Damocles swinging above her head. They'd soon fall behind on the mortgage again, with foreclosure proceedings right behind. She felt the walls closing in.

❖

Nicky passed Zoey in the hall as she returned to her office following dinner.

"I've been meaning to ask you how things are going with your new roommate?" Nicky said.

"That bitch? Thanks for saddling me with her."

"What's going on?" Nicky would love it if just once she was thanked sincerely for what she did. That was so rare she couldn't think of the last time it happened.

"Get this. She's drawn a line down the middle of the room, like little kids do. If anything of mine touches the line she has a fit."

"You are exceptionally messy. Maybe she felt it was necessary."

"It's insulting. She bought masking tape this morning and my stuff was nowhere near the line."

"I admit it's not the friendliest thing to do. Try to make the best of it, Zoey. I have nowhere else to put her."

"Of course, you don't. This place is packed tight as it is." Zoey continued on her way to the AA meeting room where the six o'clock was about to start.

Nicky went into her office and closed the door. She should have gone to the meeting herself. God knows she could use one. Being around other alcoholics always made her feel calmer. Their funny stories, vulnerabilities, and brutal honesty all resonated and made her feel stronger, less alone. Too long without one and her brain started to revert to the one that said it was okay to drink.

Instead, she fired up her computer and opened the drug testing spreadsheet. It would have to be altered to accommodate the new protocol. Her fingers hit the keyboard hard as she thought about Gerri and how she was ruining things. She felt sick at the effort it was going to take to get all ten women downtown twice a week.

How could she protest this? Gerri was the God of Olive Street House—Nicky didn't even know who her boss was. Everything came through Gerri as edicts, not as suggestions on how to solve problems in the house. It was clear she didn't care about the women's welfare. She glanced at the time on her phone and rolled her chair away from the desk. The AA meeting was over and it was time for the weekly house meeting. She'd rather be tossed from a cliff than walk into the room. She felt like a doomed gladiator entering the ring with a rubber sword.

The last stragglers from the AA meeting were leaving as Nicky entered the room. The residents stayed in their seats for the house meeting to come. She took the secretary's seat at the front of the room and looked out at her charges. They sat in groups of two or three and clearly sensed bad news coming. They looked at her through narrowed eyes.

"We're going to get started now," Nicky said. "I have two things to tell you about, and you're not going to like either one." She could see the apprehension on everyone's expression. "The first is about Lou, who left the house on Friday. She was found dead over the weekend, apparently stabbed in the heart."

The room erupted in questions, all of which Nicky waved away. "I don't have any further information. The police will want to talk to you all. I expect you to cooperate with them."

The women fell into an eerie silence. All eyes were on Nicky, waiting for more bad news to be sprung on them.

"The second bit of news is the company that owns this house is now requiring you be tested twice a week for drugs. Everyone needs to assess their schedules to insure you meet the new requirement. I've been told those who don't comply will be removed from the house."

The uproar started halfway through her speech. Heads turned to each other with looks of outrage and then they turned on Nicky. "You can't possibly be serious," Susan said. "It's hard enough getting down there for one test. This is totally fucked up."

Invectives were hurled Nicky's way. Everyone was talking at once. She sat there as impassively as she could, holding the gavel in her hand and fighting the urge to whack it down. The women needed the opportunity to protest and she didn't intend to ignore them, as Gerri would have done.

"Listen," she said. "I have no clout on this. There's nothing I can do to get the policy overturned. All I can do is help you get to the lab, either by adjusting your schedule in the house or driving you down there myself."

Madison, the newcomer, stood up. "I'm not going to listen to this." She worked her way past the women in her row and walked out the door. In the next instant all the women rose and walked out after her, not one of them saying anything to Nicky. Suddenly, the gavel in her hand felt ridiculous. She'd lost control of the crowd and didn't know if they had any intention of abiding by the new rule. It would be good if they didn't. How did Gerri hope to force them?

CHAPTER TEN

Nicky was still in bed at ten the next morning; the thought of getting dressed and leaving her room was immobilizing. She'd have to get up soon and go to the police station for her interview with Quinn and Parker, but for now she lay rigidly under the covers, pulling them over her head. She was alternately thinking about the disastrous house meeting the night before and the unexpected call from Joanne Parker.

A sharp rap on her door startled her.

"Nicky, there's someone here to see you. What do you want me to do?" It was Roxy.

"Who is it?"

"Some older woman named Sheila. I've seen her at meetings."

Nicky groaned. Sheila was not someone she could lie to—she'd see right through the artifice. If she sent word down that she was busy, Sheila would come back again. Her persistence was sometimes annoying, but she was one of the distressingly few people who genuinely cared about her. That was something worth keeping.

Sheila was waiting for her in the meeting room. When Nicky walked in she was bent over her phone, tapping out a message. She looked up and smiled and some of Nicky's pique faded away.

"I just heard about Lou," Sheila said. "How are you holding up?"

Nicky sat in a chair one over from Sheila. "I'm fine. It's not me I'm worried about."

"Poor Lou. Do you have any idea who did it?"

"How would I know? The police just started their investigation."

"I know you're investigating also, or at least you had been when she first went missing. It doesn't seem like you to stop."

"I'm not police, Sheila," she said, a little more forcefully than she intended. "They're much better equipped to find a killer than I am."

Sheila looked at her appraisingly. "If you say so. You seem angry. I haven't done anything to offend you, have I?"

Nicky blew out her breath and closed her eyes. "I'm upset, nothing more. I have a house full of women freaked out about Lou. Things are a little tense right now."

"How can I help? Do you want to talk about it more?"

"No."

Sheila laughed. "No, I didn't think you would. I'm here for whatever you need. And who knows? You might be willing to take up the investigation again. I had fun as your sidekick."

"You'll have to look for your kicks elsewhere. I'm keeping my head low." She had no such intention, but she didn't want Sheila to think they were Batman and Robin.

She saw the hurt look in Sheila's eyes, quickly covered by her usual smile and supportive look. She was being an ass. There was no need to push Sheila away. "Maybe we can catch coffee and a meeting together, something like that."

Sheila's smile widened. "I'd love that. Anytime. Do you want to pick a time now?"

"I don't have my phone with me. I'll have to check my calendar and text you."

Sheila rose and picked up her bag. She wore a long black skirt and boots, with a bolero top, looking like she was ready for a feminist bullfight. "Get up and give me a hug, at least. I'm not entirely convinced you're okay."

Nicky stood and leaned in, Sheila's arms wrapping tight around her, pulling her in. "Let's say I'm okay, given the circumstances. I feel terrible about Lou."

She pulled away from Sheila, who still held her by both upper arms.

"This is a tragedy, Nicky. We all feel terrible."

They said their good-byes and Nicky closed the door behind her, sighing with relief. She wasn't fit for human company now. All she wanted was her quiet room and a whiskey. The thought popped into her brain uninvited and scared the bejesus out of her. She needed to quit feeling sorry for herself and concentrate on the investigation. There was so much to figure out, like how to find Lou's killer. Because find him she would.

Nicky met Quinn in the waiting area of the new Rogers Park police station, a modern building plunked down on a part of Clark Street much different from the boutiques and restaurants of Andersonville. Here the station shared the block with hair salons, taquerias, quick loan shops, and criminal defense offices. He led her down a labyrinthine hallway into an interview room where memories washed over her of the untold hours she'd spent in rooms exactly like it, interviewing witnesses and drawing confessions from suspects. It was where most cases were solved. Now she sat on the opposite side of the table where metal loops were bolted to accommodate handcuffs.

Quinn left her in the room to get Parker, and five minutes later they walked in with cups of coffee in hand.

"I remember you like your coffee with lots of cream," Quinn said, putting a Styrofoam cup in front of her. "Hard to forget when you've had a million cups of coffee with someone."

Nicky didn't say anything. She'd wait for questions. Quinn and Parker got settled in across from her and Parker took out her notebook and pen, flipping several pages in before folding it over and looking at Nicky expectantly.

"Nicky's a kick ass interviewer," Quinn said, looking at Parker. "Drew more confessions than anyone else in the division."

"I don't doubt it."

"That was a long time ago," Nicky said.

"Not that long," Quinn said. "Listen, before we talk about Lou Hansen, I have some news," Quinn said.

"Oh?" It had to be bad news. What else would it be?

"A body was discovered this morning, a middle-aged woman who'd been stabbed in the heart."

"Fuck." She hadn't expected the news to be that bad.

"We have an ID," Parker said. "Ruby Schiller. Her address is in Avondale, but she was found in the alley behind a sober house in Lakeview. The manager confirmed Ruby had been a resident but had been kicked out the previous day for drinking."

Nicky felt the blood draining from her face, protecting her heart from the shock. "I knew Ruby Schiller."

Quinn and Parker stared at her, waiting for more.

"If it's the same woman, I sponsored her for a short time when she first got sober. I can't say I got to know much about her. She went back out within a week or two. We'd barely cracked the Big Book."

"But you did know her," Parker said. "That's a strange coincidence, don't you think, you knowing both victims?"

"The recovery community is small. You get to know a lot of people."

"But you think it's more than a coincidence, don't you?" Quinn said.

"I don't know yet. I'm more concerned this looks like a serial murder, someone targeting women who relapse."

"Agreed. Whoever he is, he has a thing about sobriety."

"He may be a she," Parker said. "It doesn't take a lot of strength to stab the obliterated."

"Point taken," Quinn said. "Almost all serial killers are men, but you never know. We'll get the case transferred to us, keep you as involved as we can. It looks like you may have a role here. I don't believe in coincidences."

"How did Lou react when you accused her of theft?" Parker said.

"She was terrified. She was a stoic person, but this rattled her."

"Do you think she took the money?"

"Not now I don't. It turns out Lou was innocent of the theft, but I didn't learn that until after she disappeared."

"How's that?" Parker said, lifting her head from her notebook.

"I tracked down her brother Jack and spoke to him about it. He confirmed he'd bought the laptop for her."

"See, that's what I mean about a shadow investigation," Quinn said. "Cut it out. We'll keep you as informed as we can, but you can't interfere."

Nicky stared at him blankly.

"Can I count on you?"

She smiled. "As much as you ever can."

"What do you think of the knife to the heart? It's unusual, as far as street crimes go," Parker said.

Nicky had been thinking about that herself. "It's quick and efficient, but it's only done by someone familiar with exactly where the heart is in the chest. Plus, Lou would have been wearing a jacket which makes that kind of pinpoint accuracy even more difficult. Either it was someone Lou knew who could get close to her or it was a stranger looking to take advantage of a drunk."

Parker was gazing at her. Her eyes were bright rather than interrogative, as if much more was going on in her brain than the facts of Lou Hansen's murder. Nicky took a sip of the awful coffee and waited for the next question.

"We'll be in touch," Parker said.

"We're done?"

"For the time being. I'm sure we'll have more questions for you." Parker closed her notebook and clicked off her pen.

Quinn sat back in his chair, arms folded in front of him. "Remember what I said, Nicky."

She rose quickly and said her good-byes. Outside, the wind howled down Clark Street and it was spitting rain, the first after a week of perfect September weather. She trotted to her car and sat in it for a while before starting it up. The interview had gone well and there didn't seem to be any suspicion about her role in Lou's or Ruby's deaths. She liked both of them. Quinn was like comfort food—familiar and soothing. Parker was an unknown, but with some obvious qualities—she was attractive, smart, good police. There was something in her eyes that made Nicky feel unsettled. If she was in a bar at two in the morning, she might try to pick up someone with that look in her eye, but to think that's what Parker intended was preposterous.

❖

Nicky made an appointment with Lou's counselor at Northwestern's rehab facility. When she presented herself at the nurse's station and asked for Lily Tanner, she was slammed back in time to her own stint in rehab. Women in leggings and sweatshirts marched down the hall with notebooks and brand-new copies of the Big Book hugged to their chests. They were probably going from a group therapy session to a midday AA meeting, their full schedules doing a lot to keep them upright and engaged.

Nicky's own time in rehab provided her with the biggest sense of relief she'd ever felt—the crushing, uncontrollable life she'd been living was over. It was humbling, for Nicky had to admit all her best thinking and efforts led her to becoming a bottoming out drunk. She had no choice but to listen to what others were telling her. On this subject she admitted their thinking was better than her own.

Lily Tanner entered the open space by the nurses' station and walked to Nicky with her hand extended.

"I'm sorry to keep you waiting. Shall we go back?"

They got settled in Lily's office, a pleasant, sunny room meant to put the newly sober at ease, especially those who'd never talked to a therapist before.

"You said when we spoke that this is about Lou Hansen. What should I know?" Lily had the kind of warmth that reminded her of Sheila. She filled her in on Lou's murder.

"I'm trying to get a full picture of Lou. I found it hard to communicate with her. Was that your experience?" Nicky said.

"Of course, I can't talk about anything that happened while Lou was in session."

"She's dead. There's no point to the confidentiality."

"The confidentiality survives the death of the patient, so my silence still holds." Nicky knew this, but it was worth a try.

"We're trying to find Lou's killer. Can you at least tell me whether Lou shared with you any plans she had for when she got out of treatment? Did she mention any names or places?"

Lily sipped her tea and looked thoughtful. "You might want to talk to her boyfriend."

Nicky's mouth fell open. "Her *boyfriend*?"

Lily smiled. "Does that surprise you?"

"I'm sure it shouldn't surprise me, but it does. I assumed Lou was a lesbian."

"That's fairly outmoded thinking. I would call Lou queer or gender fluid; she's not attracted to one thing. I think young people today have a much wider playing field than I did in my day."

Nicky couldn't get over the idea of Lou with a man. It was impossible to picture. "What can you tell me about him?"

"I don't know much. It came up when I asked Lou about who brought her into rehab and she said no one, that she'd come in on her own because her boyfriend didn't want her to go. That's when she dumped him, so technically he's her ex-boyfriend."

"Sounds like he's a heavy user if he's threatened by her sobriety," Nicky said. "Do you have any idea how long they'd been together? Where they met?"

"She said they met over the summer at a party. Not long."

"Do you have a name?"

"His first name is Bartholomew and that's what he likes to be called. Not Bart, according to Lou. I never heard a last name."

Nicky was thrilled over the unusual first name. It made it much easier to track a person down.

"Did Lou seem upset about the breakup? I never would have known it from when I worked with her," Nicky said.

"I think the realities of a new sober life may have pushed Bartholomew out of her mind."

They spoke a few more minutes about Lou's parents, a classic case of upper-middle-class neglect. When Nicky rose to leave, she was satisfied she'd gotten what she could from Lily, with her somewhat wobbly definition of what was confidential and what was not. Now she had to figure out what to do with the information. Her first stop should be Quinn and Parker, but they wouldn't be happy about her interview with Lily Tanner. She decided to keep news of Bartholomew to herself for the time being.

CHAPTER ELEVEN

Nicky headed to Uptown, a neighborhood immediately south of Andersonville that was famed as a pocket of resistance to the complete gentrification of Chicago's shoreline. The activists largely lost the battle, but Uptown was still known as the home of many social service organizations, mental health facilities, and a fair amount of crime, interspersed with half-million-dollar condos. A neighborhood divided.

Lou told her brother she was going to stay in an SRO, a residence designed for single guests only who needed a place to stay either overnight or for an extended period. In the way back time they were called flop houses, but now they had largely eliminated that sordid feel and provided a decent place to stay when times were hard. Nicky tried to guess which SRO Lou would go to and the one in Uptown was closest.

She pulled into the nearest parking space—a block and a half away—and hurried along to the address. It was early evening and the shadows deepened as the sun neared the horizon. The days were getting shorter. She'd thought of bringing her service weapon with her but decided against it. She guessed there'd be a metal detector at the entrance. As she approached, she saw a large brick building that was once an elementary school. It stood four stories tall and half as wide as a city block, enough to house an awful lot of people in need of help.

There was no door staff to let her in, but there was a buzzer where the residents could punch in a code to enter the building. She looked around and saw a lot of foot traffic on the sidewalk, but no one turning into the SRO. Finally, a resident came out of the building and Nicky grabbed the door before it could shut her out. Inside was a wide hallway leading to the one-time classrooms in two directions, but no metal detector. To the right was the old principal's office, now dark with a blind drawn over the main window. Whatever staff there was clearly didn't do evenings or overnights.

She moved down the hallway to the right and heard laughter. A classroom was lit up at the end and she slowly approached it. When she reached the open door, the laughter died immediately. The room was set up as a lounge. Five women were sprawled in chairs arrayed around a coffee table, each looking at her as if she were wearing a mermaid costume. The silence lasted a beat before one of the women snarled, "Who are you?" She was dressed as if she were working the streets and Nicky wondered what her story was. She was interested in all their stories of struggling to live a better life. Everyday heroism, she thought, though it wasn't recognized as such. Crawling out of the gutter didn't rank with most notions of bravery, but she knew what kind of guts it took.

The other women stared at her with unblinking eyes. She felt like a freak.

"My name is Nicky Sullivan and I'm looking for someone who may have stayed here the last few nights."

"What's her name?" said the business suit.

"Lou Hansen. But if you don't recognize the name, I have a photo you can look at."

"Bring it here."

Nicky walked into the room and approached the circle. She handed over the photo that had been in Lou's intake file.

"Haven't seen her," the woman said, passing it to the next woman. It went around the circle until one woman sat up in her chair.

"I met her! She was a total bitch."

"What do you mean?"

"She grunted when I introduced myself and walked away. I don't need that shit."

"Did she say anything to you at all?"

"Not then, but later that night I saw her coming in and tried talking to her again, just to annoy her. She looked a little shaken up. She said she'd been mugged in the alley and they'd gotten her wallet."

Nicky's heart broke. With all Lou was facing—homelessness, new sobriety, abandonment by her parents—losing her wallet felt like the final straw. "Did she say anything else?"

"No. She brushed by me and went upstairs. I didn't see her again."

Lou must have gone to see her brother after this, gotten drunk and high, and then been attacked and murdered. The mugging was a street crime, the murder anything but. After making sure no one else had met or seen Lou, Nicky left. She walked around the corner of the building to the alley behind, wanting to see where Lou got mugged. It was exceptionally dark. Both streetlights were broken. Farther down the alley there was a parking lot for the SRO and then nothing but apartment buildings with various parking spots and garages. She reached the other end of the alley and turned to go back when a figure emerged from the side of a garage and held a gun toward her.

"You're kidding me, right?" She felt more annoyed than anything.

The man holding the gun was small. Without the gun, she'd have a fair chance of taking him. His hair and beard were shaggy, his clothes filthy. He held the gun in front of him with two trembling hands, more because it was heavy than it was the preferred stance with a handgun. He was a very nervous robber. She remembered mornings being so hung over she couldn't bring a cup of coffee to her lips for all the shaking. This guy was an equal mess.

"Listen, before you take my money I want to ask you a question. Would that be okay?"

He lowered his gun for a minute in confusion. Nicky didn't hesitate to take a step and kick it out of his hands. It went skittering into the middle of the alley and she was there to retrieve it before the man could react at all. He had no business trying to mug people. A car entered the alley and Nicky shoved the man into the dark next to a garage. They stood there flattened against the garage until the car passed. She didn't want anyone calling the police.

"Now, about that question."

"Get out of my way."

"I'll be happy to, depending on what information you have."

"Information about what? I don't know anything about anything!" In his agitation he started hopping like a pogo stick. As calming activities go, that would be low on her list. Deep breaths might be a better choice. She put her left hand on his shoulder and pointed the gun at him with her right.

"You better calm down or you'll give yourself a heart attack." She pushed him back against the garage and reached into her pocket for the photo of Lou. "Did you mug this woman a few nights ago?"

"That's a woman?"

"Do you recognize her or not?"

"Never seen her."

Shit. She jammed the photo back in her pocket and as she did so, the man reached toward his belt and drew a knife, a big honking Bowie knife, and slashed toward her in an arc. The tip of the blade caught the top of her forehead and drew a line across it, effectively opening a curtain of blood streaming down her face. She was reaching for her head when he shoved her to the ground and ran off. The gun was still in her grip. At least he no longer had that to terrorize people with. She should call the police, but the hassle seemed too much. Plus, she was bleeding like a stuck pig and the jacket she had pressed to her head did nothing to staunch the flow. She tried to wipe her prints from the gun, but her DNA-laden blood was everywhere. She jammed it into her jacket pocket. By the time she got to her car, two people had seen her trotting by bleeding profusely and hadn't said a word or offered any assistance. She dropped herself into the driver's seat and swore. One thing she couldn't avoid was a trip to the emergency room. She found a sweatshirt in the back seat and pressed it to her head. It worked much better at keeping the blood out of her eyes, but it wasn't safe to drive.

Who to call was the question. She was already late getting back to the house for dinner time, and it was now going to be hours before she'd be home. Before thinking about it too much, she called Parker, who, after all, had called her once. It wasn't so odd for her to get in touch, if only for a favor.

The phone rang several times before Parker picked up. "Nicky Sullivan," she said. "Whatever the reason is, I'm glad you're calling."

"You might not be when I tell you I need someone to take me to the ER."

"What happened?" Nicky heard the concern in her voice and was thrilled.

"I got mugged and the dude got me with a knife, a nice slice across my forehead." She took the sweatshirt away and looked in the rearview mirror. The blood was still spilling enthusiastically. "You know how head wounds are—they bleed like hell. It's not serious, but I can't drive."

"Give me the address. I'll leave right now."

Parker arrived and they drove to Illinois Masonic's emergency room. Two hours later they were on their way back to Olive Street House, twelve stitches in Nicky's head covered by an embarrassingly large bandage. It was cartoonish.

"I can pick you up in the morning to go retrieve your car. My shift doesn't start until later."

Nicky looked at her auburn hair, the fine lines around her green eyes, the strong hands holding the steering wheel loosely. The attraction was strong, but didn't love need an opening to thrive? She had no openings. All systems were in overdrive.

"You don't have to. I can find someone to give me a ride."

"Let me be that someone. I'd like to."

They exchanged a glance Nicky didn't dare hold for longer than a second. She felt more nervous than she had with a gun pointed at her earlier. Parker pulled up in front of Olive Street House and put the car in park. Christ, was she going to kiss her? Nicky opened the door and put one foot on the curb, ready to bail should Parker make a move. She wasn't prepared for a kiss.

"I wanted to talk to you about the Lou Hansen case, but maybe we could wait until morning," Parker said.

"Let's definitely wait. I'm starting to fade a bit." She thought she'd better tell Parker about Bartholomew, but tomorrow would be soon enough.

The moment Nicky woke the following morning her hand went to the bandage on her forehead. The wound hurt, with a bad headache lurking beneath it. It was already after eight and most of the women should've been at their day jobs. The house was quiet. She threw on some jeans and a sweatshirt and was about to go down when her phone rang. It was Parker. Nicky had programmed her into her phone so she'd know when it was her calling.

"Good morning," Parker said. "Hate to disturb you so early in the day."

"You're not disturbing me. You can call me anytime."

Did that sound flirty? Nicky was such a bad flirt she couldn't tell. Parker was quiet for a moment, which filled her with worry she'd said the wrong thing.

"Thank you, Nicky. That means a lot to me."

They had clearly moved to the stage where two people know they're attracted to each other but no one's making the first move. Everything they said was laden with meaning, but what that meaning was was still uncertain and scary. This time Nicky was quiet.

"I have some news for you," Parker said, smoothing over the awkwardness. "We got the test results back for Lou and it looks like she was full of meth when she died."

"Her brother said he'd given her some, so I'm not surprised. It helps explain how anyone got close enough to stab her. She was too high to protect herself. It's fucking sad."

Nicky paused before shifting gears. "Have you gotten lab results from the other woman who died? I wonder if she relapsed, too," Nicky said.

"We're on it. We should get something today from the lab. Do you think it's important?"

"I don't know. It's something to keep an eye on, especially if there are more bodies of relapsed women. It might be a part of the killer's *modus operandi.*"

"Your insights into the recovery culture are very helpful. You can spot things I wouldn't think to note. Does it make you miss the job?"

"Hmm. I miss the parts I loved about the job. The catching the bad guys part. I don't miss the more toxic parts of being a detective."

"They're still there, in spades."

"How do you deal with all the assholes?"

Parker laughed. "There are a lot of them, but I'm able to compartmentalize and keep the irritating and annoying tucked away. I don't let it get to me."

"Wow. That's a seriously impressive life skill."

"I don't take it for granted. Listen, I can be over in about fifteen minutes to take you to your car. Does that work for you?"

Nicky went downstairs to grab breakfast and wait for Parker. The kitchen was empty and she ate her cereal while staring out the screen doors leading to the deck and backyard. A familiar and terrifying feeling crept over her. She was thinking of drinking and how it felt to take a drink of whiskey and have it course its way through her body. The "ah" moment of that first sip. If only she'd been able to limit herself to one or two drinks, but it was never just that. The first sip meant she'd drink until she passed out, every time. She had forfeited the right to enjoy the positive aspects of alcohol, because for her there were none. Instead of calling her sponsor she took a deep breath and shoved the drinking thought away. Sometimes good things, like the possibilities with Parker, could be as triggery as bad things.

Parker picked her up for the short drive to Uptown. Nicky told her about her conversation with Lou's inpatient counselor and the surprising news that Lou had a boyfriend.

"I see you've taken to heart Quinn's warning about not investigating on your own."

"I heard him. I'd already made the appointment with the counselor and thought I'd keep it before backing away."

"That's such bullshit," Parker said, smiling. "Should I be surprised Lou had a boyfriend?"

"Maybe not. Lou was in bad shape toward the end there. When the bars are closing, any human body seems attractive. And maybe she genuinely cared for him. Anything's possible."

"We know his name is Bartholomew, which should filter things down nicely. Do you have a physical description?"

"A shaky one. Apparently, he's short and slender. Lou must have towered over him. He has dark hair and a beard and that's all I got."

"Okay. We'll track him down. I like him as a suspect. I'll have to smooth things over with Quinn."

"Understood. But if Bartholomew killed Lou by stabbing her in the heart, who killed the other woman who died the same way?"

"Maybe Bartholomew knew her too. There are lots of questions, Nicky."

Parker dropped her at the SRO with a promise to be in touch soon and drove away in her late model Subaru Crosstrek. The air was the coldest it had been that fall, and Nicky's light jacket was unequal to the task. She sat hunched in her car, waiting for the engine to warm up enough to drive without a blood-curdling screech. For a moment she wondered what it would be like to make money again, to be able to buy a decent car and shop somewhere other than the thrift stores. She hadn't bought a new book since she'd been sober, and it used to be one of her greatest pleasures. Not that she'd been sober enough to read any of them, but their look and feel were a talisman for her.

The house was still quiet. Compared to the pandemonium that followed the announcement of twice weekly drug tests, the quiet was a balm. Nicky had tried to calm the uproar by volunteering to drive residents down as a group to get their tests. But the loud grumbling among the residents continued and Nicky despaired over what to do to increase morale. It wasn't in her power to give the residents what they wanted, which left her with very little power at all.

She went upstairs to get her laptop. It was ancient and had a battery life of about a minute. When it died she wouldn't be able to replace it, leaving her limbless in the modern world. In the hallway she heard soft music coming from one of the rooms at the end. All the women from those rooms should have been out working. She walked down the hallway and found the music coming out of Madison and Zoey's room. She knew it wasn't Zoey in there. Despite her surly attitude, she was diligent about showing up to work regularly and on time. That left Madison, the new *de facto* leader of the women. She knocked on the door and entered without waiting for a response. Madison was sprawled across her bed, face up, unable to react to the shock of someone barging in her room because she was too shit faced. She lifted her head for a moment, saw Nicky, and groaned. Next to her was a junkie's works—spoon, a tourniquet, a Bic lighter, and an empty packet of heroin.

Nicky ran to her office and opened a supply cabinet where she kept doses of Narcan, the miracle drug for opioid overdoses. She ran back up while ripping off the packaging. Madison was passed out and Nicky was able to easily administer the spray into each nostril. She grabbed her phone and dialed 911.

Soon, two fire trucks, an ambulance, and two squad cars blocked the street in front of the house. Just the kind of thing the neighbors hated about living near a halfway house. The first responders rushed upstairs where Madison was still passed out and soon they carried her down on a stretcher and took her to the hospital. She'd have to tell Gerri about this, but for once she wanted to. Gerri wouldn't mind throwing her out. Nicky suspected Gerri enjoyed the power she felt when she disrupted the women's lives. She put in the call.

Gerri picked up on the first ring. "Nicky Sullivan. I hope you're not calling with a new problem at Olive Street House."

Nicky gritted her teeth. Was it wrong to feel violence against your boss? "There's been an incident. I just caught your gal Madison with a hefty dose of heroin up her arm."

"What?"

"She's at the hospital now and I'll join her as soon as we hang up."

"Could there be some mistake?" Her voice was strained and higher than usual.

"No mistake. She passed out with the drug works right beside her. You have no choice but to kick her out."

Silence. Nicky waited impatiently for her to say something. "You are going to throw her out, aren't you? I mean, it's the number one rule around here."

More silence. Finally, Gerri cleared her throat and said, "That poor woman. She needs help; she doesn't need to be tossed out like garbage."

A white light appeared before Nicky's eyes, blinding her with rage. Lou needed help, too, you crazy bitch. She got herself under control and said with a steely voice, "You have to evict her. You have no choice."

"But I do have a choice. The decision rests solely with me, and in this case it's my opinion the good of the house would better be served by keeping her with us and helping her regain her sobriety."

"But you kicked Lou out on the suspicion of wrongdoing. You're applying the rules at your whim. Besides, Madison is the most vocal opponent of your policies. Why would you want to protect her? When the residents find out, morale will sink even lower."

"I wouldn't worry about the morale. Women will do what they have to to keep their place in the house, and when they don't, like with Madison, we can show compassion by helping her get back up again."

"This is wrong."

"Keep up the good work, Nicky. I appreciate what you do at the house. You'll be able to smooth this over with the residents."

Gerri hung up. Nicky had her head in her hands as she sat hunched over her desk, a sense of dread covering her like a cloak. How could she possibly explain to the women that Madison would not be kicked out? They'd all know she relapsed—the women working later shifts were home when the first responders started pouring into the house. They would quickly spread the word to the others. One positive thing about Gerri's decision was it likely saved Madison's life, with one less relapsed alcoholic on the streets to become a target for their killer. Too bad Lou hadn't had the same luxury.

CHAPTER TWELVE

Nicky peeled off her bandage and stared into the mirror. An angry wound crawled from the top of her forehead to beyond her hairline. A little patch of hair had been shaved to make way for the sutures. It was too ugly to leave uncovered. She inexpertly put on a new dressing and left the bathroom.

The day before had left her drained and angry that Madison didn't seem the least grateful she hadn't been thrown onto the streets. Now all the women would think they could do it too. Gerri's unequal application of the rules was impossible to explain to a group of women wondering what the hell was going on. When Madison came home from the hospital, a little wobbly but basically fine, the other women gathered around her as if they were disciples. Her sanctioned relapse was the equivalent of turning water into wine for the newly sober. If the women decided to cast their lot behind one leader, Madison was the leader she dreaded. She was spreading resistance throughout the house and she blamed Nicky for the new rules. It didn't take long for suspicious looks to replace normally friendly ones and she felt herself losing grip over her charges.

Nicky went into her office and left the door open, as she usually did to encourage the women to come to her with their problems. She was taking her first sip of coffee when Susan appeared in the door, she of the in-house love affair. Susan and Diane had broken up, causing further drama in the house as women picked sides.

"Nicky, I can't make my test today," She stood stiffly and didn't smile. "I got an extra shift at the store."

"That's okay. I'm driving everyone down on Saturday."

"I'm working then, too."

Nicky sighed. So far, only a small portion of the women were current on their tests. Suddenly everyone had work conflicts. "You have to get the test by Sunday. Isn't there a time before or after your shifts where you could sneak it in?

"Sorry. There isn't. What happens if I don't get the test?"

"I don't know yet, but it'll be something."

"You people can't play with our lives like this. You need to get your shit together." Susan disappeared from the doorway. Nicky couldn't disagree.

She was steeling herself for another fruitless conversation with Gerri when her phone rang. It was Quinn.

"Bad news," he said. "A third body's been found."

Nicky's heart hammered in her chest. "Where?"

"Down in Ukrainian Village."

"Was she at the St. Ignatius home?"

"Was being the operative word. She got kicked out last night, found dead this morning."

"She was stabbed?"

"Neat as a pin, right through the heart."

"Jesus. We definitely have a serial killer on our hands. I don't know how your bosses could deny it."

"They can't, not after this one. Parker and I will get a couple more detectives assigned to us. I'd like to get word to the press to try to warn other women, but I'm not sure the brass is willing to sound the alarm yet."

"What's her name?"

"Janelle Jergins. Do you know her?"

Nicky's coffee cup came down with a thud. "Oh, God. She was my first sponsor. How could she have relapsed? She had something like twenty years of sobriety."

"Relapse is always a risk, isn't it?"

"Yes, but more of a risk for some rather than others. She was solid in the program."

"I'm sorry, Nicky." He paused for a moment. "That means you know all three of the women murdered and that gives us something to work with."

"You don't think I did this, do you?" She was starting to feel defensive, knowing her alibis couldn't be verified by any of the residents. They'd have no idea if she left the house in the middle of the night.

"I don't think you're the killer," Quinn said with a laugh. "But you're in the middle of it. Let's talk more later. I've got to get to a meeting."

"I don't know whether to say thanks or not."

"I'm supposed to be upset with you for conducting an interview with Lou's counselor."

"But?"

"But we can't ignore you. You're too involved with the victims. And you can give us info on the recovery community. By default, you're involved in the investigation."

"Officially?"

"Well, not officially. But you'll be a major resource."

He hung up, abruptly for Quinn, but he had three murders on his hands and no time to waste. Neither did she.

By the end of the afternoon, Nicky had called all of the sober houses in Chicago to warn them about the relapse killer. The manager of the house in Rogers Park, Julie Tabor, was a friend of hers. She didn't hesitate to share the news about the murders.

"It's bizarre you'd ask me about women getting kicked out of the house. I had to evict someone last night because she relapsed. She left around eight and I have no idea where she may have gone."

"What's her name?"

"Allie Becker."

"Oh, shit. I know her too. I dated her for a while after I got sober, which I had no business doing. I was a wreck. I think we had three dates before I called it off." Nicky's heart filled with dread. Somehow, she was responsible for a rapidly growing series of murders. There was no denying it now.

"She came to us a month ago. Apparently, she'd had a massive relapse and was advised to live in a sober home for a while. When she came home yesterday afternoon she'd clearly been drinking. I gave her time to sleep it off before she left."

"Allie is in danger. Can you give me her cell number so I can track her down?"

Julie gave Nicky the number and promised to question the women in the Rogers Park house to see if they knew where Allie went and get back to Nicky.

She had to tell Quinn and Parker and decided to call Quinn again. She was nervous about Parker and wanted to keep the call completely professional. Quinn picked up and she told him about the woman out on the street in Rogers Park, possibly drunk. She confessed to knowing her as well as the others.

"I'll have patrol start going down the alleys around the house. Hopefully we won't find any bodies. I want you to come in for a meeting with Parker and me. This is escalating quickly."

No shit. Nicky felt like she was in a rockslide, with all the big rocks gaining momentum behind her. She left her office to get some air on the back patio. It was brisk out and she grabbed a blanket from the family room as she walked through. She sat in a chaise lounge to ponder what her connection to the victims was all about. The noise in her head was so loud not a single cogent thought stuck in her brain. She closed her eyes and tried to relax, but she was like a humming electrical wire. It would be a great time to meditate, if only she weren't so terrible at it. Every other month or so she'd gamely turn on a guided meditation only to be frustrated by her galloping thoughts. It was far more agitating than soothing. Just as she flung the blanket off to go back inside, Sheila came onto the patio. Nicky didn't want to see anyone but lifted her hand in greeting and settled back in her chair.

"What are you doing sitting in the cold?" Sheila said.

"I'm having a hot flash."

Sheila laughed. "You're a little young for that. Believe me, you'll know when you're in menopause." She joined Nicky at the table.

"Since you're here, you should know there have been two more murders since Lou's, women who have relapsed and been kicked out of their sober homes. A fourth woman was kicked out last night after relapsing, but no one knows where she is." She'd repeatedly called Allie's number but never reached her.

At first it looked like Sheila didn't comprehend what Nicky was saying, but then her face sharpened and she looked mad as hell. Nicky kept back a few things, like her connection to the victims.

"I think an announcement should be made before every AA meeting," Sheila said. "We have to warn people."

"That's a great idea, though I don't know how we'll get the word out." AA was not like other organizations. There was no office to help disseminate information. Each AA group was its own island, connected loosely to a central office in New York.

"I can start spreading the word. It's better than doing nothing."

"Sure. That would be great. We'll start making the announcement at our meeting here and ask everyone to spread the news."

Nicky showed Sheila out before driving up to Rogers Park to look for Allie Becker. She knew the police had probably been up and down the same alleys, but it was possible they missed something. She drove around the neighborhood, trying to imagine where Allie might have been attacked. She checked the alleys behind bars and restaurants, the beaches dotting the shoreline, the areas around the El stops. Nothing. She was glad to not find a body, but her gut told her it was only a matter of time.

CHAPTER THIRTEEN

Jack Hansen didn't answer her when she called the following day. It could be the number he gave her when they met at the diner was not the number he used now. Dealers changed burner phones like underwear. There was no voicemail for her to leave a message, but half an hour later he called back.

"Who is this?" he said.

"It's Nicky Sullivan. We talked a couple days ago about your sister, Lou."

"Right. I remember."

"Have you learned anything that might help us find who did this to her?"

"I don't think it had anything to do with me. I had it checked out. As far as I know, there are no current vendettas against me. I don't know how my colleagues in the business would even know about Lou."

"What about Lou's boyfriend? You hadn't mentioned him when we last talked."

"That little twerp. I'll tell you, that was the weirdest match in history, like an Amazon with a Pygmy."

"Who is he?"

"I don't know a thing about him, other than his name is Bartholomew. I think Lou had ended things with him when she went into rehab. They were inseparable for a while and I don't think he was happy at the breakup. Could that little fucker have killed my sister? Anything's possible."

Jack hung up, leaving Nicky holding her phone, looking at it blankly. She had to find Bartholomew, but without resources it was nearly impossible.

❖

The offices of Reardon-Malloy were abuzz. Word had gone out the company suffered another quarter of losses, and everyone was busy looking essential. Gerri put her bag in her desk drawer and made a beeline to her boss's office. She had an idea and she couldn't wait to share it with him.

Dave Edmundson looked up from his desk at Gerri hovering at his door. He was wary of her, she could see it in his eyes, as if she were there with yet another problem and not a solution.

"Good morning, Dave. I want a minute of your time to discuss an idea I have to increase revenue."

His look relaxed. "I always have time for that. What have you got?"

Gerri took the liberty of sitting down uninvited. "As you know, there are very few ways for us to increase profits given the model of the sober living house. They pay rent to be there, but the margins are small once the expenses of the house are paid. What if we were to add one more woman per room, increasing the census at each house by one-third? The cost of the bunk beds we'd need to install could be absorbed in the first month or two."

Edmundson tapped his pen on the leather, monogrammed portfolio on the desk. "I don't know. How bad do you think the backlash will be from the residents?"

"Who cares? They need us more than we need them. There are always more where they came from."

He looked at her for a moment. "I wonder if there are other houses out there that have three to a room."

"If there aren't now, there will be soon. It's the quickest way to bring in some cash, and everyone needs more of that. What do you say? Do you need to clear it with anyone?"

"No, that's my decision. If you think we can do it without losing all our residents, then I'm willing to buy the bunk beds."

"Excellent. I'll coordinate with your office and take care of our three sober houses. Can I get started right away?"

He hesitated a moment longer. "Yes, take charge of the project and give me regular updates. This is on you, Gerri. A great idea if it works, but a terrible one if it doesn't. Don't disappoint me."

Gerri left the office before he could change his mind. She was jubilant. No one else in the office could say they were working to increase profit, which put Gerri into a safe place against layoffs. Jeff had taken a freelance job that was going to allow them to make a payment on their mortgage and push the wolves back a bit, but until he got a permanent job, they would remain underwater.

She researched the best way to buy all the bunk beds. There was a discount furniture place that could deliver them in a few days. Perfect. The next step would be to tell Nicky and the other resident managers that the house census was being raised. Nicky was becoming obstreperous and this ought to render her speechless. She closed the office door and put the call in to Nicky. The other managers would be a piece of cake after her.

"Good morning, Nicky. How's everything up at Olive Street House?"

"Not good. Ever since you refused to kick Madison out for using drugs, the women have been restless, irritable, and discontent, to quote the Big Book."

"Don't quote the Big Book to me, please. This is a business and you have to start treating it like one."

"Our business is to improve these women's lives."

"No, it's to collect rent from desperate women who need a place to stay. Any business needs profit to stay open and it can't depend on the wishes of the residents. They'd have us give them single rooms with spa privileges."

"What are you getting at?"

"My superiors at Reardon-Malloy have made a new policy decision. Starting next week we'll be housing three to a room here at OSH. We're waiting for the bunk beds and then I'll start sending new women to you."

She was right. Nicky appeared to be speechless. After a moment she said, "You can't do that. The women won't stand for it. They're already rebelling at the second drug test. This will push them over the edge."

"They only have to understand one thing—follow the policies of the house or get kicked out. The women look to us as the arbiters of all decisions, and sometimes they won't understand the reasoning."

"Well, neither do I."

"No matter. You should tell your people soon so they can start figuring out who they want to room with."

"Is it possible for me to talk to your boss?"

There was no fucking way she'd let Nicky talk with Edmundson. "I'm the regional director here. I am the boss. I have the power to accept or reject the women in the houses and to fire and hire the resident managers. Something you should think about."

"I'll find a way to go over your head. You can't be allowed to singlehandedly ruin the house."

"If you weren't such a pain in my ass I would find you amusing. You have no power here. None. My patience is running thin, Nicky. If you don't fall in line, you're done."

Nicky hung up before Gerri could say good-bye. Fine. Whether Nicky hated her or not was immaterial, and if she continued to get in her face about everything, she'd fire her. That had a nice feel to it. She'd give it some serious thought.

Nicky met Parker and Quinn at Kopi Café in Andersonville, a dark, quiet coffee shop that had become her hangout place when she quit drinking. It wasn't the equal of a bar. She could stay in taverns for hours and hours, but the attraction wasn't the same in a coffee shop. There was only so much of the stuff you could drink, and the people weren't there to talk to each other. They all had headphones on and eyes locked on their laptops.

She found a table in back and soon Parker and Quinn joined her.

"Have you found the Rogers Park woman yet?" Nicky said.

"Nothing yet. She might be fine," Quinn said.

"Maybe, but it turns out I know her too."

"Of course, you do. What's your connection with Allie Becker?"

"I dated her shortly after I got sober. I'm surprised in retrospect she asked me out, given how new in sobriety I was. I thought it was a big honor, like I was a special student who got special favors. I was too much of a wreck, though. I broke it off shortly after it began."

"Was she upset you ended it?" Parker said.

"She sent me one snarky text about five years ago, so I'd say our connection is a thin one."

"But this is what we have. Lou, the first victim we know of, was one of your residents. The second woman from Avondale was Ruby Schiller, who you sponsored. Then we have the third woman, Janelle Jergins, from Ukrainian Village, who was your first sponsor. Why did that relationship end?"

"She moved way down to the South Loop. It was too hard to see her in person and you need that in early sobriety."

"And now there may be a fourth woman added, this Allie Becker who you dated after you got sober. I don't know how we can ignore such an obvious commonality," Quinn said.

"We can't," Nicky said.

"Maybe we need to understand the AA culture a little more," Parker said.

"It's not the kind of culture that would produce a killer, but psychopaths can be recovering alcoholics, too. The killer has to be in AA in order to know anything about these four women. He has to know me, though it's just as likely to be a woman."

"We'll keep an open mind," Quinn said. "I agree. I don't think a man could get close enough to the female-only sober houses to know who relapsed."

They were quiet for a moment. "I asked a friend of mine to spread the word at other AA meetings around the city that a killer is targeting women moving out of sober homes. That'll probably be more effective prevention messaging than anything the CPD could put out."

"The first thing we do is find the missing woman," Quinn said.

"What are you doing after that? I mean, do you even have a plan?"

Quinn looked at her with a small smile on his face. "We've investigated a murder or two together, Parker and me. And I don't recall you questioning my competence when we worked together."

"I didn't mean it like that. I'm getting desperate—women are dying because of me." She was wreaking havoc on other people's lives, as if she were still a drunk.

"We'll get him," Parker said.

They got up from their table and Quinn promised to be in touch with news about the Rogers Park woman. Nicky was certain she was dead, a fourth victim of whoever hated her enough to kill women she was associated with.

It was midafternoon. Almost involuntarily, Nicky pointed her car toward Laura's house, hoping she'd be able to see her as she arrived home from school. Parking on the street was tight, but she was able to squeeze into a space one house down. Five minutes after she settled in for the wait, a white van carrying disabled students pulled over in front of her. The door to Laura's house opened and a middle-aged woman dressed in jeans and a paisley-colored Henley emerged. She waved at the van but made no move to approach it to help Laura. Instead, she waited patiently with a smile as Laura struggled out of the van and slowly made her way to the house. The only thing that kept Nicky from despair was she had landed with a good foster family. They might even have adopted her by now. Still, every halting step Laura took with her crutches was a reminder of the moment she shot at Laura's father and hit her instead. Now there were four more victims placed at her door.

How would the weight of it all affect whatever relationship with Parker came about? Her ability to be happy was crippled by her own thinking and she didn't want Parker saddled to a melancholic, guilt-ridden underachiever. It wouldn't take Parker long to realize what she'd gotten herself into and put an end to it.

Laura made it to the house and exchanged a kiss with the woman holding the door open for her. Nicky watched until they were both in the house with the door closed before starting her car and pulling out. Sometimes the visits provided some relief that Laura was in good hands. Other times they sent her down the rabbit hole of remorse and lingered for days. The heaviness in her heart told her which kind of visit it was. She cranked up the radio to try to divert her thinking, but that did no good.

CHAPTER FOURTEEN

Nicky stayed near her phone, waiting for word from Quinn on the Rogers Park woman. It was close to dinner time and she wandered into the kitchen to see what there was to eat. The next day was grocery shopping so there was probably next to nothing left. Her head was in the refrigerator when her phone rang. Parker. She took in a deep breath before answering. Parker was the other big thing going on. She knew they were headed for something, but she didn't have the time at the moment to fall in love. If there was one thing she knew about new love, it took up terrific amounts of time and energy. But when she had a chance to talk to or see Parker, her heart jumped with excitement, despite her dour mood. She pressed the green button to take the call.

"Hi, Nicky." Her voice remained at its sexy alto, but also sounded bright, as if she were happy to hear Nicky's voice.

"Did they find Allie Becker?"

"Not yet. The emergency contact in her file was her mother, but she died a month ago. There was no father or siblings. We're interviewing her housemates to see if anyone knew what she was up to last night."

"I suppose it's possible she's holed up with a bottle."

"We can hope. I figured you'd be upset. Thought I might take you to dinner."

Damn. Parker was going for it and Nicky didn't want to turn down the invitation. That's the thing with a strong attraction to someone—it was impossible to ignore, whether it was the right time or not. "Sure. But we're going Dutch."

"I wanted to take you to AntePrima."

"Yeah, I can't pay a tenth of that bill, let alone half."

"Let me take you this once. You need a break and I want your company. You can't say no."

She was too tired to feel humiliated about her income. It was obvious her job wouldn't pay much and there was nothing she could do about it. Plus, she'd always wanted to go to AntePrima. Every time she walked by it at dinner time she was struck by how the diners leaned into one another, as if they were having the most intimate conversations. It almost made her feel lonely. "Okay. This once. Next time we'll go Dutch at the Honey Bear."

They rang off with plans to meet in an hour. Nicky went up to her room to consider her wardrobe options, which mainly consisted of the suits she wore as a cop and not appropriate for a date. She found some dressier black jeans and paired them with a blue sweater her mother had given her for Christmas. She killed some time playing solitaire before grabbing a jacket and walking to the restaurant.

Parker was seated in back when she arrived. Every table was full and there was a line out the door. Nicky wondered how she had gotten them in. Sometimes a flash of the badge could move your name up the reservations list. That wasn't Parker's style, as far as she could tell. She didn't use her police powers for anything other than catching bad guys. During the worst of Nicky's drinking, she inappropriately flashed her badge more times than she could count or remember. She'd always found it drew women to her, and as she grew more desperate, she used it to pick them up. Charm alone used to work, but whatever charm she'd had was long gone.

They ordered drinks—two sparkling waters with lime. "You can have a drink if you like. It doesn't bother me," Nicky said.

"It doesn't?"

Well, it did, but Nicky would never say so. The last thing she wanted to be was a killjoy. "Not at all. Please order what you normally would."

"I don't drink much, so it's fine. I'm hitting it hard if I have two cocktails a week."

"I still don't understand people like you. Having one drink and then stopping, imagine that."

"I used to drink a lot in college and my early twenties, but then my body didn't want it much. But I don't have alcoholism in my family's history. I think the two of us are programmed differently."

"Do you have anything new to report on the case?" Nicky said.

"I don't. But I thought we'd have a night of not talking about it." Parker looked right into Nicky's eyes until Nicky had to turn away. She felt her gaze like a laser beam.

"Do you think that will give us some perspective on the case?"

"I think it's good to look away for a while and come back with fresh eyes. I don't know much about your background or you mine. I want to get to know you better."

Parker had a wonderful way of being straightforward in the gentlest manner. She asked for what she wanted, and she said what was on her mind. Nicky found herself starting to trust her and wanting to open up to her. She gave up trying to tamp down the attraction.

"What do you want to know?"

"Tell me about what's going on with your job. I know there was some trouble over increasing the drug testing."

"God, you don't even know the half of it." Nicky proceeded to talk about the new bunk bed policy and how she was sure it would be the final straw for the women. She dreaded them walking out *en masse* and becoming targets of the killer.

"Is there anything else you'd like to do career-wise? This job sounds like it's coming to an end."

"I don't have a clue what I'd want to do."

"Security? Private investigations?"

Their food arrived. Nicky had been so absorbed in the conversation she almost forgot where they were. The trout piccata was better by several factors than what she usually ate and she tucked in. "I gave being a PI a few seconds' thought."

"You'd be great at it."

As the conversation surged on, Nicky realized she was having fun. The talk was easy and yet as intimate as the conversations she imagined taking place in the restaurant, though she realized everyone was leaning into each other because the restaurant was so loud. She learned more about Parker—she was the daughter of two doctors, grew up north of the city in Glenview, went to University of Illinois, and joined the police when she was twenty-two. She said she'd broken up last year with a woman she'd been with for ten years. That told her Parker had at least one ability she did not—she was able to sustain a relationship for longer than a month, which was Nicky's record. It also answered any remaining question Nicky had about Parker's sexuality, not that she had much doubt. Her gaydar lit up the moment she first saw her.

They shared a crème brûlée at the end of the meal. Parker held her spoon to her lips and said, "Why don't you come to my place for some coffee? I'm not quite ready for the evening to end."

Nicky hesitated before plunging in. "Where do you live?"

"I'm in a high-rise on Sheridan. You can park in the garage. I'll wait there for you and we can go up together."

"I should get back to the residents."

"Come on. I'm dying for some coffee."

"You drink coffee this late?"

"Decaf. I'm not superhuman."

When Nicky pulled in to the parking garage of Parker's building, her car making an ear-splitting noise as she took a tight turn, Parker stood nearby with a smile on her face as Nicky got out. "No jokes about the car, please."

"Who cares about your car? One day you'll have a nicer one. Follow me."

Parker led her to a corner unit on the thirtieth floor of the 1960s building on the lake. Huge floor to ceiling windows overlooked the pitch-black water. The room was beautifully decorated, and Nicky imagined Parker picking out each piece carefully, wondering at the nesting side of her, the parts of her she'd never seen. Butterflies bounced in her stomach as she followed Parker into the galley kitchen, which had clearly been completely redone sometime in the recent past. That was a big outlay for a cop. Parker must manage her money well, something Nicky had never done properly. It was hard to plan for retirement when your paycheck went largely to booze.

They settled into the living room with cups of decaf—Parker took hers black and had only skim milk to offer Nicky to lighten her coffee. Better to drink it black. They continued their conversation from the restaurant and Nicky wondered if Parker would lean over and kiss her. She kept waiting for it while at the same time not having the courage to start the kiss on her own. The tension was killing her and when the talk started to peter out Parker said, "I imagine you have to get back to your women."

Nicky was crushed at the dismissal. She reminded herself not everyone jumped in bed on their first date, the way Nicky did when she was drinking. They walked to the front door and stood facing each other. The question of a kiss hung between them like a pendulum. Parker leaned forward, her mouth finding Nicky's, her lips lingering long enough so no mistake could be made about the nature of the kiss. When it ended, Nicky pulled her back in for a longer one. She couldn't remember a kiss like this, not while she was drinking or sober. Certainly not with Deb, the only woman she'd had sex with in sobriety. This was different, like the slightest opening in a door to something magical.

"When can I see you again?" Parker said. Her arms were around Nicky's waist, their foreheads nearly touching. "I don't want to wait long."

"Soon. We'll have to play it by ear. Can we talk tomorrow?"

They left everything else unsaid. Nicky tipped the garage attendant well and pulled into the street, for once not worrying about her car. It was the first time she'd been properly kissed and she felt like a teenager—giddy, fully alive, a little stunned.

"There's no way in fucking hell we're agreeing to this," Madison practically spit.

The OSH women and Nicky were in the meeting room on Saturday morning. Nicky had gathered everyone and announced the decision to put bunk beds in all the rooms. Madison was the first to stand up, and all the women's eyes were on her. It galled Nicky that the woman who most abused the rules and got away with it should be taking the high moral ground here. None of the women seemed to dismiss Madison because of her relapse. If anything, she'd solidified her position as leader. There had always been one or two of the women who were stronger characters than the others, but there had not been a singular leader of the group since Nicky had been there. She didn't view it as a positive development.

"Listen, I know this is hard. I did my best to protest it, but I was overridden."

"I think it was your idea to begin with," Madison said. "Now you'll have more women to lord it over."

She wanted to hang her head in frustration but would never show that to the women. "The beds arrive in a few days. Do you want to try to make your own groups of three or do you want me to assign the rooms?"

"Leave it to us. We want as little of you involved as possible." The other women nodded.

"Fine. It's Saturday, so let's get started on the yard work." A sea of angry faces glared at her. She'd lost all credibility, all authority. All the trust she'd built up was gone. She'd failed them, failed herself.

"Come on, ladies. I think this meeting is over," Madison said.

The women stood as one and filed out of the room. All the glow from the previous evening with Parker faded under Madison's onslaught. Nicky went back to her office to decompress. The residents were no doubt concocting some act of protest. Not that Nicky blamed them. If she were a resident, she'd have found a way to leave the house, but if they were to walk out, they could all be targets of the killer.

An hour later, she went into the kitchen for more coffee. She found several of the women in the family room, standing next to their luggage, which in some cases amounted to nothing more than a garbage bag. Madison was at the center of the group which included Susan, Oli, and Diane.

"What's going on?" Nicky said.

"We're making life easier for you," Madison said. "Running a house of six rather than ten should be a piece of cake." Her smile was creepy, predatory, almost like Snidely Whiplash.

"You're leaving?"

"Bingo! Nothing gets past you, oh fearless leader." Nicky was starting to really hate Madison.

"But where will you all go? Can you at least tell me that before you walk out? There's a killer out there, someone targeting sober homes. You can't leave and wander the streets."

Madison picked up both her suitcases and the other three their cheap duffels and garbage bags. "No can do, sahib. We're outta here." And with that, the women filed out of the family room. A few seconds later, she heard the front door slam behind them. Shit. She ran upstairs to check on the remaining six women in the house, knocking first on Zoey and Madison's door and entering when she heard no response. Zoey lay in her bed, headphones on, her eyes narrowing when she saw Nicky. The masking tape dividing the room in two was fraying at the edges. Madison's side was empty. The bed had been stripped and the dirty sheets piled at the foot of the bed.

"You're probably freaking out about now," Zoey said.

"Why didn't you go with them?"

"Me? I have zero money and no friends or family to crash with. I'm stuck in this gulag."

"Why aren't you outside doing the yard work?"

Zoey looked at her scornfully. "The slave labor, is that what you're talking about? Because I think I'll take a pass on it."

Nicky left the room, needing to get the whole picture of what was going on before she could act in any way. A window on the stair landing looked over the backyard, but no one was outside working. She had a full-blown revolution on her hands.

She wouldn't call Gerri about this until the dust settled a bit. Nicky suspected some of the women would return before the end of the night, after discovering their destinations were not as welcoming as they'd hoped. She wanted a final census before telling Gerri they'd lost nearly half the house in one day.

Back downstairs, Nicky was passing through the living room when the doorbell rang. That usually meant the UPS guy and she was shocked to see Parker standing on the stoop.

"You're not the UPS guy." Despite the drama going on all around her, Nicky broke into a big smile. The sight of Parker lit up the pleasure center of her brain.

"Not yet anyway. If I have many more days like today, it may be an option." Parker was smiling, too.

Nicky led the way to her office and offered coffee. They stood by the door and Parker reached over to close it. "I want to see you tonight. Can you come over?"

It felt like someone was playing tether ball in her belly. This wasn't the nervousness of her first time with Deb. This was full-on desire. She cupped her hand on Parker's cheek. "What time? I need to hang around here until later to manage our latest crisis."

"Can you be there by ten?"

"I should be able to. I'd hate to miss it."

"It?"

"Well, you know."

"I certainly do. I'd hate for you to miss it, too."

With their plans obliquely set, Parker left. By nine o'clock, Diane and Susan returned to the house, subdued if not apologetic. They had gotten back together and announced they were going to share a room. Nicky didn't have the will to deny them. No one else returned and at nine forty-five she left to go to Parker's, after showering and dressing with care. Her nerves had settled into a quiet hum. She could do this. She wanted to do it. It.

Parker let her in, and they sat on her Crate & Barrel couch. She leaned over and kissed Nicky, a long, deeply involved kiss that made her brain cloudy. Still, there was something they needed to discuss.

Nicky leaned back. "Maybe we should think this through. You could get in trouble for seeing a witness, which I am."

Parker smiled. "Department policy isn't foremost in my mind right now."

"I don't want anything to blow back on you. Should we wait until the case is closed?"

"That could be weeks, maybe months. Do you want to wait that long?"

"Hmm. That's a tough question."

"It isn't for me," Parker said, taking Nicky's hands in her own. "The department doesn't need to know. Frankly, I wouldn't care if they did find out. A write-up in my jacket seems a small price to pay."

Nicky brought Parkers hand to her lips. "When you put it that way."

"Do you mind if we skip the preliminaries and go to bed?" Parker said.

Nicky smiled. Parker was a refreshingly straightforward person. "I don't mind in the least."

Parker took her by the hand and led her down the hall to the bedroom. Usually, Nicky did the leading, but Parker's competence in all matters made her want to follow for a change. She wanted to be wrapped up in her arms, guided by her, vulnerable to her. As they made love, Nicky felt a driving desire along with a feeling of safety. It was completely intoxicating, in one of the only ways she could feel intoxicated without breaking her sobriety. She spent the night, leaving her residents on their own and not caring she did. She could break the rules as well, and there'd never been a better reason.

CHAPTER FIFTEEN

Nicky was back at Olive Street by seven the next morning. Parker had the early shift but found the time to bring coffee to a still sleeping Nicky. She woke her with several strategically placed kisses. An hour later they left the apartment, holding hands as they walked through the lobby. Parker was out and proud, which surprised her since she seemed circumspect in all things. Perhaps she was wrong. She certainly wasn't cautious in bed.

The house was quiet. Most of the remaining residents were out, God knows where. She took a fresh cup of coffee to her office and fell into the chair. She was exhausted by lack of sleep but energized by the idea Parker might upend life as she knew it. She didn't want to bring her insecurities to the relationship. She was determined to be a full partner, to not feel aloof or clingy, both of which she had experience in. She'd clung to several relationships in the last years of her drinking, dreading being alone, unwanted. The problem with acting co-dependently was she became exactly what she dreaded— more expendable.

Her phone lit up with a call from Quinn and she got up to close the door. The remaining residents didn't need to hear anything more about dead women. They were spooked enough.

"Nicky, I'm glad I caught you," Quinn said.

"Why? They found the Rogers Park woman, didn't they?"

"I'm afraid so. Her body was sitting up, leaning against the food shack at Foster Beach. There was no blood or anything else marking a disturbance there. Forensics is saying she was moved post-mortem."

"That's new."

"Same method as the others—a knife through the heart—but you're right. No one's been moved before. The scene is still active if you want to come see it."

"That's a strong affirmative."

"Parker and I are here, but there's not much to do since the crime scene is elsewhere."

"I wonder why this is the first body to be dumped? With the others he'd managed to kill in places he could leave the victims."

"Maybe it was opportunistic—the killer unexpectedly came across a target and acted impulsively. Seems careless, which is good news for us."

"If the killer is murdering women outside of the usual pattern, it's possible mistakes will be made," Nicky said.

"We can only hope. Are you coming? I don't think we'll hang around much longer."

"On my way. It'll take me ten minutes or less."

Foster Beach was directly east of Andersonville, a place Nicky went to when she wanted some beach time, which was next to never. It sat south of Hollywood Beach where the LGBTQ community had staked a claim in the sand. When she got out of her car, she could hear music wafting from that way. It was Sunday, prime party time at Hollywood, even in late September. The parking lot at Foster was busy with patrol cars, ambulances, and unmarked cars. She hurried to a knot of people by the food shack and saw Parker and Quinn in the middle of the pack. Quinn looked her way and waved. He touched Parker on the arm and pointed her way and they joined Nicky away from the crowd. The sight of Parker made her insides jump.

"They just took the body away," Quinn said. "I'm afraid there's not much to see."

"Thanks anyway for asking. Can we walk over to where she was found?"

"There was nothing around the body that was helpful," Parker said. "No footprints, cigarette butts, blood, signs of struggle." She caught Nicky's eye and winked.

"I'm not sure a woman could move the body. It's more likely the killer is a man," Nicky said.

"We need to consider all possibilities. I think a strong woman could move it," Parker said.

"He's, or she's, careful to not leave evidence, that's clear," Quinn said.

"Any evidence Allie was intoxicated?"

"We'll have to wait until they get her blood alcohol level," Parker said. "I hope she was. I don't want the killer to expand his victim base. So far it's been a specific profile with no deviation."

"Where do we go from here?" Nicky said.

Parker had her cop face on. You'd never know that a few hours earlier she'd looked at her so passionately. "We think it would be a good idea for you to sit in on the interviews of the folks at this woman's sober house. You're in the community. I think they'll open up to you more."

"Why don't I save you some time and do the preliminary interviews myself? I know the house manager and she should be able to arrange it for me."

Quinn and Parker looked at each other. "That would be helpful," Parker said.

"Well, I'm pretty motivated to find the killer. Every death feels like I plunged the knife in myself." She hadn't meant to be so forthcoming—it fell out of her mouth. They both looked at her with concern on their faces, something Nicky hated. She always felt her mother was questioning her competence every time she said she worried about her. It was her therapist who suggested what she told herself about herself wasn't necessarily true. When people were worried about her they weren't judging her—they were expressing love and caring. Slowly, Nicky was learning she didn't have to make life as difficult as she did. What a concept.

She left Quinn and Parker at the scene and hurried home, eager to talk to the other house manager and get started on the interviews. The mail came through the door just as she walked through the foyer and she picked it up to sort. Mail slots had been set up for the women where they could leave messages as well as pick up whatever mail they received. There was an envelope addressed to her and she took it into her office. It was a standard envelope with an American flag stamp and no return address, postmarked from Chicago. She opened it to a single sheet of paper.

You and your detective pals are bordering on incompetence. Four deaths and I don't feel any nip at my heels. You haven't the vaguest idea who I am. Let's light a fire under you and see what happens. You have one week from the date of the postmark to find me or another of your sober sisters dies. I should say your not-so-sober sisters. Good hunting.

A chill ran through her as she dropped the paper onto the desk. *Holy Mother of Fuck.* Any remaining question as to Nicky's direct connection to the killings was firmly put to rest. She craved a cigarette. She thought longingly of disappearing behind a wall of booze. She should call Parker and Quinn immediately to report it. In fact, there was no way around it. But for the moment she imagined herself locked in a two-handed battle with the killer. Why was she being targeted? How could the killer know all this personal shit about her? If it were a man, was he big and strong, or would she have a decent chance against him, given her training and desperation?

These were the moments when she should call her sponsor. Bad moment equals call sponsor. That was the guideline. There were a lot of AA guidelines she hadn't been following lately. She wasn't going to meetings, she wasn't talking about her problems with another AA member, she'd started to view Sheila as more of an annoyance than an asset, and she'd had several alcohol cravings that she wasn't sharing with anyone else. A pathway to relapse, though Nicky didn't feel she was in danger. Still, she'd call Sheila, to cross it off her list of things she should be doing. When she got her on the phone, she told her about the fourth body and the note sent to her.

"What's your next move?" Sheila said.

"Tell the police and hope they have some new leads from somewhere. Anywhere. We're lost at sea."

"You said one of the cops was your ex-partner. What about the other? It's a woman, correct?"

"Yeah. Joanne Parker." Nicky hadn't mentioned anything about Parker to Sheila, but if she was going to get anything from her sponsor's advice, she had to be open about what was going on. "We're getting to know each other a little bit."

"How so?" She sounded more alert. Relationships were something a sponsor could sink her teeth in, more so than a serial killer running loose in Chicago.

"We've been on a date." She smiled to herself at the memory. "I like her."

"Doesn't the police department have some sort of rule against sleeping with witnesses?"

"I didn't say we were sleeping together."

"Are you?"

"Well, yes, but it's all very new. The department definitely frowns on any relationship with witnesses, but I figure it's Parker's job to deal with them."

Sheila was silent for a while. "You're five years sober, Nicky. I'm not going to say you're not ready for a relationship, because I think you are. Maybe not right now, given how chaotic things are. I'd advise you to slow things down. It's not a good time to make personal decisions when the pressure on you is so intense."

"Okay. That makes sense. You don't mean I should stop seeing her now, do you? Because that would be a bummer and I'd probably do it anyway, though I don't know why she'd want to be with someone responsible for four deaths."

"Oh, Nicky, you're not responsible and I know Parker can see that. In fact, everyone but you can see it. I know you'll find the killer."

"In a week?"

"You can do it. But before you do anything, get to a meeting. I know you're down on those."

"I'll get to one today. I better go. I have to call Quinn and Parker."

They rang off and she looked again at the warning letter on her desk. She wasn't misinterpreting its message, which was loud and clear. To stop the killing she was going to have to be a smarter investigator than perhaps she'd ever had to be. A stroke of good luck would also go a long way.

There was an eleven o'clock meeting at the 12 Step House she could make if she hustled. The reading of How it Works had already begun when she arrived. Not unlike millions of other meetings, this one was held in a basement where people sat around long tables, pouring coffee from carafes and doctoring it up with lumpy powdered cream and sugar. She found a chair at the end of the table and looked around to see who she knew. There were several familiar faces, women from her home group and the Olive Street meetings. There were two men from the gay AA meetings she went to. Then her eyes rested on a woman dressed in bike gear, blond, fresh-faced with rosy cheeks, energy pouring from her. She realized it was Teagan, a friend from her time in rehab. It looked like she'd managed to stay sober.

The meeting secretary came to the part in the introduction when any AA-related announcements are made. The secretary scanned the room first before picking up a sheet of paper. "I have an important announcement. The police want us to know there has been a series of murders involving women living in sober homes. If you are such a person, please be aware the killer is targeting women who get kicked out of their house for relapsing. What a great reason to not relapse! Please spread the word at other meetings you attend. Avoid being alone at night, stay out of alleys, don't relapse, and don't get kicked out of your house. If you have further questions, I don't know who to talk to."

Loud murmuring started as people turned to each other in disbelief. Chicagoans were used to hearing lots about crime, but this was different. Serial killers were rare and struck terror in the populace. The media had begun moving the story up, which Nicky was glad to see. Women needed to be warned. But it also exponentially increased pressure on the police to find the killer

It was hard to tell if the killer was for or against AA. Killing relapsers would seem to say he believed AA was the only path to sobriety and those who relapse and turn their backs on the program were targets. She'd known her share of AA extremists, people who gave their whole life to the program and believed fervently in rules, as opposed to those who used AA to live a fuller life outside the program and treated its tenets as suggestions, not absolutes. The hard-core AAs were the ones who made people think AA was a cult, something Nicky abhorred. There were a few meetings of the conservative wing she could attend and see if anything shook free.

During the meeting she caught eyes with Teagan and they both smiled. When it ended, Teagan made a beeline over to her and reached out for a hug.

"It's wonderful to see you here," Teagan said. "I'm surprised we don't see each other more at meetings."

"You look fantastic. Sobriety suits you."

Teagan flashed a hundred-watt smile. "You look great, too. I recently came across a photo of the two of us in rehab. We both looked like death warmed over."

"Felt like it, too. Do you ever see Meg around? She saw me the other day when I was at coffee with some people and interrupted us. It was awkward."

"I'm surprised she's still sober. I never see her and when we were in rehab she struck me as a good candidate for relapse. How'd she look?"

"Fine. I think she's still sober but didn't ask. I just wanted her to leave."

"What about that announcement?" Teagan said. "What the fuck is going on?"

"They just found the fourth victim, Allie Becker. Did you know her?"

The healthy glow drained from Teagan's face. "Allie Becker? I saw her the other day. How could she be dead?"

Nicky held on to Teagan's arm. "You have to tell me everything." They were alone in the basement, but for the man cleaning up the coffee service. She kept her voice low. "How well did you know her?"

"She's a good AA friend, someone I reworked the steps with. I hadn't seen her for at least a month, though, which is why I called her up for coffee. I heard her mother died and was getting worried about her."

"Do you know anything about her relapse?"

"I don't, but I'm not surprised. She didn't admit it when I saw her, but from what she said, she was isolating. I offered to take her to a meeting, but she was very evasive."

"Nothing about anyone stalking her or giving her the creeps in any way?"

"Not that she mentioned. Of course, I didn't ask. Didn't know to ask." She picked her backpack up from the floor.

"I imagine the police will want to talk to you. Do you mind if I give them your number? It might help."

"Sure, glad to help. We should get together soon, have coffee." Nicky liked Teagan but doubted she'd call, doubted she'd initiate anything either. They were buddies in rehab and got to know nearly everything about each other's sordid pasts. Closeness like that often didn't survive the end of the bubble they lived in for twenty-eight days. She hadn't seen her since they got out of the hospital.

Teagan left the basement and Nicky soon followed. When she looked at her phone there was a message from Parker—she was needed at the police station at her earliest convenience. She pointed the Buick north. Time was ticking down toward the killer's deadline and she needed Quinn and Parker more than ever.

CHAPTER SIXTEEN

The lobby of the police station in Rogers Park was redolent with the smell of Indian food. Little India was a few blocks away, a stretch of Devon Avenue that was exclusively devoted to all things India and Pakistan. Colorful sari shops, fabulous restaurants, and nightmarish traffic congestion. She approached the desk sergeant, who was opening his biryani. The order was enough to feed six and he piled it all on a paper plate.

"I'm here to see Detectives Quinn and Parker."

"I've got this, Sergeant," Parker said as she approached Nicky from behind. She felt a gentle breath on the back of her neck, but that wasn't possible. She wouldn't do that in a police station, would she? She led Nicky upstairs to the interview rooms. "I miss you," she whispered.

"I miss you, too. Can we see each other later?" Nicky said.

"Let's get through this first and then we'll make a plan."

"That sounds ominous."

"I'm sure it won't be as long as you tell the truth."

"Is there some question I won't?" Nicky said. She couldn't help feeling defensive and a little hurt.

Parker didn't answer as she led them into a room where Quinn sat waiting. He nodded to her and that was all. Something had changed and Nicky didn't think it was in her favor. She took a seat across the table from them and tried to maintain a neutral face.

"I'm going to jump right in, Nicky," Quinn said. "The brass like you for the murders. I told them it wasn't you, but that didn't hold any weight."

"We're meant to go through your alibis and do whatever it takes to nail you for the four deaths." Parker's face was pale, her low-key red lipstick now standing out like a poppy in a snow field. "I'm sorry, Nicky."

"Hey, it's not your doing. It makes sense, since I'm the common denominator, they'd want a closer look. Don't worry about it."

"I'm not too worried," Quinn said. "If there isn't any evidence against you, which I'm presuming there is not, the brass can't do much. Let's take another look at your alibis."

"My alibis are a little shaky. At the time of the first three murders I was at home at Olive Street. I could probably find some residents who would vouch for me being there, but that would be for earlier than ten o'clock, when I generally go into my bedroom."

"They wouldn't know where you were in the middle of the night, correct?" Quinn said.

"I'm afraid not."

"How about the fourth murder?"

Nicky realized she'd inadvertently led Quinn to the only alibi she had—her night with Parker. The silence grew.

"Nicky?" Quinn said.

"Yeah, I think I misspoke. I don't have an alibi for that one either."

Parker leaned forward. "Nicky, don't." She looked at Quinn. "She was with me all night. Make of that what you will."

Quinn smiled. "I'm not blind, you know. I've seen you two lock eyes. Are you together now?"

Nicky sucked in a breath and hardly dared look at Parker. When she snuck a glance, Parker was smiling, too.

"Let's say we're getting to know each other," Parker said. "But I do realize what a problem this causes. If we let the brass know about the alibi, I'll be taken off the case and reprimanded. If we don't admit it, Nicky has no alibi."

"It's a dilemma, all right," Quinn said.

"And she only needs one to turn their attention elsewhere. It's clear all four murders were done by the same person."

Quinn gazed at Parker. "If I didn't like you and Nicky so much, I'd say I was disappointed in you. Sleeping with a witness? They'll say it calls into question your objectivity and can compromise an entire case. It's a stupid thing to do."

"Gee, thanks, partner." She glanced at Nicky and rolled her eyes.

"We can't let them know," Nicky said. "We'll think of something else for my alibi."

"Nicky, we can't lie about this," Quinn said. "That's a fireable offense and I don't think Parker or I are willing to do that."

Parker shook her head decisively. "No way. I'll tell the lieutenant today."

"But that means you're off the case," Nicky said. "We can't let that happen."

"I don't think we have a choice," Quinn said. "Couldn't you have restrained yourselves while the case was active?"

Nicky and Parker looked at each other.

"No comment," Parker said.

"Ditto," said Nicky.

"Christ. You're not teenagers."

Nicky couldn't figure out if Quinn was more straitlaced than she realized or whether he was jealous, as anyone in a group of three was when the other two paired off.

"This is so new we haven't even talked to each other about what we are," Parker said.

Quinn waved a hand away. "The damage is done. You can't avoid telling the lieutenant if we want Nicky to have an alibi, which we do. I don't want to spend time digging into her background while the real killer is still out there."

"I agree," Parker said. "We don't have a choice, Nicky. I'll be okay."

"There's one more thing I need from you, Nicky," Quinn said.

"Anything." She didn't need to worry since there was no evidence against her, but she was wary. Evidence had a way of suddenly appearing. She wasn't naive about what some police were capable of. If the brass wanted her for the killer, there were ways to make the charges stick.

"I need a list of all the women you've slept with, ever, which I realize may give you a hand cramp."

"Oh, God," she said. "I wouldn't know where to start."

There was no way Parker wouldn't have some reaction to how long the list was. If they were talking only about sex she'd had in recovery, there'd be only Deb's name to put down. She'd never slept with Allie while they were dating. She'd been too petrified. But before? It was an embarrassment.

"It doesn't have to be in order or anything. Jot down names and we'll take care of finding and warning them."

"Oh, Christ. It's not like I'll remember all that many. I was a blackout drinker and there's no way to pull back those memories. Now I'm putting them all in danger."

Quinn pushed his chair back. "Do the best you can. We have four days before the deadline and I need you to do as I ask. No stone unturned. I'd prefer it if you stay here to make the list and give it to me when you're done." He looked at Parker, who made no move to leave. "I'll leave you to it."

He closed the door behind him. Nicky reached across the table and took Parker's hands in hers. "I'm sorry. How bad is this going to be for your career?"

Parker stood and gathered Nicky into her arms, apparently unconcerned what people might see through the window panel next to the door. They hadn't done much hugging yet, and the feel of Parker's strong arms around her was like sixty minutes of mindfulness meditation. She felt calm for the first time since she woke up with her.

"I don't want another detective on this case. They won't be as good."

"I'm not going anywhere," Parker said. "Quinn will keep me up to date and I'll be around you, I hope. I can still chime in."

They looked at each other from inches away. Talk of business would last only so long. Parker put her palm on Nicky's cheek and leaned in. "Can you come over tonight?"

"If I ever get done with this list, I'd love to."

"It's that long?"

"Prior to sobriety I was a tom cat. You should know that about me—my past is ugly and messy and probably shocking to a non-alcoholic."

"All I care about is the person you are now. It's not like I was a saint. I've slept with plenty of women."

"All you'd have to do is sit there and you'd have a steady stream of women throwing themselves at you."

"Is that a compliment?"

"Well, yes. An awkward one, I admit. I can't spend the night. If the residents realize I'm not there, God knows what will happen. Last night was a one-off, I'm afraid."

Parker leaned in to kiss her. "I'll take what I can get. Text me when you're done with the list and I'll come get it from you."

Nicky turned to the legal pad and wrote Deb's name down since it was freshest in memory. As she went back through her sexual history she felt increasingly anxious. The reminder of the person she used to be was humbling and triggery and a little scary. It wasn't the sex as much as the fact it was always drunken sex, unsatisfying and desperate. She knew she'd had plenty of one-night stands, but she could remember the names of only a few of them. And how likely was it they'd be a target of the relapse killer? Most were not alcoholic, and their connection to Nicky a thin one. She began jotting down the names of girlfriends, people she dated for more than a week and who broke up with Nicky as often as she broke up with them. This list was equally disturbing. Clearly, she was incapable of sustaining a love relationship, and it couldn't all have to do with drinking. Her feelings for Parker didn't belong in the same universe as these women, and she was terrified of screwing up now that the relationship really mattered. Her skills as a girlfriend were shaky at best.

Gerri stared out her office window into the gathering dark. It was only Monday afternoon, but she couldn't stand being at work another moment. Dave had announced earlier that the company audit was proceeding and they were ordered to cooperate with the accountants. She should never have implemented her landscaping scam. It didn't amount to much, certainly not worth getting caught over. Too bad she didn't think of that sooner.

She told the receptionist she was leaving early and headed straight home. Jeff was at an interview—please, God, let him get the job—and then on to a meeting and dinner with his friends. He should move into a sober house, he loved being around recovering alcoholics so much. She didn't see the appeal. All that clean living made for an insufferable group of people and she wished Jeff would leave her in favor of his friends. That wouldn't happen, as long as he was financially dependent on her. They'd stumble along with him devoted to his program and her deeply scornful of it. The tension between them grew every day as he shrank away from her perpetually foul mood.

Once home she changed into her loose sweats and plopped in front of the TV with a bag of Twix and some wine. Relief flooded her as the sugar entered her system. She turned on an episode of *The Bachelor* and put her feet up. Her phone rang and she cursed when she saw it was Nicky. Her first response was to reject the call, for she rarely heard good news from her, but she needed her to implement the new bunk bed policy. She hit the green button and took the call.

"Hello, Nicky. I was going to call you to see how things were going at Olive Street." She tried out a friendly, supportive voice, but it felt like something sticking in her throat.

"Things are a disaster at Olive Street. Your bunk bed scheme spurred a revolution and four of the residents have left the house. I tried to tell you this would backfire."

"What?" Now her throat nearly closed. This was exactly what Edmundson didn't want to happen. "What are you talking about?"

"It's like I told you—they left over the weekend, led by your favorite, Madison. Two have returned, but you have to replace two women, plus find the additional five you wanted to add. Good luck with that."

Gerri barely kept herself from sputtering and growling. She couldn't handle another problem right now, not of this magnitude. "This is your failure, Nicky, not mine. You've lost control of the house, the thing you're most responsible for."

"I'm done with your bullshit. You knew putting three in a room would cause an uproar. It's not my doing. You don't give a damn about supporting these women in their early recovery. Instead, you abuse them with the extra drug testing and now this. What did you think they were going to do?"

This wasn't good. Up until now, Nicky had followed orders, albeit reluctantly, and done what she needed to keep the house in a smoothly functioning state. Belligerence had replaced compliance and Gerri was alarmed. What if Nicky got hold of Edmundson to complain?

"I thought they'd follow direction, which you're supposed to provide. I want those bunk beds installed. They're supposed to arrive tomorrow."

"You'll have to come and supervise. I refuse to look like I'm supporting this policy."

"Who do you think you're talking to? I'm giving you this one chance to get things straightened out there. If you don't, I'll have to consider firing you. You understand that?"

"Oh, I got it. You want me to help you ruin the house. I won't do it."

Shit. She didn't want to fire Nicky. It would raise a red flag for Edmundson, who would want to know why she dismissed her. She felt backed into a corner. Usually when she was on the defensive she lashed out, but she needed to tread carefully.

"All right. I'll come supervise the installation of the beds so you can save face with the residents. Then I'll find more residents for you. I can hear you're frustrated, but you have to understand I'm only following orders from my boss. I'll save you from the dirty work, but you need to assure me you'll support our policies. Otherwise, I will have to fire you."

Nicky was silent for a moment. "I guess I'll see you here tomorrow."

Unbelievably, Nicky hung up on her, that devious bitch. As soon as things settled down, she'd make a move to replace her.

CHAPTER SEVENTEEN

Nicky's face was hot to the touch when she hung up on Gerri. Anger that had been simmering ever since Lou was thrown out finally reached the boiling point. She didn't want to get fired. It would feel like she had failed the residents in the house when things were at their most chaotic. And there was the not insignificant matter of her paycheck. It wouldn't be the last time Gerri would threaten to fire her. She'd rather leave on her own terms, but she wouldn't be silent any longer.

Her next thought was of Parker and what trouble she was in because of their relationship. Relationship? Could she call it that? They'd spent every night together since the first one and that meant something. She knew what casual sex felt like, and this wasn't that. But wasn't it too soon to be considered a couple? She realized how much she wanted to be part of a couple, how with Parker the whole idea of it seemed bright with possibilities, their life together spooling out before her on a yellow brick road. If she were to tell Sheila about it, she'd advise slowing things way down. Therefore, she wouldn't tell Sheila a thing.

She called Parker, who picked up before the first ring was done. Her radio-worthy voice sent a frisson of pleasure racing down her body.

"Nicky, I was just about to call you."

"What happened when you told your lieutenant about the alibi? Are you okay?"

Parker laughed. "As usual, you're short on the preliminaries. Tell me how you are and then I'll tell you my fate."

"You don't sound too stressed out, so you're either a buddha or the consequences were minor."

"I'm no buddha, that's for sure. It's what we expected. He took me off the case and put a reprimand in my file."

"Oh, no. I feel terrible."

"Don't. You're not responsible for my sleeping with a witness, I am. I knew what I was doing, but I thought it was worth it. Don't you? Would you have wanted to wait?"

"No," Nicky said quickly. "That would have been hard. We need you on this case, though. That's the worst thing about it."

"Can you come over? I'm on my way home now."

"Yeah, but I have to come back to the house."

"I almost wish that satanic boss of yours would fire you. Then you could spend the whole night."

"You're wish may soon be granted. She's gunning for me."

"Come soon, then. We need to make the most of every minute."

The next morning Nicky heard from Quinn. He wanted her to sit in on an interview with Bartholomew, Lou's ex-boyfriend, whom they'd located the night before. He'd agreed to come in for the interview, which told her he either had nothing to do with Lou's death or he was a crafty son of a bitch who wanted things to look that way. She was dying of curiosity about a man who Lou, of all people, chose to hitch herself to. When she arrived at the station, Quinn took her into the same interview room as before. As they got settled into their seats, a giant of a man walked through the door and looked at the two of them. He was at least six foot five and well over three hundred pounds. He held a handkerchief in his giant paw and wiped his brow.

Quinn handled the introduction. "Nicky, I want you to meet the detective taking Parker's place. This is Hector Martinez."

She stood and offered her hand which Hector ignored as he pulled out a chair and sat next to Quinn. "So this is the one Parker shacked up with?"

Nicky's heart sank with disappointment. Her time with the police came immediately to mind, where insults flew without regard to anyone's feelings and with some, the cruder the better. She was surprised he hadn't called Parker a whore. She ignored his comment. Quinn inched his chair away from Martinez. "Hector comes to us from Area One. He's been a murder cop a long time."

"Okay," Nicky said.

Martinez stared at her for a moment, appraising her, no doubt condemning her. "From what I understand, you're also the one all the victims of the Alkie murders have slept with. Tell me, do you have some kind of secret potion? Cause I wouldn't mind getting some of that."

"The Alkie Murders?" Nicky said with disbelief.

"I don't call it that," Quinn said, "but a bunch of others do. Nothing I can do."

"If you'd read your file, Martinez, you'd know I didn't sleep with any of the victims. I dated only one, in fact. Get your facts straight."

A uniformed officer opened the door and said the witness had arrived, stepping aside to reveal an elfin man with a five-day stubble and long hair swept up in a topknot. He stopped and looked at the three of them crowded around the small table and took an involuntary step back.

"Bartholomew, thanks for coming in," Quinn said. "Why don't you take a seat next to Nicky."

Nicky could hear Martinez's labored breathing and feel his eyes on her. He couldn't outrun a legless man and she wondered, not for the first time, why there were so many out of shape cops. But his physical shape wasn't what she was worried about.

Quinn turned on the recorder and folded his hands on top of his legal pad. He took Bartholomew through preliminary questions before pausing. "Take us through the night you last saw Lou, the night she died."

"I didn't have anything to do with it, I swear. I didn't even know she was dead until you guys showed up at my door."

He was a nervous witness, the best kind if they had useful information to cough up. It was the affectless witness that hid the most. You had to work to get anything out of them.

"Tell us when you first saw her that day. Don't leave anything out."

"Lou called me at about eight o'clock. I don't know if it was the same night she was killed, but it was the only time I've seen her in weeks. She broke up with me in August and then nothing until she showed up at my door. She was drunk, but not falling-down drunk. She could always handle a lot of liquor. She asked me if I wanted to party and pulled out some meth." He paused. "I don't want to tell you more if it's going to get me in trouble."

"No one's interested in whether you took drugs or not," Nicky said. She glanced at Martinez and saw he was looking at her with something bordering on hatred. What the hell had she done to him? Then she looked at Quinn. "Right?"

"We're only interested in what happened when you saw her. If you killed her, I'm afraid we can't turn our heads at that."

"I didn't kill her!" Bartholomew looked frightened for the first time. "She left after a few hours and I never saw her again."

"Were you surprised she'd reached out? I mean, she's the one who dumped you," Quinn said.

"Yeah, I was a little. She said she'd been kicked out of her rehab house and had nowhere to go. I guess I was happy she'd thought to come to me."

"What happened while she was there?"

"Nothing, man. I mean, we partied and talked some, but nothing happened the way you're probably thinking something did. She wasn't interested in sex."

"Did she tell you that?" Nicky said.

"I made a move on her and she shut me right down, said she wasn't there for that. Mostly she talked about how screwed she'd gotten by that house she was living in. Said she was set up by someone and she was pissed about it."

Nicky's heart shrank to hear Lou blamed her for her eviction. She'd been hoping against hope she didn't hate her, but that was magical thinking. Of course she blamed Nicky. Who wouldn't?

"What else did you talk about?" Quinn said. Martinez remained quiet, but for his wheezing.

"I don't know. This and that. I asked her how being on the wagon had been and she said it sucked. I could have told her that. Then I said she was welcome to spend the night, to stay as long as she wanted. As soon as I said that she was up on her feet saying she had to go."

"This is important. Did she say where she was going?" Nicky said.

"Only that I couldn't go with her." Bartholomew looked around the table with a hopeful expression. "That's all I know."

Martinez leaned forward and glared at Bartholomew. "You may be the last person the victim saw so you're going to have to do better than that. Now, where did she say she was going? Don't hold out on me. I'd hate to have to arrest you."

Quinn and Nicky looked at him in disbelief. Generally, you didn't threaten arrest unless you were prepared to back it up. They didn't have enough on Bartholomew to make spaghetti stick. Martinez was already throwing his not inconsiderable weight around and confirmed for Nicky what a pain in the ass he was going to be.

"I don't think I should say anymore without a lawyer."

And that was why you didn't threaten arrest at this stage of the game. Now they'd lost Bartholomew's cooperation.

"That's up to you, of course, but it's going to look bad if you refuse to talk," Quinn said.

Bartholomew looked dejected. "I don't have anything else to tell you and I'd like to go now."

Quinn turned off the recorder. "We're going to want to talk to you again. You're free to go."

Bartholomew stood up and quickly left the room. Martinez remained hulking over the table and glared at them both.

"Why the fuck do we have a citizen taking part in an official police interrogation?"

"Nicky was one of us, my partner in homicide for a long while. She's also in the center of the investigation. We'd be fools not to tap into what she can bring. Don't be a dick about it, Martinez."

"Don't be a dick? How about don't be a fool? Does the lieutenant know you're treating a witness, a person of interest, as a co-investigator?" He turned to Nicky. "You may think you can sleep with a detective on the case and play buddies with us, but that's over. Unless you want me to talk to the lieutenant about it?"

Nicky leaned back in her chair and tried to project her indifference to his threat. But the threat was real and she feared being cut off from the investigation because of the massive asshole staring at her from across the table.

Quinn tossed his pen down. "Listen, Martinez, we have a deadline to catch a serial killer or he'll strike again. We need every resource available to us, and Nicky can give us insights into the recovery world and information about the victims we wouldn't otherwise know."

"She knows that shit because she's a drunk. Do you want to trust a drunk? I know I don't."

"That's enough, Martinez." He barked out the words in a tone she'd only heard Quinn use when talking to the bad guys.

"Don't bother, Quinn. He's not worth it." She stood and put her notebook and pen in her jacket pocket and moved toward the door.

"I'll call you," Quinn said.

Nicky closed the door behind her with a little more force than necessary. She'd talk to Quinn later and ask they continue to share information, even if it was behind Martinez's back. She was sick at the thought of him ruining everything. He hated her and she wasn't accustomed to being hated. It wasn't hard to hate him back. The deadline was looming and she was no further along in discovering who the killer was. She was almost done with warning the women on her list. Most were unreachable, some she didn't remember their full names, others didn't show up through any internet search she did. The cops had more sophisticated databases and would have better luck. She needed to reach Deb to warn her as well. As soon as she was back in her car she called her.

"It's Nicky, Deb. I need to talk to you."

"Nicky Sullivan. I thought we would have crossed paths by now, but I haven't seen you at meetings."

"We've been going to different meetings, I guess." This was a fabrication. She'd not been going to meetings regularly, which she knew made her more vulnerable to relapse. "Are you aware of the series of murders that've taken place recently, all the victims somehow connected with the recovery community?"

"I heard an announcement and couldn't believe it. What do you know about it?"

"I know you're going to hate having spent any time with me. All of the victims were somehow connected to me, one because we dated. You need to be extra careful."

"Why, because we dated for five minutes? There's not much to connect us, Nicky."

"There's enough. You need to lay low until I tell you you're in the clear."

"What do you mean by lay low?"

"Don't go out at night, don't talk to strangers, and above all, don't relapse. The killer seems to have a thing about women who relapse."

"Well, I wasn't planning on relapsing, but I guess you never know. I can't stay in every night. I work late most nights and on others I try to make a meeting."

"You'll have to change that. Go straight from work to home and use every lock you have. Maybe you can go to one of the noon meetings downtown for a while."

Deb was silent for a moment. "I should have known you were trouble, Nicky."

"I don't think there's any way either of us would know a serial killer was targeting people I know. Almost all of the women were from before I got sober. You're the only one I've dated in sobriety. You need to take care of yourself until we catch whoever is doing this."

"I'll do what I can. I can't promise I'll be tucked up at home every night."

"I can't police what you do, but this is serious. I don't want anything to happen to you."

"Since I have you on the phone I want to ask you what you think happened between us? It seems like we had one misunderstanding and that was it. I never heard from you again."

"I never heard from you either." Nicky hoped Deb wouldn't insist on processing their brief relationship. She didn't have the capacity now.

"I want to understand it better." Deb's voice was gentle, as if she didn't want to startle a nervous animal.

"I'm afraid you won't get much help from me. I think it wasn't meant to be—if it was, one of us would have reached out. Anyway, I've met someone."

"I wasn't asking for another chance, Nicky." Now there was an edge to her voice.

"Listen, take care of yourself, be safe, be well. Call me if you notice anything weird, like if you feel you're being followed."

"Jesus."

"Take my advice, Deb, and lay low. I'll let you know when we've caught the killer."

They hung up as Nicky pulled into the Olive Street garage. It was just starting to rain. She walked into the house, fully expecting another problem to present itself. It wasn't yet noon, plenty of time for more catastrophes.

❖

Nicky stared out the living room window at the steady downpour of rain. Temperatures had fallen and the last vestiges of summer were gone. She felt as gloomy as the weather. A large moving van from Steve's Discount Furniture pulled up to the curb in front of the house—the fucking bunk beds had arrived. The truck was too big to enter through the alley so they'd have to tromp through the front foyer and up the carpeted stairs in their wet shoes. Gerri was supposed to be here when they arrived, but unsurprisingly she was nowhere in sight. A man jumped down from the cab and walked toward the front door. She was tempted to turn him away but there was no point. Gerri would have them come back. She propped open the door, signed a piece of paper, and felt grateful at least that Angela was the only resident in the house. Even she was upset with the powers that be.

Gerri's car pulled up behind the van and parked. She unfurled an umbrella and struggled out of the car holding a briefcase in her other hand. Nicky left the door open and went to get her jacket and car keys. She wouldn't stay for the installation, wouldn't back down from her refusal to support the policy. Let Gerri fire her. That couldn't be any worse for her than the way things now stood. Between her mother and Parker, she wouldn't be homeless while she got back on her feet. Humiliated, yes; homeless, no. She slipped out the back and drove off, leaving Gerri to figure out what to do. The assembly of the bunk beds was going to take a while and Nicky needed to make good use of the time.

When she walked into Kopi Café she saw Quinn at one of the front tables. He was dressed in his usual neatly pressed suit from Men's Warehouse, his face haggard. Working a case with no leads would do that to a detective. Intense worrying about how they'd find the killer before he struck again was the anti-Botox. Lines deepened and skin grayed. The pouches below the eye became pouchier and bruised looking. She'd caught a glimpse of herself in the mirror that morning and turned her head when she'd seen the same on her own face.

Parker wasn't with him, but thankfully neither was Martinez. Quinn had called to arrange the meeting and she was curious what he wanted. She plopped into the chair opposite him and shrugged out of her wet slicker. Quinn smiled at her, but it was the smile of someone listening to a bad joke. Pain was involved.

"Thanks for coming, Nicky. I wanted to talk to you away from Martinez."

"That guy is a total dick. He hated me before he even saw me. What's up with him?"

"Old old school. Probably doesn't like you because you're gay, but he hasn't said that. He also thinks we've not looked into you enough as a suspect. Says you probably got the cut on your head when a victim fought back."

"But there's no evidence any of the victims fought back. Zero defensive wounds. I have an alibi, you know."

"I know. He thinks Parker could be lying to protect you, that since you're together now her word is suspect. Do you want coffee, by the way?"

"You think Parker and I are together?" The idea alarmed and delighted her in equal measure.

"I don't know what you're calling it, but the alibi is you were together the night of the last murder and he's drawing his own conclusions. What he's most upset about is you being in on our investigation. I think he'll talk to the lieutenant about it."

Nicky got up to use the bathroom, her face flushed with anger. When she returned she was calm enough to not take her frustration out on Quinn. "We can't have both me and Parker off the case. Left with Martinez, the killer will never be found."

"I won't cut you out, Nicky, but we must go on the QT. No more sitting in on witness interviews or meeting with us at the station. But I'm always available by phone."

"It sounds like you're cutting me out." Quinn had a case to solve and a boss to obey. She knew she shouldn't take it personally, but she did.

"I'll keep you as informed as I can about leads we're following, elusive as those may be. Martinez is going to be in the way, though. I may not get to you as quickly," he said.

"I suppose he might be able to bring some fresh ideas. It seems we're all stuck. I've warned everyone I can think to warn, including outpatient programs and other sober houses. I wasn't able to get hold of most of the women on the list."

"We have a detective working on that."

"Before you cut me off, can we review where everything is?"

"Why don't you ask me what you want to know." Quinn picked up his coffee and leaned back in his chair, more relaxed than he'd been when she arrived. She still sensed a slight distance and it depressed her.

"Where are you on forensics?"

"Same weapon used on all victims, a long thin blade like a boning knife, impossible to trace. None of the victims showed defensive wounds, so they were either surprised by the killer or they knew who it was and didn't suspect they were in danger. All victims had evidence of drugs and/or alcohol in their systems, most in high dosages. There was no DNA left behind. The killer wears gloves and is careful to not leave trace evidence."

"What about their families?'

"None of the families knew the other victims so it's unlikely, though not certain, the victims knew each other. No link there. Other than Lou's parents, all the families said they would have welcomed their daughters into their home. They were upset but not surprised that they had relapsed prior to their death."

"Looking for other connections doesn't get around the fact that the main one among the women was their connection to me."

"Which is why Martinez thinks of you as a suspect. From the outside looking in I can see his point. But from the inside I know it's not you, couldn't be you."

Nicky looked through her notebook. "Nothing on the national databases?"

"All we could do is search on similar modus operandi and didn't find anything. There were plenty of knife attacks, but none with this kind of blade and manner of death—a single stab to the heart. Multiple stab wounds is more the norm."

She flipped a page. "Have you looked any further into Jack Hansen, whether anyone in his world was targeting him through his sister?"

"I think that became a non-starter once a second body was discovered that had nothing to do with the Hansens."

"Which means we have nothing. No current leads, only our working theory the killer is someone who knows and, clearly, hates me. It could be someone I put away while I was on the job. Is there a way to compile a list from department databases?"

"I put a detective on that. In the five years you were in homicide, nearly all your perps are still in jail or are heavily alibied. Even if there was anyone who was out and seeking vengeance on you, how would they know all these women? And that they relapsed? If any of them did it, I would expect a messier kill. Our killer is more refined, their profile different from any of the ones you sent to jail."

Nicky threw her pen on the table. "We're left with waiting for the killer to strike again, which he will do soon if the threat is legitimate, and we can only hope he'll make a mistake. It's a high price to pay for evidence."

"Too high."

"What about a profile? Is anyone working on developing one?"

"I got it this morning and skimmed through it."

"Give me the highlights," Nicky said.

"The usual. The precise nature of the knife to the heart suggests someone who wants to be in total control at all times. What serial killer doesn't want to be in control? The report is inconclusive as to whether the killer is male or female, which surprised me. I thought there'd be some marker the profiler would identify, but I guess not. I'm still leaning toward it being a woman. What about you?"

"The jury's still out. Cases of female serial killers are so rare."

"It's in the report—only about fifteen percent are women, but that's not nothing. The profiler mentioned the lack of a sexual component to the killings, which also points toward a woman. The other thing the report talks about is almost all female serial killers are motivated by profit or revenge, with profit by far the most dominant. None of our victims was robbed, so there goes the profit motive. I can't speculate about revenge. That may be part of this."

"Someone has it in for me, they want revenge for something. The four women are collateral damage. I wonder if the murders would stop if I killed myself."

"Nicky, stop. That's nothing to joke about."

"Who says I'm joking? Is my life worth more than those four women's lives? Is it worth ten or twenty? We have no idea how long the killer will keep this up."

"Don't be ridiculous. A killer will find a reason to kill. If it wasn't you it would be something else. It's not your fault."

"I don't know. It seems the right thing to do." She almost laughed at the distressed look on Quinn's face. "But I'll think about it some more if it makes you happy."

"Relieved is more the word. What would Parker say if she heard you talking this way?"

"Don't tell her. I don't need a lecture from her, too."

They were quiet for a while. Nicky finished her coffee.

"I'm open to any new ideas you may have," Quinn said.

Distressingly, she had none. They parted ways. When she was back in her car she took a call from an unknown number. She couldn't afford to dodge calls with so much going on, but every ring of the phone threatened bad news. Unless it was Parker calling. She was all that was good in a sea of bad.

"Is this Nicky Sullivan?" Whoever it was spoke with a high, clear voice that sounded young. "My name is Ashley Martin and I'm a reporter with the *Chicago Reader*. Do you have a minute for some questions?"

Nicky wasn't familiar with the name. Her experience with the press during her time as a detective had been generally good, but she didn't have much hope this would be a repeat. The *Reader* was known for its in-depth investigative pieces. She wondered how they'd gotten her name in conjunction with the serial killings. "What about?"

"I understand you're the resident manager at Olive Street House, is that correct?"

"It is, but why are you asking?"

"We've been contacted by some former residents about some activity at the house we'd like your comments on."

Madison strikes again. She was taking the bunk bed news as a call to arms. "I can't comment on anything that goes on in the house, but I'm happy to give you the name and number of my boss. Do you have something to write with?"

"I'm working on an article on the recovery industry in Chicago and coincidentally was forwarded a call to our news desk from a former resident of yours who claims the house engaged in abusive practices. Are you sure you don't want to comment and get in front of that?" Ashley had the slightly urgent tone of voice that reporters all seemed to have.

"I'm very sure, but as I said, my boss is the one to talk to. She oversees all the company's sober houses in the city and will probably be a very good source for you." Nicky gleefully gave her Gerri's name and number and got off the phone. She'd have a fit when she learned Nicky had sent a reporter her way. It almost put her in a good mood.

When she returned to Olive Street, she found Gerri holed up in her office, typing furiously on her phone. She didn't look up until she'd finished. "Good, you're back. They're almost done assembling the bunk beds. Would you please sign off on them for me? I have to get back to the office on the double."

"As long as you know it's under protest."

"How can I forget when you keep bringing it up?" She got up from the desk and stopped in front of Nicky. "I've got seven new women coming to the house over the next few days. You'll have your hands full."

Nicky didn't respond. The idea of the house overflowing with women made her sick. Maybe the threat of the investigative piece in the *Reader* would get Gerri to rescind the bunk beds and second drug test. She could only hope. After she'd gone, Nicky saw she'd forgotten her briefcase. It was sitting on the floor next to the desk, a beat-up leather bag with an open top. She paused for a moment to think about whether it was the right thing to do to go through it. Her sponsor would say no, that any dishonest behavior was wrong. But Sheila wasn't there to argue over it.

She peered into the case and saw several file folders and a plastic baggy full of double-stuffed Oreos. A folder labeled Budget was in front and she took it out, along with one called Mortgage, doubtful either would be of much interest. Gerri would return soon when she realized she'd forgotten the briefcase, so Nicky quickly opened the budget folder and took out a spreadsheet dense with text and numbers. There was a section for each sober house owned by R-M in the Midwest, and she scanned the page until she reached Olive Street House. She'd never seen the whole picture of sober house economics. Among the line items were groceries, utility costs and the like, but her eyes stopped at the expense line for Trujillo Landscaping Services. She checked the date of the budget and it was for the current year-to-date, squarely in the time frame when the residents were made to perform the landscaping chores themselves. The cost per month was five hundred dollars for their biweekly service. Nicky skimmed the sections on the other sober houses Gerri oversaw and confirmed they also had line items for landscaping. Nicky knew those houses weren't receiving any landscaping because she and the other resident managers had all bitched about it when Gerri announced the change. She was skimming or embezzling or whatever you wanted to call it. Nicky had just been handed a giant cudgel in her fight against Gerri.

She was almost giddy at the discovery. If she could get the bunk bed and testing policies changed through blackmail, she wouldn't hesitate to do so. She perked up at the thought of holding the cards for once rather than always being subject to Gerri's increasingly erratic whims. She kept the budget folder out and skimmed through the mortgage one. There was a pre-foreclosure notice at the top of the file and for a moment she thought Olive Street House was in trouble. Then she saw the address of the property and realized it was Gerri's own house that was about to be lost. That would explain the motive for her embezzlement, but Nicky was hard-pressed to feel sorry for her. She'd done too much against the welfare of the residents to garner her sympathy. The foreclosure news underscored how vulnerable Gerri would be to Nicky using the information against her.

Gerri returned to the house a half hour later and looked ready to growl.

"I left my briefcase." Nicky nudged the case toward her but put her hand flat on the two file folders on her desk. Gerri glanced at them and froze. "You went through my briefcase? I'll have you fired for that."

"That's fine. Fire away. But we're going to discuss you stealing from both your employer and the house. I saw the line item for landscaping. You're in a world of trouble if I tell your boss about your scheme, don't you think?"

Gerri's eyes narrowed and she reached for the files. Nicky pulled them close, out of her reach, and took the spreadsheet out. Gerri tried to snatch it away. "You deceitful bitch. Give it to me."

"What will your boss say, do you think? I think he'll say you're fired, which won't help your mortgage situation, will it?" It was clear to her now that Gerri stole the cash boxes, too.

Gerri stood still and glowered at her. "What do you want?"

Nicky smiled. She felt happy for the first time in memory. "I want the twice weekly drug tests returned to once a week and the bunk beds removed. Do that and I'll overlook what I see on the budget. Don't mistake me—I'll turn you in at the first sign you're not cooperating."

"It can't be done, not without me getting fired myself."

"That's probably better than jail, don't you think?"

"You're way out of line, Nicky. You're dreaming if you think you have any power over me."

"You're dreaming if you think I don't." She folded the spreadsheet and slipped it into her back pocket and pushed both file folders back across the desk. "It's your choice which way this will go."

Gerri looked like a wild dog backed into a corner. If Nicky reached a hand toward her she was sure she'd be snapped at. She was desperate and angry—a dangerous combination. "You're fired. I want you out of here by the end of the day." She grabbed the folders, shoved them into her briefcase, and picked it up.

"So be it. I'll still be talking to your boss."

"I don't give a shit who you talk to. The word of an alcoholic who's been fired from another job isn't going to go far."

She spun on her heel and left the office, the front door slamming behind her a moment later. All her fear of being fired evaporated, for now it seemed like a strategic battle won. She didn't worry about what would happen to the residents for she had every intention of getting Gerri fired and her policies changed. She'd do all she could for them and beyond that she had no control. She felt light, as if a yoke had been lifted from her shoulders, though now she was without money or any job prospects. There were still the murders to worry about, but she'd take what she could get. Today was a win.

CHAPTER EIGHTEEN

Parker chose that moment to call, just as the reality of being jobless started to sink in. There she was, whenever Nicky needed her. Their love happened too quickly—everything about it was too something. Too soon to be trusted, too wonderful to be believed. Yet, that meant nothing next to the central truth that Parker felt absolutely right to her. She dreaded what she'd feel when she broke up with her, but Parker was in too much danger because of her relationship with Nicky. She stabbed at the green button on her phone and closed the door to her office.

"I have news," Nicky said.

"Surely you know most people answer the phone by saying hello. Did your parents not teach you that?"

"I got fired."

"What? How's that possible?" Parker's voice seamlessly changed from teasing to concern. It was the gentle tone of her concern that got to Nicky, made her yearn for something that was suddenly within reach. She filled Parker in on the embezzlement she'd discovered and her confrontation with Gerri.

"What kind of notice did she give you?"

"The immediate kind. I have to be out by tonight."

"I've got you covered. Come over to my place when you're ready. We can figure things out from there."

Nicky hesitated. "I can't stay with you. I'm sorry."

"I don't understand. You've been here most of the past week and now you need a place to stay. The good news is you don't have to go back to Olive Street in the middle of the night. I can finally wake up with you."

"It's too soon to move in with you. I know you know that."

"Who said anything about moving in? It's not a permanent thing, at least not yet, but you do need a place to stay tonight. I thought you would want to stay with me." There was no mistaking the disappointment in her voice.

Nicky tried to sound convincing and gentle, a subtle fusion of emotion that was probably above her pay grade. Whatever her tone of voice, it was killing her to say it. "I can stay with my mother. I won't be homeless. But the truth is we need to stop seeing each other altogether. I can't risk something happening to you. With the killer's deadline coming up, it would be crazy to have you be associated with me."

"We're already associated, as you call it, and the killer almost certainly knows you're my girlfriend."

"I must have been absent the day you decided we were girlfriends."

Parker was quiet. "I'm going to cut you some slack because you're under enormous pressure."

"The more we're together the greater the risk. Do you think I could live with myself if anything happened to you? As of now, the only people who know we're interested in each other are Quinn and others in the department. We have to be extremely cautious."

"Nicky, I'm police. Do you think I can't take care of myself? I'm not even a candidate as a victim. It's not like I can relapse and I promise you I won't get drunk until the killer is caught."

"You don't get drunk anyway," Nicky said.

"Exactly. I don't have the same profile as the other women."

"I'm not at all sure the profile won't be expanded. A killer needs to kill, right? He's going to run out of relapsing alcoholic women who are associated with me in some way. He's going to turn to non-alcoholics in order to keep up the action."

"You don't know that," Parker said. Nicky heard her frustration.

"You don't know that he's not. I can't take the chance."

"I don't get why this is a unilateral decision. Isn't it something we should discuss?"

"We're discussing it now."

Now Nicky heard her anger. "You brought this to me as a fait accompli, as if your opinion was the only one that mattered."

This was one of those relationship skills she was terrible at, but in this matter her opinion *was* the only one that counted. "I hope you'll still be there when the killer is caught, but until then I can't see you."

"It's like you're breaking up with me."

"The only thing that matters to me is you not dying. I'm sorry if that means you're mad at me. Even sorrier if you won't want to resume once this is all over."

"I don't like the way you've handled this, Nicky. You don't fight well."

"Are we fighting?"

"Damn right we are. You do what you have to and I'll do the same."

She hung up. Nicky threw her phone onto the desk, scared to her toes it would be the last time she talked to Parker. Just as a spark could produce a fire, a bucket of water could put it out. Parker was capable of handling herself, as Nicky was. They'd had the same training in the police academy. But the risk was too great. She wasn't wrong about this. Why couldn't Parker see it? Was the cost of Parker's safety the relationship itself? An exquisite pain grew behind her eyes as she fought off tears. She simply couldn't handle another death, especially not Parker's. Her life could not be more screwed up. One of the promises of AA was life would become manageable with sobriety, but that was a promise unfulfilled.

Something had to be done to find the killer and it needed to happen quickly. She went upstairs to pack her things while a plan started to form. When she came down a half hour later, the residents were gathering in the meeting room for the six o'clock AA meeting. Nicky decided to not tell them about her dismissal, at least until the next day. She had no idea if Gerri would send someone over immediately to take charge of the house, or at least chaperone the residents until a new manager could be found. The women who remained after the walkout were perfectly capable of taking care of themselves. It wasn't her job any longer to worry about them. She felt hollow, as if all the work she'd done at Olive Street was meaningless.

Sheila arrived for the meeting and caught sight of Nicky as she was crossing the living room with her bags in hand. Everything she owned fit into a small roller bag and backpack and the garbage bags she'd stuffed with her useless suits. Sheila followed her into the kitchen.

"What's going on? Are you on another vacation?"

Nicky turned, not surprised she was there. She'd have to tell Sheila about losing her job. As her sponsor, she'd want to know all about it to make sure Nicky wasn't going to drink over it. The thought hadn't occurred to her, but now it flashed in her brain in vivid detail. A quiet tavern with comfortable barstools, a bottle of Pabst open in front of her, no glass, and a shot of tequila next to it, no lime. A Bears game on the television, a smart bartender who liked to talk about interesting things, a newspaper folded to the crossword, and snow falling gently out the window. That had been her world for a long time and she suddenly yearned for it—the familiarity of it, the comfort of knowing where she belonged, talking and laughing with friends. And most of all, obliterating all of her uncomfortable emotions. Thoughts like this were not frequent, but they scared the bejesus out of her. She turned to Sheila.

"A permanent vacation is more like it. I got fired today."

Sheila stood motionless as if Nicky had sprouted two heads. "Has Gerri lost her mind? You're the only thing holding the place together."

"I think Gerri lost her mind some time ago, but that doesn't mean she can't fire me. There are things I need to update you on, but I don't have time right now."

"I could skip the meeting and we could talk. It's important, Nicky. Big events like this can be triggery."

Triggery, smiggery. She knew she could trust herself not to drink. "Later, I promise. I'll call you."

She walked away from Sheila and through the back door to the garage. It was fully dark but only six o'clock. The air had become nippy, hinting at a first frost. She drove to the Closet, a gay bar in the middle of Boystown. The Closet was one of the few bars with a mixed clientele of all the letters in LGBTQIA+. She hadn't stepped in the bar for five years, but there was Addy, the same bartender who'd cut her off on more than one occasion. She was wearing the same ponytail, though her hair was a little grayer, her middle a little chunkier. She still had her killer smile.

"Nicky Sullivan," Addy said. "I haven't seen you for a long time."

"It's been about five years."

"Where've you been?"

"I've been busy not drinking." Someone got up from a barstool and Nicky grabbed it. The feel of settling into it sent a shimmer of fear through her. She knew being there was dangerous, but so was the person who'd killed four women. She'd rather drink again than have anyone else lose their life.

Addy wiped the bar in front of her. "What can I get you?"

"I have a favor to ask and you're going to think it's crazy. Have you heard about the women being murdered recently?"

"Sure. A few people here have known them. What about it?"

"I have a vested interest in finding the killer."

"Well, sure. You're a cop."

"Not any more. But I'm working with the detectives who are on the case. I could use your help."

"What can I do?"

"I'm going to sit here all night drinking rum and Cokes, minus the rum, and pretend I'm drunk when I leave. I know that sounds absurd. You'll have to trust me there's a reason for it. I need you to pretend you're putting rum in my glass each time I order a round. And try not to laugh when I act like a drunk."

Addy laughed. "What the hell?"

"Play along with me. I'll give you an enormous tip."

"One rumless rum and Coke coming up."

The plan was on the pathetic side, but it was something. It only made sense the killer would be keeping tabs on her movements. It was also likely Nicky knew the killer, who wouldn't want to be recognized by her if he came into the bar but would likely follow her when she came out. She wanted him to think she was drunk to draw him out. She spent the next two excruciating hours sipping her Coke while trying to appear increasingly inebriated, a ruse that required more subtle acting skills than she was capable of.

When she was drinking, Nicky could handle a lot of booze. Two hours wouldn't make much of a dent, while six rum and Cokes would make most people legless. She chatted with Addy, then with a guy who sat on the stool next to her, spent some time at the pool table. She used to be an excellent pool player, but no longer. She couldn't sink the easiest shots and she noticed the smirks and rolled eyes of the women standing in a ring around the table.

A woman sitting alone at the opposite end of the bar looked approachable and Nicky swaggered over to talk to her. She felt guilty as she flirted with the woman, thinking how it would make Parker feel. What if it was really over with Parker? What if that were the end of things? It would be the quickest she'd ruined a relationship, nosing out countless others. The riff didn't seem big enough to break up over, but they were so new and unestablished she didn't think it would take much for Parker to see what she was getting into and run like hell. The more time that passed by without a call from her, the more Nicky was convinced they were through. She tried to flirt with the woman, but stone cold sober, her skills were pathetic. Soon she found herself enmeshed in a discussion of the woman's job at a food bank.

When she returned to her barstool she found a fresh drink in front of her. The idea of drinking another plain Coke repelled her. It would be much more palatable with rum in it and so easy to do. The smell from the beer in front of the person sitting next to her quickly brought her back to the whitewashed version of her drinking days, when everything was still fun and she didn't hate herself. Facing all her problems sober seemed like a stupid way to go. Why writhe in pain and anxiety when a few drinks would smooth things over? She'd learned from others in recovery that when you have an urge to drink, think through the disaster that would inevitably follow—the Olympic hangover, the embarrassment and shame, the hair of the dog that led to another full day of drinking, the utterly predictable cycle of drunkenness and remorse that would become her life again. At the moment, the price she'd pay for drinking again seemed worth it.

She signaled Addy to bring her a beer when the door opened and in walked Colleen, the woman she'd talked to at Donna's the night she went there looking for Lou. Nicky still had no clear memory of her from the drinking days, though it was likely they'd had sex and neither remembered it. Should she warn her of the killer out there, how he was targeting people connected to her? Colleen scanned the room, looking for friends or an empty barstool. When her eyes landed on Nicky, she smiled and made her way over to her. The bar had gotten even busier than when she'd first arrived and she had to wend her way through all the people standing in front of the bar.

"We meet again," Colleen said. "For a non-drinker I sure see you in a lot of bars."

"It's a weird coincidence. I haven't been in a bar since I saw you at Donna's."

"What are you doing here now? I mean, I'd love to buy you a drink and it doesn't have to be alcoholic."

"If I drink another Coke I'll throw up." Just then, the bartender plunked a bottle of Pabst in front of her. Colleen raised her eyebrows.

"What's this?"

"It's a beer. I thought I'd hold it in my hand for a while."

"That's bullshit. You can't drink it. It'll ruin everything."

Nicky looked at her closely. "What would you know about that?"

The stool next to Nicky's became open and Colleen sat. "I was in AA for about three months a few years ago. I couldn't hack it—all the higher power talk and strangers giving me their phone numbers. It wasn't for me. I wanted to drink way more than I wanted to work those fucking steps, so I drank again. I felt shitty about myself and it'll be the same for you if you drink that beer. It's not going to make you feel any better."

"Why don't you quit again?"

Colleen frowned. "I keep trying, but I never make it more than a day. Maybe I missed my one shot at it. You've been sober how long?"

"Five years."

Colleen picked up Nicky's beer and took a long swallow. "Don't blow it. Not that you seem like the happiest sober person I've met, but it's better than where you were before. I mean, neither of us can remember whether we slept together. I know what kind of drunk you were."

They were silent for a while, Colleen finishing the beer, Nicky weak with relief she hadn't put the bottle to her lips. She slipped into her jacket and threw some bills on the bar. "I better get out of here. Thanks for showing up."

"If you ever want to look me up, you'll find me here or at Donna's." She looked down the bar for the bartender. She wouldn't want to be without a drink for too long.

"Do you know what's going on out there, the serial murders of female alcoholics? You should be careful when you leave the bars at night. This is no joke."

"It's all the talk at Donna's. One of the women was a regular there."

Nicky sat back down. "Who?"

"Allie Becker. She tried to get sober after her mom died but didn't make it and went into rehab. She got kicked out of her sober house and made a beeline to Donna's. I used to drink with her a lot before she went into treatment."

"Did you see her the night she was killed?"

"I'd say yes. I'm in the bar most nights, and I remember Allie drinking that night. Fucking sad."

Nicky's nerves jangled with the five Cokes in her system and now the scent of a lead. "Tell me everything."

"Not much to tell. She sat a couple stools down from me, but I could hear the conversation. She said she'd come back to the sober house drunk and they kicked her out. They were going to let her sleep it off, but she grabbed her shit and left. That's when she got to Donna's. Not much to tell beyond that."

"Did she tell you where she was going when she left the bar?"

"She said she had a bone to pick with her sponsor. She left and I think that was the last anyone at the bar ever saw her."

"She didn't happen to mention the sponsor's name, did she?"

"Nope. That's all I know."

"Thanks, Colleen. You've been a big help. More than you know."

Nicky left the bar and came out onto Broadway. The street was busy, mostly with gay men on their way to restaurants and bars. She didn't have the heart to pretend she was drunk and stagger up the street, trying to draw out the killer. It felt ridiculous. She went to Donna's instead.

The bar was relatively quiet. The music was turned down the way she liked it. She could hear the crack of a pool cue hitting a rack of balls. Women at the bar were watching Loyola play DePaul in women's basketball. She waited for Donna to finish up with other customers.

"I thought you were supposed to stay out of bars."

"That's what they say. I have some questions about Allie Becker, the woman who was killed the other night. I understand she was here the night she was murdered."

"Yeah, that was fucking tragic."

"It was. Did you hear any of her conversation? We're trying to figure out where she might have gone and whether she left with anyone."

"She said she was going to talk to her sponsor, which I can't imagine goes over well when you're drunk. I thought it was weird, but maybe she was having second thoughts about having started drinking again. She was alone when she left." Donna looked around and frowned. "Do you think the killer might have been here?"

"I wish I knew." She tore a sheet out of her notebook and scribbled her number on it. "If you see any of the women who were with Allie that night, will you let me know and also give them my number? Maybe she said something useful to one of them."

Out on the Andersonville streets she decided to walk home to see if anyone followed her. She walked slowly up Clark Street and turned west on Olive, where the dark would be more inviting for an attack. She went into the alley to approach the house from the rear, but there was no one following, no one leaping at her from a hiding place. Deflated, Nicky straightened her posture and returned to her car, wondering what plan would succeed in drawing out the killer. There were none she could think of.

CHAPTER NINETEEN

Still no word from Parker. Nicky didn't want them to see each other at least until the end of the killer's deadline, the day after the next one. If she didn't call her, would Parker think she wanted to be away from her for good? If only she knew the right thing to do.

It was getting late. She'd called her mother earlier to see if she could crash with her for a few days and she was delighted to have her. Nicky's old bedroom was now a guest room and that's what she intended to be—a short-term guest. She'd have to find a job quickly or she'd be out of ready cash. It was one thing to stay with her mom and yet another to ask her for money. She'd shamelessly done that when she was drinking, and she cringed at the thought of it. When she got to the house she rang the bell—letting herself in with her key seemed wrong.

Her parents lived in North Center, a neighborhood of single-family homes and excellent public schools, away from the lake but still centrally located. She'd grown up in a two-story bungalow, a dormered attic turning the upstairs into a master suite and additional bedroom. There were two smaller bedrooms on the first level, where unpainted woodwork and original stained glass made the house feel warm and welcoming. She loved it but hadn't planned on ever living there again. When her mother answered the door she put on a smile and tried to act normal, not like her life was falling apart.

"Why didn't you use your key?"

"I didn't want to chase your lover away." She walked into the foyer and threw her coat on the rack.

"I wish," her mother said. "I could have gentlemen callers every night of the week and I don't think your father would notice." She picked up Nicky's bag and grabbed her by the hand. "Let's get you settled. It's late."

"It's nine o'clock, Mom. That's like breakfast time for you."

"Well, I know you go to bed early. Let's have a drink." Her mother seemed to always forget Nicky was sober, which annoyed the hell out of her.

"You drink, I'll watch."

"What would you like? Some herbal tea, perhaps?" She made it sound like she was offering her baby food, pablum that shouldn't be of interest to an adult. Her mother always paid an appropriate amount of lip service to her sobriety, but with a slightly disappointed tone of voice. She wasn't an alcoholic, but she was a firm believer in the power of a cocktail.

They settled into the two chairs placed in front of the fireplace. Nicky tried to explain what had happened at Olive Street House. She was worried sick about the women who'd left the house in the walkout. If the killer had been aware of Lou, he must be aware of the other OSH women leaving the house. It wasn't making a lot of sense to her that a male killer would know so much about her life. Who could that be? Quinn was the only man close enough to her to fit that description, and she knew he was no killer. Her mind stuttered and stopped and stuttered again.

"I say you're better off out of that place," her mother said. "You can do so much more, Nicky."

Here we go. Next would be the pep talk about how it wasn't too late to start a new career, something that reflected what she was capable of, something that wasn't embarrassing like living in a sober house at forty years old. She forestalled it by going to bed, leaving her mother in front of the fire with her second large scotch and the TV remote. When she was in her room she looked at her phone. Still nothing from Parker. She climbed miserably into bed with no comforting thought of a better day tomorrow. It would be miserable, too, as would the next day and all the days it took to catch the killer—man or woman.

The next morning at Olive Street House she found Angela knitting at the desk in the office. She dropped her needles when she saw Nicky.

"What are you doing here? You were fired."

"What are you doing in here?"

"Gerri has me supervising while she finds someone to replace you." Nicky could hear the pride in Angela's voice.

"Okay. That's a little weird since you're only a year sober."

"You don't have any say in the matter, Nicky."

"I'm here to clear out my stuff from the office and return the keys. Can you give me the room, please?"

"I don't think I should leave you alone with any official files and such."

Nicky took a step into the office. "Get the fuck out of the room, now."

Angela hesitated and Nicky took another step. She towered over her. "I'm calling Gerri. You can't threaten me."

"Be my guest but give me the fucking room." She took a final step in and stood immediately in front of Angela, who grabbed her knitting and eased her way around her and out the door. Nicky slammed it shut. Why was everything a confrontation? She opened the desk drawers, some of them with a key, and took out the few things she kept there—some lip balm, a copy of the Big Book, a half-eaten bag of Cheetos, a charging cord, and, in a locked metal box in a locked drawer, her holstered Glock and ammunition. She clipped the gun and holster to the rear of her jeans and put the ammunition in her pocket. It was how she wore her weapon when she was a detective and the feel of it at the small of her back made her miss her old job, the one she could never go back to. What was she going to do with herself? How long would she have stayed at this small desk in this cramped office before moving on to something else? It might be a good thing she was being forced to do something different. Being a resident manager wasn't meant to be a permanent job.

She called the Reardon-Malloy general number and asked for Gerri Thomas's supervisor. She had to wait five minutes on hold before he picked up.

"This is Edmundson. How can I help?"

"Mr. Edmundson, this is Nicky Sullivan, the resident manager at Olive Street House. It's important I have a word with you."

"I know who you are, Nicky. What can I do for you?"

"Gerri Thomas fired me yesterday."

"I hadn't heard that. Why did she? You've been with us some time now, haven't you?"

As if she needed a reminder. She told him about Gerri's drug testing and bunk bed policies and how they worked against the atmosphere they wanted for the residents, but his reaction to that was muted. It was less so when she told him of the walkout and that the house census was down. Then she moved in for the kill.

"Yesterday I saw a copy of the budget for Olive Street House and discovered Gerri's skimming profits by setting up a dummy landscaping company. The women here have been doing the landscaping themselves for over a year."

He was silent for some time. "Is there anyone at Olive Street to manage the house?"

"Gerri put a resident in charge. She'll have no authority over the others. I'm at the house now."

"I'm reinstating you effective immediately. Thank you for bringing this to my attention. We'll have a discussion in the near future about the bunk beds and testing, but for now try to get things as settled in the house as you can."

"I don't think I can work for Gerri. She's destroying the place."

"Have you seen her there today? She hasn't come into work and we don't know where she is. After hearing all this, I'm wondering what's going on."

Nicky tried to dredge up concern for Gerri and found she had none. "We need to have that talk soon. I can't work here unless things change."

"Understood. Get hold of me if you see or hear from her."

They rang off. Gerri might be out of her life or she might rise like a phoenix from the ashes. She wouldn't put anything past her. At least she wouldn't have to sleep at her mother's that night. Nor would she be sleeping at Parker's. With the killer's deadline up the next day, Nicky wanted to be as far from her as possible. But was that the right way to look at it? Wouldn't it make more sense to be near Parker, in case she was attacked? They had a better chance against an assault if it were two of them instead of Parker alone. Or Nicky alone, for that matter. Perhaps she should talk to her about it, as she'd suggested in the first place.

She heard someone come in the front door and went out to see who it was. Angela was taking in some packages piled on the front porch. The residents loved Amazon. They bought everything cheap enough to buy and most of their closets were stuffed with crap.

"I've been reinstated, Angela. Your heavy burden has been lifted." The frown on her face was almost comical. "Is there anyone else home?" Nicky asked.

"There are a few in the family room, a few upstairs."

"I'll talk to them in a little while and we'll have a meeting when the others get home."

The door opened again and Sheila walked in. She seemed surprised to see Nicky and broke into a smile. "Great, I caught you. Do you have time for lunch?" She nodded at Angela, who made no move to excuse herself. God, she was annoying.

"I don't think so. There's an awful lot going on right now."

"So I gather. I ran into Madison and her group at a meeting last night."

"Let's go into my office." They walked past Angela and got settled in their chairs.

"Talk to me. I'm worried about you," Sheila said.

"Why? Because there's someone out there killing alcoholic women? Or because there's been a mutiny in the house and my boss is insane?"

"Because all those things together are a recipe for drinking."

"Oh, for God's sake. Isn't every day in this fucking life a recipe for drinking? Have I done something that makes you doubt me so much?"

Sheila sat back in her chair as if pushed. Nicky felt guilty immediately but not enough to apologize. She needed people to leave her alone.

"Have I done something to deserve that?" Sheila said.

"I'm under a lot of stress. I don't need you stressing me more with your worry."

"I see." She reached to the floor for her bag. "I'll get out of your hair, then."

"One more thing. Keep your head low and don't go out at night for a few days. It's possible the killer will strike again soon and, like it or not, you're associated with me."

"For how long remains to be seen."

"What's that supposed to mean?" Nicky felt the flush of anger rise to her cheeks.

"It means I can't sponsor someone who refuses to be sponsored."

"I think you need to leave before this conversation gets out of hand."

Sheila stared at her a moment before rising to go. "Be very careful, Nicky. You're on dangerous ground with your sobriety."

At the moment, she didn't care. Her sobriety was getting a lot of women killed. She watched Sheila leave and hoped she wouldn't see her again. She felt something squeeze her heart as she realized how alienated she was from the people in her life. She'd just shunned her sponsor, her lover wasn't talking to her, and what friends she had were out of the picture completely. She had no control over her life. It was simply a series of reactions to terrible events. She took her gun holster off and put it back in the drawer, wishing the killer was lined up in her sights. She'd sworn to never again pull a trigger, but she'd make an exception for that.

Later in the afternoon, Nicky went to the grocery, glad of something to do. Buying groceries for the house was no small task and the short days meant it was dark by the time she returned. A couple of women lounging in the family room helped her put the food away and promised to start making dinner. She retreated to her office, only to find Gerri sitting behind the desk, the chair tilted back and her feet up on a pulled-out drawer. Nicky immediately recognized the drawer as the one she kept the gun in. Had she forgotten to lock it? Her heart started to hammer.

"Come in, Nicky. Close the door and have a seat."

"I'd rather stand. Actually, I'd rather have my chair back. Why don't we switch places?"

"You're fired, don't you remember? You no longer have a seat in the house. But I'm glad you're here. We have some unfinished business to discuss. Now, close the door. You don't want your residents to hear our conversation, do you?"

She closed the door. "Our business is done. I've told your boss about the embezzlement and he reinstated me. He's wondering where you are. Have you gone AWOL?" Nicky was tall enough she could easily see there was no gun in Gerri's lap. Maybe it was still in the drawer. Gerri's eyes narrowed and her grip tightened on the arms of the chair.

"A simple accounting error."

"If you say so."

Gerri lowered her feet to the floor. "I'm his best director and he knows it. He's going to listen to me, not to some disgraced house manager."

"Reinstated, not disgraced. As soon as I explained the situation to him, he told me to report straight to him. You're not my boss anymore. I bet that hurts."

If Gerri wasn't such a terrible person, Nicky would feel she was being cruel. She'd never been one to kick a person when they're down, but down was not necessarily out where Gerri was concerned. Suddenly, Gerri's hand plunged into her brief bag on the floor and came out with the Glock, gripped in both hands like she knew what she was doing.

"Dave might reconsider giving you your job back when he hears you have a gun in the house," she said.

Nicky quietly drew a breath and focused on the gun. It wasn't the first time she'd had a gun drawn on her, not by a long shot. But it was the most blood-chilling one. Unlike the confrontation with Laura's father, this time it was entirely personal. Gerri hated Nicky, loathed her, and, most of all, feared her. She feared her now more than anything and would want to eliminate the threat. Nicky slowly raised her hands and adopted a placating voice.

"Let's take this a step back. If you think your life is fucked up now, wait until you see what shooting me will do to it. Your entire future hinges on what you do in this moment. I wouldn't give me that much power, if I were you."

"You have no power over me. None."

Gerri's eyes looked crazy—big and bright and moving from side to side. What were the chances she'd pull the trigger? Nicky thought they were pretty high and she felt adrenaline course through her body. "You have a good life, Gerri. Don't blow it by doing anything insane."

"Let's see—no money, no job, thanks to you, no husband, no house. It doesn't sound good to me. In fact, it's no life at all." Her face was twisted in rage.

If Gerri felt she had nothing to lose, taking out Nicky would be her first option. It would eliminate so many of her problems. "What do you mean no husband?"

"He left me. I got home yesterday from being blackmailed by you to find a note from him saying he'd have a lawyer get in touch with me. His closet is empty. It's so like a man to run when things are hard, don't you think?"

"Some men, yes. I'm sorry he left. I'm sure it hurts."

"Hurts? I don't give a fuck about that loser. But even his unemployment checks were helpful. He's left me with a house that's about to be foreclosed on."

Gerri lowered the gun a bit. It was hard on the arms holding a gun steady for any length of time. Nicky took a seat across from her and waited for her opportunity.

"Either give me the gun or let me walk out of here. Those are your choices. Shooting me is a crap option for you. You'll only hurt yourself."

"Oh, no. I'll most certainly hurt you, preferably hurt you dead. It's the one thing that feels cheery right now."

There was a rap at the door. Gerri dropped the gun below the desk. "Make them go away," she hissed.

Nicky got up and faced the door. "I'm busy now. You'll have to come back."

"It's Parker, Nicky. When will you be free?"

The last person she wanted in the line of fire was Parker. "I'm not sure yet. I'll call you." She could feel the strain in her voice and wondered if Parker could hear it.

"Everything okay in there?"

"Ten-four-zero. Talk to you soon."

She could see Parker hesitate through the opaque door and then move quickly away. She turned back to Gerri, who was again aiming the gun directly at her.

The number ten-four-zero in cop code meant a hostage situation, close enough to the familiar ten four to slip unnoticed by Gerri. She hoped Parker would pick up on it and send in the troops.

"What do we do now?" Nicky said. She sat and adopted a casual look, as if they were deciding whether to go to a movie or not. "What do you want from me?"

Gerri stared at her but kept quiet. Her eyes changed from shrewd to empty and Nicky wondered if she saw the hopelessness of her situation. That made her desperate and dangerous.

"I don't know yet what I want from you. Groveling would be good. You can start there."

"I think I'll pass."

The air in the office was thick and still. Gerri had started to wheeze, and each breath sounded like something scraping against sandpaper. It would take about a half hour to get a SWAT team and negotiator to the door, long after Gerri might decide to shoot. Nicky would rather not die yet. She'd miss out on everything that might happen with Parker. Her coming to see Nicky was a good sign they'd work something out. Maybe the thing to do was deal with Gerri in another way and throw some sugar on the problem. "I'm sorry about your husband. I've been there and I know how much it can hurt."

"Oh, please. You have no idea what I feel like, though I'm not surprised you've been dumped before. You're almost as bad as my sanctimonious husband, who lost most of his value the day he got laid off."

The gun was quivering in her hands and she brought it down to the desk. "I'm better off without him." She was trying to convince herself. Her voice lost some of its venom and she brought a hand to her eyes and squeezed, desperate to keep a tear from leaking out. "Don't think I'm in some sort of vulnerable emotional state."

"Anyone would be upset in your situation."

"I'm not upset! I'm furious, mainly with you. Things ran smoothly in my sober houses until you got a firecracker up your ass. Now it's one problem after another. It never stops."

Nicky could point out she wasn't the cause of all of Gerri's problems, but that might get her shot. "Listen, holding me against my will, whether you shoot me or not, brings some serious time and, frankly, I don't see you doing well in prison. Why don't you leave now and I won't say anything about it?"

"I don't think so." Her eyes focused intently on Nicky, looking her up and down, the gun following suit. "You're so tall I'd have to be blind to miss." She pulled back the slide and chambered a round. She knew how to use a gun. "If I'm going down, you're going with me. I could use the company." She smiled sardonically. "Stand up and say your whatevers."

She could see in her eyes Gerri felt she'd already lost everything and dying was not a hardship. A murder/suicide solved the problem of going to jail. She had to keep her talking or she was dead. She didn't question Gerri's resolve to shoot. When the phone on her desk rang Gerri almost jumped out of her chair. "What the fuck?"

"It's a phone, Gerri. They ring on occasion." The only window in the tiny office faced the building next door and on a good day let in a minimum amount of light. Now she could see reflected blue lights flashing against the other building's wall. The troops had arrived. "You better answer it. The police are right outside the door."

"What?" The phone continued to ring as Gerri looked behind her and saw the police lights. "Fuck."

"Pick up the phone. It's the only way you're going to get out of here in one piece."

Gerri scowled and grabbed the receiver. While she listened, Nicky saw a text come into the cell phone she held in her hand. *We'll take it from here. Hold tight. I won't let anything happen to you.* It was Parker. It seemed much more likely she'd avoid getting shot with Parker on the job. Nicky had some experience as a hostage negotiator. She knew her job was to avoid antagonizing Gerri while the police tried to get her to put her gun down and come out of the building, but everything she said only pissed her off more. The residents would be gathering in the living room to see what was happening out front. She prayed no one would come to the office.

Gerri slammed the phone down without having said a word and glared at Nicky. "They want me to come out with my hands up or at least let you and the residents go. There's not a chance of that."

Nicky heard the voices of the women in the living room and then the squeak of the front door opening. She guessed the women were being led out of the building by members of the SWAT team, who then were taking up position at the end of the hallway her office was in. The phone rang again.

"God damn it. Why can't people leave me alone?" Gerri picked up the receiver and listened for a moment. "What I want is to walk out of here and drive my car away." She listened some more. "I'll think about it," she said, then slammed the phone down again.

"You're in a no-win situation, Gerri. Cut the best deal you can and let me go. You don't have a police record, at least I don't think you do. You've been under tremendous stress. It might not turn out too badly."

"Like hell it won't. And I no longer give a fuck." The gun came up and Gerri fired, clipping Nicky in the shoulder and knocking her out of her chair. A second shot was fired at the same time the SWAT team burst through the door, slamming it into Nicky, who was quickly dragged out into the hall. There was no further sound from Gerri.

Parker appeared, kneeling next to her and applying pressure to her wound. Tears glistened in her eyes and she let them fall. "Thank God, you're not dead. I was so scared."

Nicky raised her head and looked toward the desk. Gerri wasn't visible, but brain matter speckled the wall behind the desk. "Jesus Christ. She was worse off than I thought."

Quinn appeared overhead, grinning down at her. "Luckily, she was a lousy shot."

"Yeah, lucky me."

Everyone made way for the paramedics who were already on the scene. They started an IV on the spot and put her on a stretcher. Parker followed her to the ambulance. "Can I ride with you?" Her eyes were uncertain but hopeful.

"Please. I don't want you to leave me." Their disagreement vanished, rendered silly by much greater things.

"I won't."

"I mean ever." She didn't care if it was too soon. Being shot made her bold. It also hurt like hell. They sped to the hospital holding hands, stunned and yet somehow happy.

CHAPTER TWENTY

Nicky insisted on being released from the hospital that night. There was no one at Olive Street to make sure the house wasn't in chaos after all the upheaval. She'd been shot up with Demerol and was no good to anyone, but Parker took her back to Olive Street, put her in bed, and told the residents Nicky needed to rest. When she woke the next morning, Parker was still by her side, dozing in the chair next to the bed. Her eyes fluttered open.

"Good morning." Parker's voice was sexy as hell, even to someone lying in bed with a hole in her shoulder.

"Was I dreaming, or did I get shot last night?"

"No dream. How're you feeling?"

It hurt like hell and she wondered if she'd gotten any pain pills. "A little uncomfortable. Not too bad."

Parker produced a bottle and rattled the few pills in it. "You've got a limited quantity of OxyContin here. Do you want one now?

Nicky considered. She'd done her share of drugs before she got sober and the oblivion of narcotics was a siren song—perhaps distant but still heard. "No, but I think there's some ibuprofen in the bathroom."

Parker got the pills and some water and sat on the bed to give them to her. "I thought I'd call in sick today so I could stay with you."

"Do you think I'm going to stay in bed all day?"

"Probably not. But you did just have a bullet removed from your shoulder. It's not like you have the sniffles."

Nicky carefully scooted herself to a more upright position and tried not to grimace. "You know what today is, don't you?"

"It's the killer's deadline. Everyone's on high alert, Nicky. I hate to say it, but there's not much you can do to change whatever he, or she, plans to do."

"Wow. That's not the vote of confidence I'd hoped for." She smiled wanly, taking Parker's hand into her own.

"It's not only because you're wounded. Quinn and Martinez aren't any closer to finding who's doing this than we are. We have nothing to work with."

"Well, I can't lie here all day. I'll go nuts. Gerri arranged to send some new residents over and I'll need to deal with them."

"It's not because you don't want me here, is it?" Parker's voice was soft, unsure, and unlike her usual confident tone. Nicky squeezed her hand.

"Not at all. I'd love to spend a whole day with you, but there's so much going on it wouldn't be any fun. What am I going to do with my office, for instance, the mess left in there. "

"I know a company that cleans up crime scenes. I'll put you in touch."

"Jesus. I still can't believe Gerri killed herself. I didn't like her, but I didn't want her dead."

"Of course not. I guess if you're okay, I may as well go to work."

"I never said I don't need you, but I have a hard time admitting it."

"I'm here if you do. You only need ask."

They looked at each other for a moment before Parker helped her get up and put her arm in a sling. When she left, Nicky made her way downstairs for coffee. She hoped there was some already made—she didn't know if she could cope with doing it on her own. None of the eight remaining residents seemed to be around. Did they all flee after last night's violence? She needed to talk with Dave Edmundson and tell him what happened. She could almost feel her blood pressure rising, flushing her face and making her feel dizzy.

Two hours later, she found herself at the eleven o'clock meeting in the basement of the 12 Step House. They'd already started with the lead speaker when she arrived. She took a seat at the table, elbow to elbow with her neighbors, and tried to relax. She hoped the meeting would calm her. Her shoulder hurt, her head throbbed, and the bottle of OxyContin left in her room kept coming to mind. She felt anxious to get to it. Was it the pain she wanted diminished or her anxiety? She remembered the Demerol they'd given her in the hospital, the way it made its way down her body, relaxing each muscle it passed through and rendering almost everything inconsequential.

At the far side of the room she saw Meg staring at her with a big smile on her face. Meg was not what she needed at the moment.

As soon as the meeting ended, Meg sped over to Nicky and put a hand on her good shoulder. "Nicky, it's good to see you. What happened to your arm?"

"A little mishap. Nothing serious."

"So we meet again. Good to see you're still making meetings."

"Why? Is there a reason you think I wouldn't be?"

Meg looked horrified, as if aware of a giant *faux pas*. "No, not at all. You always seemed like a winner to me, unlike some of those chicks in rehab with us. You could tell they were never going to make it."

That was all very rich coming from her. "Good to see you, Meg. I've got to scoot out of here."

"Wait a sec. I'd love to get together with you. Can you have dinner tonight?"

She'd rather poke herself in the eye. "Sorry, I've got plans."

"How about some other night this week?" Meg's face was bright. She didn't look like she feared being turned down. Nicky looked her in the eye.

"I'm busy all of those nights, too."

Meg frowned and took a step back. She'd been inside the cusp of Nicky's personal space. "I see. Is it something I did?"

"No, I simply don't have the capacity for people right now. I have a lot going on. Maybe I'll run into you again sometime."

"I'm sure we will."

An uneasy feeling spread through her as she walked away, taking the stairs as quickly as she could with her bad arm strapped to her side. There was something slimy about Meg, the way she insinuated herself and ignored all the signs she wasn't welcome. She thought for a minute before calling Parker from her car.

"Everything okay?" Parker said.

"I may have something. Remember the woman who came to our table that first day we met? I just saw her again. What I didn't tell you at the time was Meg had a thing for me in rehab and apparently still does."

"Can't fault her for that."

"Can you run a check on Meg Antoniou? Could be Margaret, I suppose."

"Sure. What pinged for you?"

"It's been five years since I first met her and she still seems to be interested in me. She's periodically gotten hold of me throughout that time. It's worth a look. She's still in AA and said something about women relapsing."

"I'll run it now. Sit tight."

Parker called twenty minutes later. "Interesting. Meg Antoniou has a jacket. A couple DUIs and disorderly behaviors, which is expected with her alcohol history. But two years ago she had an order of protection taken out against her by a woman in Evanston who claimed Meg was stalking her."

"Oh, Christ. Is there contact information for her?"

"I have a street address and phone number for Meg and for the woman who was stalked."

"I'll go talk to her."

"We should probably tell Quinn and Martinez."

"I'm not telling Martinez squat, not yet anyway. I have an idea, if you're game."

"I suppose that depends how close it comes to getting me fired. What are you thinking?"

Nicky's speech was rapid, her grip tight on her steering wheel. "Let's camp out at Meg's place and see what she does over the course of the night. If she's the killer, this would be the night she'd take another victim, especially if she was pissed off at me for turning her down when I saw her today."

"That's throwing all our eggs in one basket, isn't it? Meg probably isn't our killer. I think she would have shown up before this, interacted with you somehow prior to this chance meeting today."

"First of all, what else are we going to do tonight? We don't have any other leads. And secondly, we don't know she hasn't been watching me this whole time. She's a stalker, right?"

"I'm game. It's not like I have a better plan," Parker said. "I'm glad to have any plan at all."

Before setting up the surveillance on Meg, Nicky and Parker detoured to Evanston, a suburb just north of the city limits. Parker had set up a meeting with Hope Dentino, the woman who'd taken out the order of protection against Meg. She lived in an attractive small house in the town's southwest side and answered immediately when Nicky rang the doorbell.

Hope was so petite Nicky had to look straight down to address her. She wore a white dress that dramatically contrasted with her dark skin. She had full makeup and jewelry on.

"Thank you for seeing us, Ms. Dentino. We'd like to talk to you about Meg Antoniou."

"As I said on the phone, I'm happy to do anything that will keep her from stalking another woman." Her voice was surprisingly deep for one so small.

She invited them in and they sat in her sunny living room, where all the seating was facing the large TV hanging on the wall, theater-style. They sat on either side of her.

"We'd like to know more about how Meg's stalking of you began," Nicky said. Parker sat back, giving Nicky the lead.

"God, it's embarrassing now to admit I dated her. I should have known from the start she was trouble. Meg was possessive—wanting to be together all the time, to know where I was and what I was doing when we weren't together—but I chalked it up to the enthusiasm of new love. It was after we'd been together a few months that I caught her watching me. One time I'd insisted I needed a night alone in my apartment and she grudgingly accepted it. At the time I lived in a condo building on the third floor. Around nine that night I was closing the blinds when I saw her car on the street below. You couldn't mistake it—she had a lime green Kia Portage with a bike rack in back."

"Do you know why she was there?"

"To spy on me, of course. To make sure no one else was coming to spend the night with me."

"Did you confront her about it?"

Hope was becoming more agitated as she spoke. "I immediately went down to the street, but she drove away before I could get to her. I went back inside and called her, but she didn't pick up. I don't know if she thought the whole thing would go away if she just ignored it. I left her a voicemail message that it was over."

"It must be a disturbing memory," Nicky said.

"That was nothing compared to what was to come. She tried to get me back with flowers, poetry, and quite a bit of begging, but I was done. That's when I started to notice her watching my building most nights of the week. She'd turn up wherever I was, like if I were in a Starbucks I'd see her behind me in line. She didn't talk to me, she just wanted me to know she was there."

"Did she do anything else?"

"She started posting photos of me on Instagram, shots she took while stalking me. She followed my grandmother into the grocery and helped with her bags, introducing herself as a friend of mine. There's lots of other things and they didn't necessarily end when I got the order of protection."

Nicky wondered if she'd been stalked by Meg and she never noticed it. She was more observant than that, though. "When was the last time Meg harassed you?"

Hope relaxed and gave Nicky a rueful smile. "I think she's finally gone off me. It's been about a year since I've noticed anything."

They talked for a few more minutes before Nicky and Parker said their good-byes. Parker spoke first on the drive back into the city.

"Meg is dangerous and very disturbed. I can easily see her as the killer."

"Me too. It's so weird, though. Talking to her, she seems like she's reasonable, if not a little eager. I wouldn't have pegged her as an obsessive. I mean, she's had a thing for me for a few years now, but I never thought of her as a stalker."

"You never know about a person. Not really. You saw that a lot when you were on the job, didn't you?"

"All the time. The world is filled with Jeckles and Hydes."

They set up across the street from Meg's building in Parker's Subaru. They were in the Lakeview neighborhood just off the busy Broadway corridor. By late evening, pedestrian traffic on Aldine Street had trickled down to a few people walking quickly up the long block lined with three flats and courtyard buildings, with old-growth trees hanging on to life along the public parkway. Lake Michigan was a quarter-mile to the east and the wind was whipping off it at thirty miles an hour. A man's baseball hat flew off his head and they watched as he awkwardly chased after it.

When they'd arrived at five, they saw a slew of people walking up the street from the El station and ducking into their buildings, but no Meg. She finally arrived at eight, and judging from where a light popped on shortly after, she lived in the front east unit. She was dressed as she had been at the meeting—tiny denim jacket under a light puffer coat, short skirt and leggings, knee-length boots, everything in black.

"If she's our person, she'll likely go back out late tonight," Nicky said.

"Could be earlier. We don't know how long she stalks the victims," Parker's eyes were firmly on the entrance to the building. Their hours together in the car had been difficult and wonderful at the same time. Parker had insisted they process the disagreement they'd had, which Nicky would have paid good money to avoid. She'd much rather get on with things and not poke at feelings too much. Somehow, she knew that life strategy wasn't going to work with Parker.

"I'm sensitive to people making decisions for me," Parker said. "It has a lot to do with my parents and my ex-husband."

Nicky turned quickly to look at her and her injured shoulder lit on fire. The hours without as much as an aspirin were starting to take their toll. Her face felt greasy with sweat. "You were married to a man?"

"Yep. Five years and the best thing I can say about it is it was a revelation. It convinced me of what I already knew about my sexuality and it helped me break from the controlling people in my life."

"You think I'm a controlling person?" Nicky tried not to react defensively, but geez.

"I don't know yet, but I don't think so. You're not a narcissist, at least."

"Thank you very much. How much therapy have you had?"

Parker grinned. "A lot. It's good, though. I was a mess before, filled with fear of everything. I don't feel that way anymore."

"No, you don't seem the least bit fearful to me."

"You think I'm not scared of what's happening between us? I'm afraid it's all an illusion of some sort and reality will wipe it away. I'm afraid it's happening too quickly and will sputter to a stop."

"There'll be no sputtering on my part. I can't stop thinking about you, even with everything going on. I don't know if it's attraction or obsession," Nicky said.

"Let's go with attraction."

"You never feel far away. Why is that?"

"Probably because I'm always thinking about you. It's some sort of cosmic connection."

"Don't go all New Agey on me. I like to have my feet on the ground."

Parker laughed and whatever tension had been between them evaporated. The rest of their time in the car was spent holding hands and keeping their eyes peeled, trying to not give into the urge to start making out. They saw Meg emerge from her building around ten thirty, still wearing the same clothes and carrying a sling bag draped across her body. Parker started the car and they watched as Meg walked to the end of the block before unlocking a Mini Cooper and pulling out, luckily in the same direction they were pointed. She headed north through Buena Park and Uptown and then into Andersonville where she pulled over in front of Donna's bar on Clark Street.

"Figures she'd go to Donna's," Nicky said. "I wonder if you should go in and watch her. She'd recognize me in about a second."

"Gladly. I need to stretch my legs."

Nicky watched her stride toward Donna's and open the door, envious of her assignment. Sitting in the car was torture. She got into the driver's seat in case she had to pull out quickly and waited. And waited. Finally, Parker returned to the car and she didn't look happy.

"I lost her. Did she come out to her car?"

"I haven't seen her. What happened?"

"She was at the bar this whole time, chitchatting with a group of women, drinking coffee. She went to the bathroom once and came back. Then she headed back there a second time and never came back. It took me a minute to realize she'd been gone too long. I went into the bathroom and she wasn't there. Where could she have gone? Did she twig to you watching her?"

"I don't know. There was a back room in the hallway near the bathroom and I imagine an exit to the outside from there. Let's drive around to the alley and see. Fuck. I can't believe it. I should have followed her."

Nicky was almost glad to see Parker as fallible—it made her even more attractive. She probably should have followed her into the bathroom, but there was nothing to be done about it now. "I would have done the same. Let's see if we can find her. It's strange she hasn't come out for her car. She's either walking or Ubering, which doesn't make much sense."

They waited a few more minutes to see if Meg would return to her car and then drove around to the back. It was a typical grungy alley running behind a row of businesses, lined with dumpsters smelly from the restaurant garbage. A door behind Donna's was propped open but there was no sign of Meg.

"Let's drive back to Lakeview and see if she's come home," Parker said. The front east unit was dark when they got there.

"What's our next move?" Nicky said. "She may be out there stalking her victim now." A sickening thought overcame her. "Deb's place is within walking distance of Donna's."

"Who's Deb?"

"A woman I dated for a very short time. I'm worried she's a potential victim."

She fished her phone out of her jacket pocket and called Deb. The phone rang and rang. She was about to hang up when Deb's blurry voice came on the line.

"What the hell, Nicky. This better be an emergency."

"It might be. I lost a suspect I was following and I'm worried she was headed for your place."

"You're still going on about that? I'm fine. No one's getting in here. You need a code to enter the courtyard, another code to enter the building, and I have double dead bolts on the door."

"That's good, but I'd rather you stay somewhere else the rest of the night."

"That's not going to happen. Good night." The call was disconnected.

Nicky looked at Parker. "She's secure, but I think she's still a likely victim number five."

"Deb hasn't relapsed, has she? I'd hate to think the killer is starting to widen the list of potential victims." Parker peered at her. "I think we should call it a night. You look like you're about to pass out."

"All I need is a painkiller and I'm good to go. Let's go back and watch her place. We may see her return and we can roust her, have the police pick her up for questioning."

Parker was having none of it. She insisted Nicky get some rest. "Let's call Quinn on the way and tell him about Meg. They can watch her place. He's going to be pissed off we didn't tell him about her earlier."

Parker called Quinn through the dashboard speaker while Nicky tried to think about something other than the stabbing pain in her shoulder. Quinn was not happy to be woken, but he agreed to put a BOLO out. There were extra patrol vehicles driving around the city's sober houses so there was some chance they'd pick her up. He'd have a couple of them cover Meg's car in Andersonville and her home in Lakeview. Then he addressed Nicky.

"Why the hell was this Meg Antoniou not on your list? The order of protection taken out on her would have got our attention."

"It was a big fucking mistake on my part and I don't have an excuse. I never was involved with her, even a little bit. That's probably why she didn't come to mind, though she should have. I have an idea, though. I'll call her in the morning and ask her to coffee. We can follow her from there."

"What time will you meet?"

"I'm going to suggest eleven at Kopi Café."

He planned to be in the café as well, ready to pick her up the second she left. Parker started the car and drove toward Olive Street House, deaf to Nicky's urging they continue to look for her on the streets. As soon as Parker dropped her off she got in her car and headed to Deb's, a better place to stand watch than Meg's building. She knew without knowing Deb was tonight's victim.

Staying alert was the problem. The earlier stakeout with Parker and the searing pain in her shoulder had wiped her out. She had no partner to fetch coffee or talk to keep herself from nodding off. She shook herself awake several times but stayed until eight in the morning without seeing anyone entering the gated courtyard. She hoped she hadn't missed anything.

CHAPTER TWENTY-ONE

When Nicky returned to Olive Street she picked up the bottle of Oxy and opened the top. Parker had suggested she take one earlier, but she still hesitated. She was afraid if she took one she'd want more, triggering cravings she'd mercifully been free from for five years. After her sleepless night she admitted it was time to call her sponsor.

"Take the damn medicine," Sheila said. "We're not in the business of choosing pain over comfort. As long as something is prescribed and then taken strictly as prescribed, there's no breach of sobriety."

"What if it makes me want more?"

"Have someone hold the medication for you, like me. That way you can't get your hands on it until you're due for a dose."

"That would be a pain in the ass for you."

"I'm happy to do it. I'll either drive over to you with a pill or you can find me at the library." She sounded eager to be of service.

"I like the idea, but I think Parker's the better person to hold it."

"Do you see her that often? I didn't realize things had progressed so much."

"With the case going on, we're together quite a bit."

They talked a little more before she was able to end the call. The first thing she did was find her bottle of Oxy and down one with the stale water on her nightstand. She was surprised by how much pain she was having and somewhat mortified she couldn't gut it out. She thought about asking Parker to hold her pills and it seemed more problematic than she initially thought. What would she think of her? An addict/alcoholic with five years of sobriety who couldn't be trusted to take drugs as prescribed. She'd think she was bad news, that's what. Nicky looked inside the bottle and counted the pills. There were only seven left. She couldn't get into much trouble with seven pills.

It was close to ten thirty when she called Deb to check on her. The call went directly to voicemail, which probably meant Deb was avoiding her calls. Still, she didn't like it. She needed to hear her voice to be sure nothing had happened to her. She googled the name of the company Deb worked for and called their main number. When she was transferred to Deb's assistant, she introduced herself as a friend.

"I don't know where she is," the man said. "Usually, she's in the office before I am and she's never late. I'm going to give it another hour before panicking. She may have overslept."

"But you don't think so."

"It would be entirely out of character."

Nicky said she'd be in touch and hung up. She wasn't waiting to panic. She called Quinn and asked him to break into Deb's apartment, but he declined.

"She needs to be gone longer than this before I can get the paperwork authorizing us to enter her apartment."

"We both know what this means. I talked to Deb late last night and she was fine. The perp must have gotten to her after that, probably when I'd nodded off. If he entered the apartment to attack her, it would be a complete change from his usual MO."

"Did Deb relapse?" Quinn said.

"I'm almost certain she did not, another change in method."

"Let's do this. It's almost time to meet your friend Meg for coffee. If Deb hasn't shown up by the time that's over, I'll talk to the lieutenant."

"Thank you. I hope I'm wrong, but I have the worst feeling about this."

Nicky got to the café in plenty of time for her eleven o'clock date with Meg, but she was already there waiting for her. Quinn was stationed across the room from them, next to the shelves of travel books. He wore a brimmed hat and glasses so she wouldn't recognize him from their brief meeting in the café. Meg jumped to her feet and gave Nicky an exuberant and extremely painful hug. She wasn't wearing her sling, which was simply stubbornness on her part. She didn't want to be impeded in any way.

"I'm happy you asked me here. You're a hard woman to pin down," Meg said. She had a megawatt smile, bright enough to feel insincere.

"Don't you work downtown? I was surprised you were able to meet me."

"I work from home most of the time, which is wonderful if it means I get to see you."

"Seeing you at the meeting yesterday reminded me we should catch up," Nicky said.

Meg was dressed in business casual—a crisply ironed shirt and well-tailored gray trousers. She bombarded Nicky with questions. Where did she work? Had she had any relapses? Did she work with a sponsor? What did she do in her free time? Was she seeing anyone?

"I ask because I saw you with a woman at AntePrima. I was walking by and you were in the window table. It made me wonder if you're in a relationship."

Had she just happened to see her as she was walking down the street, or was she following Nicky, stalking her? The last thing she wanted was for the killer to see Parker with her.

"No, that was a friend. You should have come in to say hello."

"I didn't want to interrupt. It looked like you were having an intense conversation."

Nicky didn't know how to respond to that so she changed course. "Tell me what you've been up to. I don't want to make this all about me."

Meg's demeanor changed from super charged, as if she were on amphetamines, to subdued. "Mostly I take care of my mother."

"Oh? Is she sick?"

Meg clasped her hands together. "Cancer. She probably doesn't have much longer to live."

"I'm sorry to hear that. Is she in hospice?"

"Home hospice through Northwestern. They're amazing, but it still means we have to cover around-the-clock care. My siblings and I work shifts."

Nicky saw where this was going. "When do you stay with her?"

"Most nights I cover midnight to eight in the morning. She's asleep most of the time, so it's not too bad."

"Were you there last night? I hope I'm not interrupting your sleep."

"Yeah, I was there, but don't worry about me. I'm glad to see you."

"Where does your mom live?"

"She's a block from here. At least it's convenient."

Crap. When Parker lost track of Meg in the bar it was because she left to walk to her mother's house. It would have been easier to leave her car in front of Donna's on Clark Street than try to find parking on the densely populated side streets and closer to go out the back to reach the side street. If the killer struck last night, it probably wasn't Meg, though her alibi wasn't solid. She could have left her mother's house in the middle of the night without anyone knowing better. She glanced at Quinn. He seemed to be fully engaged with a newspaper. She wouldn't need him after all. There was no pretext for bringing Meg in for questioning, nothing tying her to the previous murders except for her interest in Nicky. While she considered that suspicious, it didn't mean Meg murdered anyone. It didn't mean she didn't either. They'd have to keep an eye on her.

"I have to shove off," Nicky said, reaching for the jacket draped behind her. "It's been good to see you."

Meg looked like a child who'd just opened a bad Christmas gift. Gloves or socks or something equally disappointing. "Already? I was hoping for a nice long chat."

"Maybe some other time, but I have to get back to Olive Street."

"Why don't we make it dinner some night you're free?"

Nicky looked Meg in the eye and saw the hopefulness there. It wasn't the look of a cold-blooded murderer, but then a serial killer as elusive as this one would be unlikely to give much away. "Are you asking as a friend?"

"Well, sure, I want us to be friends. But if there was something more, that would be fantastic."

"I don't want you to misconstrue anything. It would have to be friends only."

She saw a flash in Meg's eyes that looked like bitterness, but it was so brief she couldn't be sure. She gave her a brief hug before leaving the café. Quinn followed and they ducked into Alamo Shoes next door to talk. She told him what Meg had said about being at her mother's overnight.

"That explains her movement, but her alibi still has holes," Quinn said.

"In the meantime, we're sitting on our collective asses waiting to see if someone else was murdered last night."

"I'm worried about that, too."

"Hang on a second." She pulled out her phone and called Deb, still with no answer. She called her assistant, who reported Deb still hadn't shown up at work or called in. "We have to break into her apartment, Quinn. Now."

"I'll talk to the lieutenant about a wellness check, but he's not going to want to enter without a warrant. At this point there's not enough to justify breaking into a private residence."

"What, do you need the smell of a decaying body before you'll enter? Given everything going on, it's obvious Deb's in danger."

"Give me some time, Nicky."

That left Nicky with one course of action. She said good-bye to Quinn and drove the three blocks to Deb's apartment. She reached into her glove box for her set of lock picking tools, hoping she still had the touch necessary to do the job. Her uncle was a locksmith and taught her how to do it years ago when she first joined the police. The courtyard door and the building door had electronic keypads, but their locks were still in place for those using a key. The street was empty of people as she fumbled a bit waiting for her pick to find the pin locking the door. It sprang open. She did the same at the building door.

Deb's apartment was on the third floor. After knocking and hearing nothing inside she inserted her pick and felt both locks had already given way. Adrenaline surged through her. She pushed the door slowly open and stepped into the living room off the foyer. It was a large room with French windows overlooking the street, decorated straight out of a HGTV show. She didn't remember much from the night she'd been here and had sex with Deb. She'd been too nervous. There was no sign of a struggle, everything was neat and tidy. On the other side of the foyer was the hallway leading back to the kitchen, with two bedrooms located along the way. The first bedroom was set up as an office and was also exceedingly neat. The door to the second bedroom was closed. She tapped on the door before pushing it open, her heart hammering against her chest, and there was the sight she knew on some gut level she'd find. Deb lay motionless on her back, the bed covers pulled away to show her bare legs, her white T-Shirt marred with a small circle of blood over the heart. Nicky's knees almost gave way and she slid against the wall until she sat on the wood floor. An animal noise escaped, one she didn't recognize as coming from her, and her hands began to tremble. Of all the deaths that could be laid at her door, this seemed the most immediate, the most damning. She hauled herself up and placed the tips of two fingers against Deb's carotid artery and felt nothing. She didn't dare touch anything else.

She pulled out her phone and called 911, her eyes roaming the room looking for anything the killer may have left behind, but it appeared as perfectly kept as the others. The killer must have approached without waking Deb, flung the covers aside and plunged in the knife before she had any chance to react or defend herself. She'd taken no precautions after Nicky's warning phone calls, hadn't even put the chain in place on her front door. What Nicky told her must have sounded preposterous, the ravings of a paranoid ex-cop who'd given her no reason to trust her.

She backed out of the room and went downstairs to meet the first responders. In minutes the entire courtyard of residents would be looking out their windows as police, fire, and paramedics poured in the building. Nicky led the uniformed officers up to the apartment and stepped aside. She'd called Quinn first and then Parker. Both were on their way. She told the officers she'd wait for Detective Quinn to arrive before giving any statement and was ordered to stand in the living room to wait.

Parker arrived before Quinn and used her detective's shield to enter the crime scene. She found Nicky staring out the windows over the street. "Oh, Nicky, I'm sorry."

Quinn and Martinez entered the room, Martinez with his usual scowl. "What's she doing here?" he said, pointing at Parker.

"She's helping a friend. Do you have a problem with that?" Parker turned to face him directly.

"I have a big problem with both of you. Sullivan, you found the body, right?"

"That's right."

"Maybe now the lieutenant will take you seriously as a suspect. We have you at the scene of a crime, which has made my day. Stand over there until I question you."

Nicky looked at Quinn, who shrugged and looked apologetic. "We do need to talk to you, Nicky."

"Fine, but I want Parker with me."

"No way," Martinez said. "She's out of here, unless you want me to call your lieutenant."

"Listen, you slimy fucker, I'm not leaving unless Nicky asks me to. Call whoever you want." Parker had both hands on her hips.

Nicky watched in quiet admiration as Parker dug in her heels against Martinez, who was definitely a slimy fucker.

Everyone looked at Quinn to arbitrate. "Parker can stay, but we need to talk to you alone, Nicky. You know that. First, we need to take a look at the body. Don't go anywhere."

When they returned, Parker stepped aside and the three sat at the small dining table on one side of the living room. Martinez and Quinn took out their notebooks.

"How did you get in the apartment?" Martinez said. Quinn was letting him take the lead, which was bad news for her. "Is this another girlfriend whose key you have?"

Nicky didn't take the bait, which required more control than she thought she had. "I was worried about Deb. I broke in."

"Broke in how? Don't tell me you picked the locks."

"I picked the locks."

"I like that." He smiled with genuine pleasure. "Now we can take you in on a B&E charge."

"We're not doing that," Quinn said. "Stick to asking the questions."

"You should go private," Martinez went on, "like all the other washed-up detectives in this city."

"I might do that." She walked them through entering the apartment and finding the body.

"You're a person of interest, Nicky," Quinn said. "Everyone who finds a body is. We'll see what the ME says, but Deb died sometime between when you called her last night and when you found her today. What do you have for an alibi?"

It wasn't good Quinn was questioning her this way, but if he didn't, Martinez would. The problem was she once again was without an alibi. "I was outside Deb's apartment, waiting for the killer to approach. I didn't see anyone coming or going."

"It could have happened before you got there. Did you fall asleep at all?"

"I may have dozed for a little while. I didn't dare leave to get coffee."

"Is there trouble between the lovebirds? No Parker to vouch for you?" Martinez said.

"Not last night. Oh, and, Martinez? Fuck you." Nicky wanted to hit him, but her fist would merely bounce off his blubber. Her ears felt hot.

Martinez barked out a laugh. "That's more like it. People lash out when they're backed into a corner."

"You're an idiot. If I did the murder, why would I call it in and stay around for the police to come? It would be the first serial killer I ever heard of doing that."

Quinn put his hands up. "Let's chill for a minute. Nicky, you're going to have to come to the station to give your statement."

"Of course."

"And, Martinez, keep things professional or this time the call to the lieutenant will be about you."

"You do that, because I'm sure he'll back me when I bring her in for questioning."

"You mean arrest me?" Nicky hadn't contemplated a life in prison.

"No one's getting arrested," Quinn said. "Nicky will come in voluntarily."

"That's bullshit. What does she have on you, Quinn? Because you're bending over backwards to protect her." He was practically spitting.

"Show some respect, Martinez. Nicky was an excellent detective. one of us. She closed more cases in five years than you'll close in your career."

"What's that got to do with collaring a serial killer?"

Nicky was touched at how protective Quinn was being. Were it not for him she'd be handcuffed to a table in an interview room.

Martinez was so mad she was surprised he didn't take a swing at Quinn. "You'll leave her free to kill again. Brilliant move."

"My case, my decision. Don't worry, Martinez. Nothing will blow back on you."

"The brass and the media are looking for an arrest. I mean to give it to them. See you in the lieutenant's office." He left the apartment, with Quinn following a minute later.

Nicky found Parker standing outside on the back deck. "Martinez is going to try to pin this on me. What a giant asshole he is."

"Don't let him get to you. There is no evidence against you— your lack of alibis isn't enough to charge you. And you have me as an alibi for one of the killings."

"Maybe they should bring me in. I feel like I killed them all anyway."

"Stop."

Nicky looked at her with a crooked smile. "Luckily, it's time for another pain pill."

CHAPTER TWENTY-TWO

Parker had to return to her open cases and Nicky needed to get back to Olive Street. Before she died, Gerri had arranged for some new women to come to the house, and two of them were about to arrive. She felt as if her entire existence was bifurcated—one half functioning, doing her job, conversing like a normal person, the other half in the midst of a primal scream from a fetal position. Nothing had changed in the years since Laura was shot, for she was responsible again for the harm done to others. She was a public menace. She'd been to the funerals of each victim and felt like the Grim Reaper skulking by the door, not quite willing to sit among the mourners, not quite willing to leave. Would the honorable thing be to kill herself? She knew that was crazy talk, but she felt crazy. No matter what she did, the deaths kept coming. Maybe if she was dead, the person doing this would stop. She wished the killer would come for her. Why hadn't he? Or she? She pulled into the garage and rested her head on the steering wheel until she could pull herself together.

The media had been increasing their coverage of the murders. It was anemic in the beginning, no doubt because the victims were alcoholics, high-risk people whose deaths didn't stir the audience into enough of a ghoulish frenzy. Deb's death would be different. She was an alcoholic, yes, but she was still a sober one and also worked in a high-end job downtown, a low-risk victim whose death would send a frisson of fear into the community. Two of the victims had been black, furthering the implication that for the press and the police, some deaths were more worth covering than others. Every aspect of the situation was sickening.

She went straight to her office and closed the door. The room stank of the chemicals used to clean up the mess of Gerri's suicide. She'd have to repaint to remove the last evidence of what had occurred. She'd hardly thought about Gerri, other than to speak to Edmundson a couple of times, getting him to agree to rescind her punishing policies. She'd even gotten him to agree to hire a landscaping company. There was a knock at the door and Zoey stuck her head in.

"There're two women here who say they're new residents. Do you want me to send them back?"

"No, I'll meet them out front."

Zoey looked at the wall behind Nicky. "Jesus, is that where her brains splattered? Can't they clean that shit up?"

"We have to paint. Want to help?"

"No fucking way. I'm glad that bitch is gone, though, no disrespect intended. It feels like we can breathe again."

Zoey had warmed up to Nicky since Madison departed and she looked to her to become more of a conduit with the rest of the residents.

"I heard from Oli," Zoey said.

"Oh?"

"She wants to come back but doesn't know if you'll take her."

"Of course I will." She didn't know what her authority was at this point, but doubted Edmundson would deny any request of hers. All she wanted was a house full of women who wanted to be there, who wanted to stay sober, and who didn't want to make her life hell. Was that too much to ask? Probably. At least Madison seemed to be gone for good.

She followed Zoey out of the office and found two women sitting on folding chairs in the meeting room. The older woman was about forty, black, neatly dressed and poised. A new roller bag was at her side and she smiled politely when Nicky entered the room. The other woman was closer to twenty, dressed in blue jeans and a baggy T-Shirt, with a grimy nylon duffle bag at her side and a sullen look on her face. Nicky introduced herself and turned a chair around to face the two.

"I am Amelie," said the older woman with a soft Caribbean accent. "Are you the house mother?"

Nicky almost snorted out a laugh. "That makes me sound very old or like this is a sorority. I'm the resident manager here." She turned to the younger woman. "And you are?"

"Lori."

Nicky waited to hear if she had anything else to say, but she did not. Saying her name alone seemed to take quite an effort.

"I'm going to show you to your rooms in a minute and have you fill out some paperwork, but first I want to explain a few things about the house to you." She proceeded to tell them everything—the temporary nature of the bunk beds, Gerri's suicide (they'd hear about that soon enough without her so it was better to get in front of it), and what some of the ground rules were. Amelie watched Nicky's face closely and raised her eyebrows a few times. Lori slumped in her chair and appeared to be listening to a recital of the phone book. She couldn't be more bored. Nicky figured they'd fit right in. There were women like both of them already living there and hopefully they'd make friends, start to view Olive Street as a home. Nicky would give anything to have the refrigerator food fights be the biggest problem she faced in the house. Those were the days.

She got the women settled and returned to her office. She spent a couple of hours working with Edmundson arranging to get the bunk beds removed and other administrative matters. With Gerri gone, she had even more duties than before. She put a sign up in the kitchen announcing a special house meeting for the next morning. She kept busy and tried not to think of Deb. Quinn would have contacted Deb's family by now and she ached to think of what they were going through. By four o'clock her shoulder was excruciatingly painful and she went upstairs to get a pain pill from her room. So far, she hadn't taken any extra pills. But as she rattled the remaining pills in the bottle she thought of how much she'd love to fall into a cloaking sleep where she could pass the rest of the day in oblivion. But everything would still be there when she woke up—Deb and the other women would be as dead as they were before. She took one pill and swallowed it dry, just as her phone lit up with a call from Quinn.

"Tell me something good," she said.

"I don't know if it's good, but I have some news. We brought Meg in for questioning. It was like you said—her alibi for each killing was being in her mother's house all night, no witnesses. She could easily have snuck away and had plenty of time to kill the women and return before her mother woke up or a replacement carer showed up. She claims to not know anything about it. But here's the good part. We executed a search warrant and guess what we found?"

"Tell me it's a thin boning knife with splotches of blood on it."

"No such luck. But we did find a box full of photos and other information on you."

"What?" Nicky felt a chill.

"Looks like your Meg was obsessed with you. The photos are candids taken from the street, as if she's been following you."

"God damn. For how long? I haven't felt anyone on my tail."

"Not all of the photos have a time stamp, but there are some as far back as three years ago and up to the present."

She sat abruptly on her bed. "It's her. It's got to be."

"Maybe. If she's obsessed with you, it may be the motive we're looking for. She had the opportunity on any of the nights the murders occurred. And anyone could have a boning knife, so there's the means as well. We've placed her under arrest."

Nicky would have expected to feel a great surge of relief, but the news made her uneasy. Quinn interrupted Nicky's silence.

"We took the boning knife in her knife block. We can hope against hope the ME is able to identify it as the murder weapon. But even without that, I like her for the killer."

"I'm still surprised it's a woman. She'd have to be strong to move Allie Becker's body to the site where we found her."

"Meg looks fit to me," Quinn said. "It wouldn't be impossible. She's asked for a lawyer and won't talk more without one. The state's attorney tells me we need more to get a conviction, but at least they agreed to hold her."

"Yeah."

"You're not happy about this?"

"I guess I'm still in shock, but it's good."

Quinn sighed. "I was hoping for a better reaction, but whatever. I still need you to come in for your witness statement on Deb's murder."

"Maybe Martinez will shut up about arresting me."

"That's not going anywhere. He doesn't have enough on you to convince the lieutenant."

They agreed on a time and rang off. She frowned as she thought of Meg as a stalker. Since rehab, they'd seen each other a few times at meetings and a couple of times at coffee. Meg called periodically to ask her out. Nicky discouraged it each time they saw each other, and she assumed Meg had moved on. Surely if she'd been stalking Nicky, she would have tried to see her more often than that, wouldn't she? Something didn't sit right. Would this woman who was irreverent about sobriety kill women who relapsed? She rotated her neck from side to side, back to front, and several satisfying pops were the result. Maybe that was the best she was going to feel—a moment's release and then the pressure started building again. She had a hard time believing it was over.

❖

Parker ordered pizza to celebrate Meg's arrest and set the table with plates thrown by a local potter. She lit candles and put some Patricia Barber on her turntable. Nicky lay on the sofa with an arm thrown over her face, watching Parker with one eye.

"I shouldn't be here," she said. "I have two new residents at the house. I'll have to go back soon to make sure they're all right."

"I'm sure they're fine. Do you want some pizza?"

Nicky hauled herself up to a sitting position and put her hand to her sore shoulder. The injury was a pain in the ass and made everything she did twice as hard. She deserved worse. Parker put a plate in front of her on the coffee table and handed her a Diet Coke.

"Do you want to watch a show while we eat?" Parker said.

"I wouldn't be able to concentrate. What do you watch? I'm trying to guess, but I can't. *Masterpiece Theatre*?"

Parker laughed. "Sometimes, but I can go way lowbrow from there. I've been known to watch *Judge Judy*, sort of a busman's holiday."

Nicky sputtered. "You're kidding."

"And *Alone*. I like wilderness shows for some reason. How about you?"

"I don't watch much, but I like cop shows. They're more like comedy to me."

"Now I know something else about you."

"You know way more about me than I about you," Nicky said.

Parker picked up some pizza. "What do you want to know? I thought we'd covered the basics."

"Have you ever had a true love? You haven't told me much about your relationship past."

Parker chewed for a while. "I had my heart broken, but whether it was true love is debatable."

"What happened?"

"It was when I was in uniform, after my divorce. I fell for an ER nurse, which is a bit of a cliché. She was charming, upbeat, happy. It was like getting a vitamin shot every time I was with her. We got together, lived in a shitty Uptown apartment, and had a life for close to ten years. Then she fell for a different female cop and I found myself alone in the shitty apartment. That was a kick in the teeth, but I think the pain had more to do with the abandonment than with losing the person who was perfect for me. There was plenty that wasn't perfect."

"It's some kind of right of passage to get dumped, isn't it? Nothing else hurts in the same way. Did you start dating again right after that?"

"There've been some other women between then and now, but nothing mind-blowing. Not like this."

Nicky put her good arm around Parker's waist and pulled her close. "You think it's mind-blowing?" She leaned in and kissed her cheek, her neck, her collarbone.

"It is for me."

"Me too. Despite everything that's going on, I still feel the hum of this, of us."

They made love on the couch, Nicky trying to swallow the pain she felt every time they switched positions. Still, it was glorious. They ended up with Parker resting her head on Nicky's good shoulder, both in that boneless haze that comes with particularly good lovemaking.

"I have to go," Nicky said.

"I knew you were going to say that."

"I have to. I can't let anything bad happen in the house."

"How long do you think you'll work at Olive Street? This going home stuff is already old."

Nicky felt defensive, as if Parker didn't realize how important the women at the house were to her. "I hadn't thought about it. As long as it feels right, I guess."

"It's your job, of course. Only you can know."

"The PI idea is interesting."

"What do you think of it?"

Nicky gently pushed Parker out of the way and sat up. She drank some of her warm Diet Coke and searched around for her clothes. "I can see it. I like the idea of being able to help people."

"You could help all sorts of people. I have a friend who left the force and set up shop. Do you want to meet him?"

Nicky was wary of being pushed into anything. "Maybe down the line a bit. I have a lot to do at the house right now."

She wouldn't leave the women now, not with so much upheaval in their lives. But it would be nice to spend a whole night together with Parker. It didn't seem like something she could do without for long.

CHAPTER TWENTY-THREE

All the residents were present for the impromptu meeting Nicky called. She introduced the new women and then rallied them all for one last day of yard work, promising the company would rehire the landscapers they once employed. There was surprisingly little pushback. She also promised the bunk beds would be gone by Monday. The women seemed like they were in a good mood, talking amongst themselves, laughing. Nicky almost couldn't believe it. She got them started on raking the lawn and clearing out the flower beds. She planned to make pancakes when they were done.

She could almost believe things had turned a corner. All Quinn and Martinez needed to do was get a confession from Meg and the horrible pressure of the killings would be over. She had plans to go out to dinner with Parker. The day looked promising.

She needed a shower and to do some laundry and she reveled in the quotidian tasks. As she gathered clothes to head to the laundry room, her phone rang.

"Is this Nicky Sullivan?" a woman's voice said. Nicky could hear a loud hum of activity behind her.

"Speaking." It sounded like a hospital and the grip on her phone grew tighter.

"You're the emergency contact listed for Joanne Parker?"

"Am I?" She couldn't say anything else. Her voice box froze.

"We have Ms. Parker here in the Illinois Masonic ER. You should get down here."

She felt completely disassociated from her body. This can't be happening, not Parker, too. "What happened?"

"We're not sure. She was brought in about an hour ago. Witnesses saw her collapse on the street and an ambulance was called. The doctors are with her now trying to figure it out. We think she's been poisoned."

"Poisoned! I'm on my way."

Nicky hung up and ran through the house to the garage, not telling anyone where she was going. Nothing else mattered. She was with Parker until late last night; how could anyone have poisoned her? As far as she knew, Parker was running errands that morning. When she arrived in the ER she was told she could not go back to see her because she was being decontaminated.

"Decontaminated from what?" she asked, trying to keep the screech out of her voice.

"You'll have to talk to the doctor about that. A resident will come out soon to talk to you."

"Is she in any danger?"

"I'm sorry. I can't say. I'll tell the doctor you're here."

The triage nurse picked up the phone and murmured into it as Nicky staggered into the full waiting room. A mother and her four kids sat quietly in one corner; a soccer player held a towel to a cut over his eye. Other children ran around the room, not listening to their imploring parents. One guy had a book open with snacks in little Tupperware containers spread out on the seat next to him. Nicky took a seat as far from others as she could find and called Quinn. He picked up on the second ring.

"Parker's been poisoned," she said. Her breathing felt labored.

"Fuck. How bad is it?"

"I don't know. No one has talked to me yet. Can you get here with your badge so we can get some answers? We're at Masonic."

"On my way."

By the time Quinn arrived, Nicky had been up to the desk twice and still not learned anything. He flashed his badge and asked to talk to the doctor as soon as possible. Fifteen minutes later, a middle-aged man wearing a long gray medical coat came out and led them into an empty part of the hallway. He was graying at the temples and looked like he ran marathons.

"Doctor, what's happened?" Nicky said.

"And you are?"

Quinn took out his badge. "Doc, I'm Parker's detective partner and this is Nicky Sullivan, her partner partner."

The doctor nodded while Nicky stood stock still. Being called Parker's partner made her panicked heart nearly break.

"The patient came in at eleven hundred presenting with symptoms consistent with sarin poisoning. She's been decontaminated and is being treated with a course of atropine and pralidoxime and is showing signs of responding. The twitching is slowing, as well as the sweating and eye tearing and drooling, all of which were severe when she came in. We haven't had to support her breathing, which is very good news. We'll keep her here to monitor her, but I think she'll be okay."

"How could someone poison her?" Quinn said. "I mean, did she get poked in the leg with an umbrella? Something like that?"

"Like in the spy movies? It's possible. It's more likely someone sprayed something in her face or passed the liquid onto her skin or clothing. Sarin is not a substance used for any purpose other than harm, so she didn't pick it up in the environment. I'll take you back and you can see her. We'll be taking her to a room soon."

They followed the doctor through the double swinging doors that led to the interior of the emergency room, as busy and chaotic as any big city ER. The doctor hierarchy was on display—white short jackets for medical students, white long coats for residents, long gray coats for attending physicians. There was a large group of coats gathered around Parker's bed.

"We don't get many sarin poisonings here so you've got a lot of curious doctors."

"Please, can we see her now?"

The doctor cleared the others away and Nicky was able to see Parker for the first time. She gasped, shocked at what she saw. Parker lay sprawled in the bed as if all the life force had left her. Her eyes were open, but she didn't seem to see anything out of them. She and Quinn approached the side of the bed. Parker turned her head to them and put both hands to her eyes to dry them.

"My eyes won't stop watering," she said. "I can barely see you."

"My God, what happened?" Nicky said. She reached for Parker's hand.

"God knows. One minute I was walking down Clark Street and the next minute I'm here. They say I've been poisoned."

"Do you remember anything right before you collapsed?"

"Unless you aren't up to talking," Quinn said. "We can come back later."

Tears continued to fall down Parker's face and she was sweating profusely. "No, if you can stand looking at me I'm ready to talk. The only thing I remember is walking by the bookstore and being stopped by a woman who asked me for directions to Taste of Heaven. I pointed her up the street and then she said she'd spray some aromatherapy crap on me as a thank you. I leaned back and tried to tell her not to, but sure enough her hand came up and she sprayed something in the air. About a minute later I collapsed."

"It's got to be our killer," Nicky said. "She knew she couldn't come after you in the same way as the others. You wouldn't be as vulnerable because you were police and could fight back. She completely changed gears and tried to poison you."

"You've got to tell us everything you can remember about this woman," Quinn said. He took out his notebook. "What did she look like?"

Parker closed her eyes. More tears streamed down her face. The poison stuck neurotransmitters in the on position. Some of her muscles were twitching at will.

"She was about five feet five inches tall, maybe one hundred and thirty pounds. Her hair was parted on the side and hid most of her face. It was long, blond, and straight and could easily have been a wig. The only thing I noticed about her face was her horned rimmed glasses and bright red lipstick. Sorry."

"No, that's excellent," Nicky said. "What else? Do you recall what she was wearing?"

"She wore a short trench coat, tied at the waist and carried a big bag on her shoulder. I think the jacket was green and I don't remember anything about the bag other than it had some sort of decoration on the side. Right before she sprayed, she'd reached into it and then shifted it to her other shoulder."

"Was the spray bottle in her right hand?"

"No, she's a lefty."

Parker smiled limply and closed her eyes. "I think I'm going to pass out for a while."

"I'll be here when you wake up," Nicky said. Parker squeezed her hand briefly and then loosened her grip. She fell asleep almost immediately. Quinn and Nicky retraced their steps to the ER waiting room.

"She could have died from that," Quinn said, his face grim.

"No shit. I bet the killer wasn't banking on her surviving, which is points in our favor."

"You know what this also means, don't you?"

"That Meg is no longer a possible suspect. She's been in jail this whole time. I suppose she could have hired someone to do the sarin poisoning, but that doesn't seem likely. Why let anyone else know what you're up to?"

"I think I'm going to have to release her," Quinn said. "This is my day off, but I'll go in and take care of that."

"You take days off in the middle of a serial killer case?" Nicky found that shocking, not like the Quinn she'd worked with years ago.

"Don't be judgy. I've got a wife and kids now, need I remind you. Anyway, I have my phone with me while I'm pushing the kid on the swing. I answered your call, didn't I?"

"True enough. Obviously, we're now dealing with a female killer—"

"Not so obvious. The killer could have hired out, as you pointed out."

"True. But I think she did the poisoning herself. Poisoning is often associated with female killers. And she's not letting up. Attacking Parker was a high-risk situation which tells me she's willing to take the risk for her high-value victims, which Parker certainly is."

"This may increase our chance of finding her," Quinn said.

"Considerably. Now we have a description. I don't know if Parker saw enough of her face to do a sketch, but it's something."

"Everything she noticed could easily have been a disguise. Probably is."

"True. But how many people could find sarin to use?" Nicky said.

"The dark web makes it possible. Anyone good with a computer could probably find it."

"That's comforting."

"We'll post an officer outside her door, in case she returns to finish the job."

Quinn left to call Martinez and tell him about Meg's release. Nicky returned to Parker in the ER. The cubicle was empty and she was pointed to ICU on the fifth floor. A nurse was getting her settled when Nicky walked in the door. For now, Parker had a single room.

Parker was partially leaning up in her bed, tissues to her face. "You found me." She sounded lost and Nicky hurried to her bedside to take her hand. The nurse finished up and left the room, telling Parker to keep drinking fluids.

"Apparently, I'm quite dehydrated, probably because every liquid in my body has come out of my face."

Nicky almost laughed, but caught herself. "God, I was so scared."

"So was I. I thought I was going to die when it hit me full on."

"Luckily, there was a doctor on the floor who could tell it was sarin poisoning. That may have saved you."

They were quiet for a few moments as Parker rested her eyes. "You were right, after all," Parker said.

"How's that?"

"You said the killer would come for me and I didn't believe you."

"I'm very sorry to be right in this case."

Parker fell asleep and Nicky took the seat by the bed. It was nearly six. She figured she could go to Olive Street and come back before Parker woke up. She needed to check on things and arrange to be gone all night. She planned to spend the night in the hospital. Even though there would be police guarding her door, she didn't want Parker alone.

A football game was playing in the family room and most of the women were there, either watching the game or flipping through magazines or talking animatedly to each other. Nicky told them she'd be gone all night but that Zoey could get hold of her in any emergency. She took some teasing about having a hot date and left the room, grateful the group seemed to be in good shape. As she passed through the living room to her office, she saw an envelope sitting on the floor below the mail slot in the front door. *For fuck's sake, not another one.*

She picked up the envelope like it was a dead rat and took it into her office, flinging it onto her desk and closing the door behind her. She found some latex gloves in her desk and opened it.

This last loss was a big one. Maybe we should cool things off for a while. You must feel the noose tightening, but don't worry, dear Nicky. You won't swing for long.

Rage coursed through her system as she read. The killer thought Parker was dead, had tried to kill her simply to make Nicky hurt. She'd succeeded. Nicky was hurt by each of the deaths, but Parker's would have been the worst. She called Quinn to tell him about the note.

"I'll ask the women here if anyone saw the person dropping off the note. It's possible."

"It's another reason for releasing Meg. She's plenty pissed off."

"Let her be. She should have been scared for stalking me. She's a creep."

"But she's not the right creep."

"We're right back where we started, with no idea of when the killings will begin again."

"We've got a BOLO out for the woman Parker described, but I don't expect anything to come of that."

"Okay."

"She's coming after you, Nicky. We need to figure out some protection for you."

"I'll be safe in the hospital tonight. At least there's that."

Nicky walked into the meeting room at six and took a seat toward the rear of the full room. All of the women living in the house appeared to be there, along with women from the community. Sheila sat next to the meeting chair and would be the lead speaker for the meeting.

After the preliminary readings and assorted business, Sheila began to tell her drinking story—how she came into AA at age thirty after nearly destroying everything in her life. The night of her last drink she was homeless and had been picked up by the police on a prostitution charge. Every time she heard Sheila's story Nicky was hard-pressed to imagine her with a john, or homeless, or strung out for that matter. They were two different people, the old Sheila and the new and it was true of herself as well. She wasn't the same person she was when she was drinking and it took every single day of sobriety to bring about the change. It didn't happen overnight.

When the meeting was over, Nicky went up to the front. Sheila was surrounded by women thanking her for her talk, many of them her own sponsees. She went to meetings all over town and collected sponsees from all quarters. As soon as there was an opening, Nicky stepped up and gave Sheila a hug.

"Do you have time for a coffee?" Nicky said. She wanted to get back to Parker's bedside, but she would be asleep for some time yet. She needed to reconnect with Sheila and her sense of belonging to AA, instead of feeling cast away from the mothership.

"I'd love it. Where should we go?"

"Somewhere quiet and private. I have a lot to talk about."

Sheila looked happy and sporty. She was wearing athletic pants and a shirt zipped to the top of the neck. "Why don't you come to my place? I'll make us some tea and I think I have some cookies left."

That was more of a commitment than she'd bargained for but she agreed. By the time she got there, Sheila had the water on to boil for tea. They sat in the living room, Nicky on the old slip-covered couch, Sheila in the worn easy chair to the side. Her apartment had a cozy shabby chic vibe, lots of color and texture masking the cheap furniture

"Tell me what's been on your mind," Sheila said.

Nicky twisted in her seat and moved a pillow from behind her back. She was about to put it beside her on the couch when she noticed a blond hair sticking out. She pulled it out from the pillow. It was long and perfectly straight.

"Sheila, you devil. Have you been dating someone?" Sheila looked embarrassed as Nicky waved the hair in front of her.

"Stop."

"Seriously. I'm happy for you. Tell me about her." Sheila looked nonplussed and Nicky decided to give her a break.

"Whoever it is, she has a nice head of hair, I can tell that. As long as it's someone who makes you feel good, then I'm happy."

"There's no one. I don't know where that hair came from."

"If you say so."

Nicky switched gears and filled her in with the latest about the hunt for the serial killer and about Parker's poisoning. Soon, she stood and said she wanted to return to Parker's bedside.

"Wait a minute. I have something for you to give to her." Sheila went into the kitchen and Nicky sat back on the couch. Her eyes fell on Sheila's bag. The woman who poisoned Parker had a bag she shifted from one shoulder to the other. Alarm started in the pit of her stomach as she thought about it. She quickly found her phone and took a photo of it. The idea was ludicrous, but she'd ask Parker whether it looked like the bag used by the woman who poisoned her. Then she thought of the blond hair she pulled off the pillow and how Parker reported the woman had blond hair. Now her belly clenched. She looked around the room and saw Sheila's desk with a box of number ten envelopes on the top and a decrepit printer to the side. Nicky was so stunned she didn't notice Sheila had come back in the room.

"I have some tea for Parker that's excellent for healing," she said, handing over a baggy filled with loose tea. "I know you think it's a lot of nonsense, but what can it hurt? Have her drink it throughout the day. It may help."

Nicky stood and took the tea from her, slipping it in her jeans pocket so Sheila wouldn't see her shaking hands. She reminded herself everything she was now seeing was circumstantial at best and not conclusive evidence Sheila killed five women. But she sure as hell wasn't giving Parker any tea from Sheila. She'd give it to Quinn for analysis. Circumstantial or not, the facts rained down on her. Sheila was in a position to know a lot about Nicky's life because of working the steps together, including reviewing her entire relationship/sex history. She knew AA women from all over town because of the great number of meetings she attended and would hear when people relapsed. She matched the body type described by Parker of the woman who sprayed the poison in her face. She was also a librarian with deep research skills—she could easily navigate the dark web where sarin was available on the black market. The blond hair found on the pillow was damning; it was unlikely Sheila had a date with anyone and the hair had the uniform look of something pulled from a wig. The envelopes and printer meant nothing on their own but were significant when added to everything else. They could have produced the two anonymous letters she'd received. It all seemed to point a steady finger at Sheila as the killer and Nicky was having a hard time wrapping her head around it.

"I'd better get going."

"Of course," Sheila exclaimed, a false note of gaiety in her voice. "You wouldn't want Parker to feel left out."

Nicky looked at her curiously. "I wouldn't want her to feel all alone the day someone tried to poison her."

"I understand completely. Go to her. I'm sure she'll be thrilled to see you."

Nicky picked up her jacket and moved to the door. "Thanks for listening to me. You're a good friend."

"I'd like to think the relationship goes beyond sponsor/sponsee. Thank you for saying that."

Everything Sheila said creeped Nicky out a little more. She couldn't wait to be away from her. She gave her a quick hug and then slipped out the door, running down the stairs until she burst out of the building into the cool, moist air. She turned her car south to the hospital, hoping Parker was awake. She needed to see if she recognized Sheila's tote bag.

Parker's eyes were at half-mast when Nicky arrived in her room. She sat quietly in the chair next to the bed and Parker turned her head toward her. It was hard to tamp down the excitement of finding the killer, even though she was her sponsor. Talk about breach of trust. Sheila had been one of the few people she trusted intrinsically, with Quinn and Parker being the others. Now Sheila was only one thing to her—a monster.

"I can't believe I was poisoned today," Parker said in a soft voice. "And I finally know who did it."

"What?"

Nicky told her about what she'd discovered at Sheila's and showed her the photo of Sheila's tote bag.

"It looks just like the one carried by the woman who sprayed me with sarin."

"That woman was Sheila in disguise. I'm certain of it."

Parker's eyes were fluttering and Nicky settled into her chair to allow her to sleep. She was tired and her shoulder hurt, but she felt a thrum coursing through her system, a familiar feeling from her detective days when a case was solved and the perpetrator about to face their undoing. She'd call Quinn first thing in the morning.

CHAPTER TWENTY-FOUR

The next morning Nicky woke suddenly in the chair next to Parker's bed. She sprang to her feet, her phone clattering to the floor as it slid off her lap. She looked at the bed and saw Parker looking at her through one open eye.

"Did a bomb explode in your dream?" she asked.

"No, sorry. I don't know why I leapt up like that. I think I'm excited to know who the killer is."

"Who you think the killer is."

"I'm right about it, though it's still a shock. I thought she and I were close, but I never suspected a thing."

"She wouldn't have killed as many people as she did if she wasn't clever."

"Still. You'd think I'd have figured it out sooner." She took Parker's hand. "How are you feeling this morning?" Nicky said.

"I'm practically fine. There's no reason I shouldn't be at home. Or back to work, for that matter."

"The doc said he'd discharge you today, right?"

"I think he will. Can you come and spend the evening with me?"

"I'll take you home after you're discharged, which probably won't be until late this afternoon. They take forever to discharge patients."

"What are you going to do now?"

"Call Quinn and get Sheila's arrest in motion."

"I hope you're right. It's going to ruin your relationship with your sponsor if you're not."

Nicky kissed her and left. Quinn picked up on the first ring as she drove to Olive Street House.

"I haven't heard from you lately," he said. "Do you have anything for me?"

"Do I ever. I found the killer, right under my nose." She filled him in on the evidence against Sheila. "You have to arrest her now."

"Hold up a minute. I'll bring her in for questioning, but we don't have enough solid evidence for an arrest. Not yet."

"That's bullshit. What more do you need?"

"A confession would be good. Maybe all that circumstantial evidence will force one out of her."

"She'll lawyer up before that happens. When can you pick her up?"

"Not until a little later. There's the funeral for Officer Shelton this morning at eleven."

"Who's Officer Shelton?"

"Didn't you hear about this? She's the tactical officer who got shot in Rogers Park. Gangbanger shootout and she caught one in the head."

"That's terrible."

"Yeah, I knew her. She and her husband just had a baby."

"Christ. There's no way you're not going to that."

"I'll call you as soon as I'm clear. In the meantime I'll put an unmarked car in front of her address in case she does a runner. If she doesn't agree to come in, I'll arrest her."

"Good."

They rang off as Nicky pulled into the garage. There was no way she'd leave Sheila on her own until Quinn got there. She might be spooked Nicky found the blond hair on her pillow and decide the better part of valor was to leave town. She wanted the confession and who better to get it than she? She ran into the house to change clothes and get her gun. A plan was formulating. She called Sheila and asked if she could bring some lunch over. She agreed, but without her usual enthusiasm.

Nicky arrived at Sheila's at noon, nodding to the officers in the unmarked car in front. She pressed the buzzer next to Sheila's name and the door clicked open. She was waiting for her at the top of the stairs.

"This is a surprise," Sheila said, "but a very nice one. Come in." She took the bag of food from her and the smell of curry quickly filled the room.

Nicky didn't know how she'd do faking she was drunk. She was no actor, but her experience in being drunk was so extensive she figured it would help. She held herself up by the doorframe and gave Sheila a big smile. "I haven't been spending enough time with you." She pushed herself off the doorframe hard enough to make her sway.

"Whoa there," Sheila said, putting her hand out to catch her. "You okay?"

"Fine, fine." Nicky walked with deliberate care into the kitchen ahead of Sheila. "I got everything you like, I think. Do you want me to dish up?" She kept her voice loud, as drunks do. Inebriation tells the brain the whole world has gone deaf and one must shout to be heard.

Sheila took charge of the food and handed Nicky a plate, which she grabbed with two hands and almost dropped. "Oops. I better get to the table with this."

"Something is off with you," Sheila said. "Are you sure you're feeling okay?"

"I've never been better. Maybe it's that you've never seen me in a good mood before. God knows they're few and far between."

"This is you in a good mood? I'm surprised, given your girlfriend has been poisoned."

Nicky didn't slur her words, didn't want to be a slapstick drunk. She tried to give herself the sound of someone attempting to control their pattern of speech. "Parker's going to be fine and that's all that matters. When she's better, I'd like you to meet her."

Sheila didn't look enthusiastic at the idea and went back to her meal. Nicky picked up the water pitcher in the middle of the table. "Can I pour some water for you?"

"Sure." Sheila moved her glass to the side of the table and Nicky held the pitcher high as she poured toward the glass. Water spilled everywhere.

"Oh, shit." Nicky grabbed Sheila's napkin and started blotting up water around her plate and on her shirt sleeve. Sheila scooched her chair back and stood.

"Nicky, have you been drinking?" Sheila looked at her with horror dawning in her eyes. "Shit, you're drunk."

Nicky stood with ersatz dignity. "I am not drunk." She swayed slightly back and forth as she watched Sheila carefully. "It's the middle of the day. How can you accuse me of such a thing?"

"Because you're obviously drunk, that's how. I can't believe you'd do this to me."

"To you?"

"You should have talked to me if you were tempted to drink."

"I can handle a few drinks. It's no big deal."

"It's called a relapse, Nicky, and it's a big fucking deal."

"Not to worry. I'll be back in a meeting tomorrow."

Sheila threw her napkin onto the table and brushed by Nicky on her way to the kitchen. Her face was contorted in anger. "What's your girlfriend going to think? Or is she the one you were drinking with?"

"You don't have to bring Parker into this."

"Why not? You've brought Parker into everything else we've talked about. In fact, I'm a little sick of hearing about Detective Parker. I guess she has the kind of glitz a humble librarian can only dream about. I never stood a chance against someone like her."

Nicky stood in the kitchen as Sheila filled a kettle and slammed it onto the stove. Sheila was attracted to her? Another piece of the puzzle fell into place. "I didn't know you felt that way. I'm sorry."

Sheila had her back to Nicky, her arms braced against the counter. "You wouldn't know, would you? I'm your sponsor and I don't come on to my sponsees. I believe in the program's suggestions, but obviously you do not."

"I never meant to hurt you, Sheila. Parker was a surprise to me, too." She stood next to Sheila and put her hand on her shoulder. "I care about you. I hope you know that." She kept her voice loud so the endearment sounded sloppy and insincere.

"Get away from me," Sheila pushed Nicky away and she stumbled as she moved backward and fell on her ass.

"What the hell?"

"I said get away from me. I want you out of here." Sheila's face was red, her hands in fists at her side.

"No, you don't."

"You're abhorrent to me. I want nothing more to do with you."

Nicky awkwardly stood and faced Sheila. "I never thought of you as someone who would kick a person to the curb for making a mistake."

"I can't abide relapsers. They're weak. You're weak. It's as if you hadn't heard a thing I've said to you all this time."

"You hate me, don't you?"

"I hate you right now."

"No, you've hated me for a while, enough to hurt people because of it."

"What are you talking about?" Sheila grew very still.

"Somehow, you've conflated your hatred of relapse and resentment of me into a reason to kill. I know it's you. And now I have proof of it."

"I doubt that's true unless you've falsified evidence. I'm not interested in your drunken accusations, Nicky. I only want you out of here."

It was time to lose the drunk act. She took her phone out of her back pocket and scrolled for a moment. Then she handed the phone to Sheila. "Recognize that bag? It's yours, right? Guess who else recognized it? Parker says it's the same bag worn by the woman who sprayed her face with poison yesterday. That woman had long straight blond hair, and guess what I found on your couch? A long blond hair. Forensics can easily identify the hair as being from a wig. If I looked around here would I find a wig? Or how about a knife? A long, thin knife used to kill five women. Can you provide alibis for the five nights these women were murdered? The walls are closing in on you, Sheila."

Sheila burst out in hysterical laughter. "Oh, my God. What an imagination you have. Maybe you should write mystery novels. That bag was bought at Target, so I don't think it's the least bit rare. I could have brought that blond hair home on my own clothing, picked up from anywhere. Whatever evidence you think you have is all in your head. Now, get out of my sight."

How could she draw a confession from her? She was supposed to be good at that, but no ideas came to mind.

"I'm going to the police with what I know. Now, as a matter of fact."

She went into the living room and stopped with her back to Sheila as she took her coat off the peg by the front door. When she turned around she found Sheila lunging at her with a knife. She managed to move enough that the knife plunged into the soft tissue of her shoulder instead of straight into her heart. The tip of the knife lodged into the drywall and pinned her in place. Nicky glanced down at the knife stuck in her shoulder and her knees buckled, putting more strain on the wound. Black dots appeared in her vision. It was the same shoulder she'd been shot in by Gerri.

"I wish you hadn't done that," Nicky said. The pain was searing.

Sheila looked at her with undisguised hatred. "I was stupid to think you were any different than the rest of them."

"Rest of who?"

Sheila began to pace in front of her. Nicky was trying to get to her gun holstered in the small of her back without giving herself away, but it was impossible. Every time she moved all she could see was white. Sweat broke out on her brow.

"Sponsees—they're like you, happy to take what I have to offer and then quick to spit it back in my face. They relapse, they fire me, they drift away with no explanation. Am I supposed to be okay with that? Because I'm not."

"But I'm not like the others. I was only pretending to be drunk."

"But you have drifted away, ignored me. Eventually you would have fired me or relapsed or both."

"You can't mean you killed all those women because I'm a lousy sponsee."

"It wasn't all about you, though I'm not surprised you'd think it was. The world doesn't revolve around you. I can't abide relapsers— they're weak and lazy and refuse to do the work necessary to stay sober. I knew Lou was connected to you, but it was pure luck the second woman was. I liked it as a theme and went on with it. Lou wasn't the first, you know. The police didn't even notice my other conquests among all the dead addicts and alcoholics."

Nicky tried to keep track of what she was saying. How to get out of this mess? No one knew she was there, a big mistake in retrospect. The cops who'd seen her go in the building might not know she was visiting Sheila. She had little chance now of defending herself, not with being pinned to the wall. She should never have turned her back when getting her coat. Another big mistake.

"How much does this have to do with you wanting something more from our relationship?"

"I wanted to fuck you, but you never looked at me twice."

Nicky nearly dropped her jaw at Sheila's language. It wasn't the Sheila she knew.

"It never occurred to me you were interested in that way."

Sheila stepped forward and wiggled the knife back and forth. Nicky howled. Enough of this. She kicked her in the shin. Sheila stumbled back a few steps and looked at her with narrowed eyes before she stepped over to the coffee table and picked up a quartz geode the size of a hat. She came at Nicky with her arm ready to strike, but Nicky moved her head just in time to avoid getting crushed. The stone slammed into the wall, leaving a dent. She forced her leg high enough to hit Sheila in the belly with her foot and violently push her away. She fell hard on the floor and quickly sprang to her feet.

"Nice move. Let's see how strong you are after another hour with a knife stuck in you."

Time was running out, her strength ebbing by the minute. She felt close to blacking out. "You're insane."

"That's a difficult term, don't you think?" Sheila tilted her head to one side, as if she were at a museum studying a painting.

"You probably tortured animals as a child," Nicky said. "Isn't that what psychopaths do?"

"I'm no psychopath. They had me tested when I was young and I passed with flying colors."

"Let me go, Sheila."

"I don't think so. It must be humbling for you to be helpless like this. Such a stark contrast to your usual attitude. You're the most arrogant person I've ever met."

"I am?" That was news to Nicky. Maybe she should take a look at it.

"Arrogant and heartless. How could you not know how I felt about you?"

"I would have to be a mind reader. You never said anything."

Sheila approached again and grabbed the knife in Nicky's shoulder. Nicky raised her leg, ready to strike and she backed off.

The knife ripped into her skin, widening the wound. She could feel trickles of blood, nothing compared to what would happen should she remove the knife.

"Well, if you're not going to let me have the knife, I have plenty of others," Sheila said as she walked toward the kitchen.

Nicky wasn't about to let herself be stabbed while pinned to the wall. Taking several deep breaths, she grasped the knife firmly by the hilt and yanked it out, just as Sheila returned with a big chef's knife in her hand. Nicky's scream stopped her where she stood, giving her time to remove her gun from the holster at her back and point it at Sheila, who looked amused.

"You'll never shoot me, Nicky. You're too spooked from crippling that young girl you shot."

She walked slowly toward Nicky, brandishing the knife in front of her.

"There's a world of difference between a serial killer and an innocent girl. If you come any closer with that knife, I won't hesitate." She wondered how long it'd be before Quinn arrived. She thought of the cops on the street, oblivious to the drama taking place on the third floor. There was one way to get their attention. She shifted her aim to the left of Sheila and fired.

Sheila screamed and hit the floor, curling herself into a ball with her arms around her head. In the silence that followed, Nicky could hear her whimper.

"Stay where you are and you don't have to die."

More whimpering. The gun shot had obliterated Sheila's overbearing confidence. Nicky reached over to the intercom and buzzed the door open downstairs. Then she opened the door to Sheila's unit.

"Up here," she yelled, knowing the police from the unmarked car would be trying to get into the building. Soon she heard them running up the stairs. She kept her gun trained on Sheila. They burst through the door, guns drawn, and immediately aimed them at Nicky when they saw her gun.

"Drop the weapon," the female cop said. Her partner was an older man who stood behind her.

Nicky put her gun on the floor. "She was coming at me with a knife. She already got me once. I shot to the left of her; she isn't wounded."

"Call Quinn," the woman said and the other cop took out his cell phone. "We were told there was a murder suspect up here, not that there was anyone else. I'm trying to figure out who the suspect is."

"She is. Quinn can clear this all up. I'm Nicky Sullivan, former police, and I've been helping Quinn on this investigation."

"Then you'll know we need to cuff you until Quinn tells us different." While the other cop talked to Quinn, the female, who's badge read Whiting, pulled Nicky's arms around her back and put her in cuffs. Then she stepped over to Sheila to see if she was okay. "Are you injured, ma'am?"

Sheila appeared to be catatonic, her eyes wide and unblinking. She didn't respond to the question.

"I don't see any blood. She seems fine physically. That corroborates your story," she said, looking back at Nicky. She knelt down and pointed to the chef's knife next to Sheila. "So does this. I'll let Quinn sort out the whys and hows. Hansen, what did Quinn say?"

"He'll be here in ten."

"Thank God," Nicky said. She wanted to call Parker to tell her it was all over, but she'd have to wait until she was out of cuffs and Quinn had cleared the scene. She heard Hansen call for an ambulance. Nicky had almost forgotten about her own wound and Sheila was going to need a psych check. But it was over. Nicky knew Quinn would be furious she'd come to Sheila's place on her own, but she'd drawn out a confession. She wasn't quite sure it was enough for a conviction, but Sheila's stabbing her would not play in her favor. At this point she was confident Quinn could get an official confession from her. The killings would stop and Nicky would be able to take a full breath again. She could feel herself start to uncoil from weeks of high tension.

A few hours later she was back with Parker, both of them worse for the wear but happy to be back together. From the midst of horror there'd come this one very unexpected thing—love.

CHAPTER TWENTY-FIVE

Six months later

Nicky was bent over a practice test book, gnawing on her pen when she wasn't ticking off an answer to a question. She hadn't counted on a test. She thought starting a career as a private investigator was as simple as hanging a shingle and bringing in clients. That was way wrong. The state required private investigators be licensed, which meant passing their test. They also required she apprentice with a licensed investigator, which forced Nicky to ask one of the PIs known to Parker and Quinn whether they'd allow her to shadow them. Kelsey Novak volunteered and she was happy to be under the wing of one of the city's few female private detectives. Her apprenticeship would be short. The state gave her credit for being a former detective.

She stood and stretched. Parker was at work and Nicky had the place to herself. She'd moved in shortly after Sheila was arrested, after she'd come to the difficult decision to leave Olive Street House. Her time there was over. She wanted to be able to spend the night with Parker, to have a more normal life than living with ten women who constantly needed her help. She didn't have the money to get a place of her own, but she wasn't sure she'd have wanted one. Moving in with Parker was the best thing she ever did, even if it was too soon.

The Olive Street residents were distraught at Nicky's departure, enough to have her reconsider her decision. They held a party for her, gave her cards and gifts. Some of them were crying. It was hard to leave them—the welfare of the women had been her primary concern for a long time. It was time now to pay attention to her own.

At three o'clock she went to Kopi to meet Parker and Quinn for afternoon coffee. Quinn seemed genuinely interested in keeping a friendship with Nicky alive and he supported her desire to become a PI. "Usually, PIs are a pain in the ass. I hate it when they're investigating the same thing we are, but for you I'll be more cooperative."

Nicky wanted the relationship to continue as well. Not only did she like Quinn, but his cooperation with her investigations would be crucial. Being an ex-cop gave her an edge, but having friends among the detectives gave her a real advantage over many of her fellow Chicago PIs. She was discovering how competitive the field was and wondered how she'd make enough money to live on. She'd reluctantly borrowed money from Parker to set up a glitzy website, something she needed on day one.

"How are things going with Kelsey?" Quinn said as soon as Nicky sat down. She leaned over and kissed Parker on the cheek. She didn't care who knew about them—the more the better. Then she turned to Quinn.

"Hello to you too," she said "Didn't anyone tell you about making small talk first? It's the polite thing to do."

"You've never liked small talk."

"Give me the update on Sheila then." She held Parker's hand on the tabletop and spotted at least three other lesbian couples in the café. It was Andersonville, the gayest neighborhood outside of Boystown.

"Trial is set for two months from now. She's still in Cook County Jail and apparently not having an easy time of it."

"What do you mean?" Parker said.

"She got shivved by someone, not sure why. They've got her in isolation now."

"I like the irony of her being knifed. I've tried, but I can't find any sympathy for her."

A companionable silence fell and Nicky concentrated on her coffee. She'd learned from Parker silence wasn't always something that needs to be filled, that when people can sit in silence, there's a deep connection between them. There was so much to be learned from Parker, who frequently reminded her there was a lot she could teach her as well. The biggest thing she learned was she was worthy of Parker's love. She figured if someone like Parker could love her, she must not be all bad. Not everything bad was her fault and not everything she'd done was done poorly. For the things that were, she'd have to learn to forgive herself. For the first time, it felt possible. When she'd driven to Laura's house the day before she felt the need to keep torturing herself lessen. She could wish her well without all the self-flagellation.

Parker put her hand on Nicky's thigh under the table and leaned in close to kiss her. Even that innocent touch made her feel fluttery and anxious to get her back in bed. Pronto.

"Eyes forward, ladies. I fear you'll spontaneously combust if you look at each other."

"Are we embarrassing you, Quinn?" Nicky said.

"No, of course not."

Nicky laughed. "Your face is awfully red."

"Let's make one thing clear. If the three of us are going to continue working together, there can't be all this kissy-face stuff. It's not professional."

"Not a problem," Parker said. "We wouldn't want to be unprofessional." The corners of her mouth moved up and she looked at Nicky.

"Don't worry, Quinn," Nicky said. "We won't embarrass you. Now that we have more alone time together, there's no need."

"Well, thank goodness for that. You make a guy feel very left out."

Nicky looked at both of them sipping their lattes and thought it was the first time in a lot of years where she didn't feel left out at all. She picked up her coffee and made a silent toast to love.

About the Author

Anne Laughlin is the author of six novels for BSB. She has won four Goldie awards for her work and been short-listed three times for a Lammy Award. Her short fiction has appeared in numerous anthologies. Her story "It Only Occurred to Me Lately" was a finalist in the Saints and Sinners short fiction contest. Anne has attended writing residencies at Ragdale, Vermont Studio Center, and others. She was named an emerging writer by the Lambda Literary Foundation in 2008 and asked to return in 2014. She lives in Chicago, the setting for many of her novels, with her wife, Linda Braasch.

Books Available from Bold Strokes Books

A Heart Divided by Angie Williams. Emmaline is the most beautiful woman Jackson has ever seen, but being a veteran of the Confederate army that killed her husband isn't the only thing keeping them apart. (978-1-63679-537-9)

Adrift by Sam Ledel. Two women whose lives are anchored by guilt and obligation find romance amidst the tumultuous Prohibition movement in 1920s California. (978-1-63679-577-5)

Cabin Fever by Tagan Shepard. The longer Morgan and Shelby are stranded together, the more their feelings grow, but is it real, or just cabin fever? (978-1-63679-632-1)

Clean Kill by Anne Laughlin. When someone starts killing people she knows in the recovery world, former detective Nicky Sullivan must race to stop the killer and keep herself from being arrested for the crimes. (978-1-63679-634-5)

Only a Bridesmaid by Haley Donnell. A fake bridesmaid, a socially anxious bride, and an unexpected love—what could go wrong? (978-1-63679-642-0)

Primal Hunt by L.L. Raand. Anya, a young wolf warrior, finds herself paired with Rafe, one of the most powerful Vampires in the Americas, in an erotic union of blood and sex. (978-1-63679-561-4)

Puzzles Can Be Deadly by David S. Pederson. Skip loves a good puzzle. Little does he know that a simple phone call will lead him and his boyfriend Henry to the deadliest puzzle he's ever encountered. (978-1-63679-615-4)

Snake Charming by Genevieve McCluer. Playgirl vampire Freddie is on the run and a chance encounter with lamia Phoebe makes them both realize that they may have found the love they'd given up on. (978-1-63679-628-4)

Spirits and Sirens by Kelly and Tana Fireside. When rumored ghost whisperer Elena Murphy and very skeptical assistant fire chief Allison Jones have to work together to solve a 70-year-old mystery, sparks fly—will it be enough to melt the ice between them and let love ignite? (978-1-63679-607-9)

A Case for Discretion by Ashley Moore. Will Gwen, a prominent Atlanta attorney, choose Etta, the law student she's clandestinely dating, or is her political future too important to sacrifice? (978-1-63679-617-8)

Aubrey McFadden Is Never Getting Married by Georgia Beers. Aubrey McFadden is never getting married, but she does have five weddings to attend, and she'll be avoiding Monica Wallace, the woman who ruined her happily ever after, at every single one. (978-1-63679-613-0)

Flowers for Dead Girls by Abigail Collins. Isla might be just the right kind of girl to bring Astra out of her shell—and maybe more. The only problem? She's dead. (978-1-63679-584-3)

Good Bones by Aurora Rey. Designer and contractor Logan Barrow can give Kathleen Kenney the house of her dreams, but can she convince the cynical romance writer to take a chance on love? (978-1-63679-589-8)

Leather, Lace, and Locs by Anne Shade. Three friends, each on their own path in life, with one obstacle…finding room in their busy lives for a love that will give them their happily ever afters. (978-1-63679-529-4)

Rainbow Overalls by Maggie Fortuna. Arriving in Vermont for her first year of college, an introverted bookworm forms a friendship with an outgoing artist and finds what comes after the classic coming out story: a being out story. (978-1-63679-606-2)

Revisiting Summer Nights by Ashley Bartlett. PJ Addison and Wylie Parsons have been called back to film the most recent Dangerous Summer Nights installment. Only this time they're not in love and it's going to stay that way. (978-1-63679-551-5)

The Broken Lines of Us by Shia Woods. Charlie Dawson returns to the city she left behind and she meets an unexpected stranger on her first night back, discovering that coming home might not be as hard as she thought. (978-1-63679-585-0)

Triad Magic by 'Nathan Burgoine. Face-to-face against forces set in motion hundreds of years ago, Luc, Anders, and Curtis—vampire, demon, and wizard—must draw on the power of blood, soul, and magic to stop a killer. (978-1-63679-505-8)

All This Time by Sage Donnell. Erin and Jodi share a complicated past, but a very different present. Will they ever be able to make a future together work? (978-1-63679-622-2)

Crossing Bridges by Chelsey Lynford. When a one-night stand between a snowboard instructor and a business executive becomes more, one has to overcome her past, while the other must let go of her planned future. (978-1-63679-646-8)

Dancing Toward Stardust by Julia Underwood. Age has nothing to do with becoming the person you were meant to be, taking a chance, and finding love. (978-1-63679-588-1)

Evacuation to Love by CA Popovich. As a hurricane rips through Florida, so too are Joanne and Shanna's lives upended. It'll take a force of nature to show them the love it takes to rebuild. (978-1-63679-493-8)

Lean in to Love by Catherine Lane. Will badly behaving celebrities, erotic sex tapes, and steamy scandals prevent Rory and Ellis from leaning in to love? (978-1-63679-582-9)

Searching for Someday by Renee Roman. For loner Rayne Thomas, her only goal for working out is to build her confidence, but Maggie Flanders has another idea, and neither are prepared for the outcome. (978-1-63679-568-3)

The Romance Lovers Book Club by MA Binfield and Toni Logan. After their book club reads a romance about an American tourist falling in love with an English princess, Harper and her best friend, Alice, book an impulsive trip to London hoping they'll each fall for the women of their dreams. (978-1-63679-501-0)

Truly Home by J.J. Hale. Ruth and Olivia discover home is more than a four-letter word. (978-1-63679-579-9)

View from the Top by Morgan Adams. When it comes to love, sometimes the higher you climb, the harder you fall. (978-1-63679-604-8)

Blood Rage by Ileandra Young. A stolen artifact, a family in the dark, an entire city on edge. Can SPEAR agent Danika Karson juggle all three over a weekend with the "in-laws," while an unknown, malevolent entity lies in wait upon her very skin? (978-1-63679-539-3)

Ghost Town by R.E. Ward. Blair Wyndon and Leif Henderson are set to prove ghosts exist when the mystery suddenly turns deadly. Someone or something else is in Masonville, and if they don't find a way to escape, they might never leave. (978-1-63679-523-2)

Good Christian Girls by Elizabeth Bradshaw. In this heartfelt coming of age lesbian romance, Lacey and Jo help each other untangle who they are from who everyone says they're supposed to be. (978-1-63679-555-3)

Guide Us Home by CF Frizzell and Jesse J. Thoma. When acquisition of an abandoned lighthouse pits ambitious competitors Nancy and Sam against each other, it takes a WWII tale of two brave women to make them see the light. (978-1-63679-533-1)

Lost Harbor by Kimberly Cooper Griffin. For Alice and Bridget's love to survive, they must find a way to reconcile the most important passions in their lives—devotion to the church and each other. (978-1-63679-463-1)

Never a Bridesmaid by Spencer Greene. As her sister's wedding gets closer, Jessica finds that her hatred for the maid of honor is a bit more complicated than she thought. Could it be something more than hatred? (978-1-63679-559-1)

The Rewind by Nicole Stiling. For police detective Cami Lyons and crime reporter Alicia Flynn, some choices break hearts. Others leave a body count. (978-1-63679-572-0)

Turning Point by Cathy Dunnell. When Asha and her former high school bully Jody struggle to deny their growing attraction, can they move forward without going back? (978-1-63679-549-2)

When Tomorrow Comes by D. Jackson Leigh. Teague Maxwell, convinced she will die before she turns 41, hires animal rescue owner Baye Cobb to rehome her extensive menagerie. (978-1-63679-557-7)

You Had Me at Merlot by Melissa Brayden. Leighton and Jamie have all the ingredients to turn their attraction into love, but it's a recipe for disaster. (978-1-63679-543-0)